WHEN YELLOW LEAVES

WHEN YELLOW LEAVES

JAMES REISS

SPUYTEN DUYVIL
New York City

ACKNOWLEDGMENTS

Thanks to Eric Arthur, Margaret Eleanor, and John Maxwell. I'm grateful to Crystal Reiss who illustrated this book's map. Bob and Tim helped out with some tricky logistics.

ISBN 978-1-941550-89-2

Library of Congress Cataloging-in-Publication Data

Names: Reiss, James, author.
Title: When yellow leaves : a novel / by James Reiss.
Description: New York City : Spuyten Duyvil, [2016]
Identifiers: LCCN 2015044655 | ISBN 9781941550892
(alk. paper)
Classification: LCC PS3568.E52 W48 2016 | DDC
813/.54--dc23
LC record available at http://lccn.loc.gov/2015044655

For David James and Ethan Jude

They call him the Guv'nor
(God bless the Guv'nor)
He's trained to kill
(God bless the Guv'nor)
Make way make way for the Guv'nor
(Make way for the Guv'nor)
Give yourself a thrill

Look at the dude
He's got the world, he got it made
He got attitude
He got a fist like a switchblade

—"The Guv'nor," Brian May

***

*They kissed again, with more deliberateness, a more
conscious savoring of their lips and tongues in contact.
What was it about kissing? Adam thought. How could it
seem so important, this meeting of four lips, two mouths,
two tongues?*

—*Ordinary Thunderstorms*, William Boyd

***

Note

Blue-collar Britons use the slang term "Guvnor" or "Guv'nor" to mean "Boss." Typically, a London cabby will politely address a customer as "Guv'nor." In this book the British "Guv'nor," spelled and pronounced "Guv'na" to rhyme with "love the" (see page 296), sounds quite different from our trisyllabic American word "Governor." In this novel "Guv'na Brush" has absolutely nothing to do with a former governor of the Lone Star State. Any resemblance to that afore-mentioned governor is mere coincidence. Readers attempting to see this book as an allegory or satire about a particular US president will be guilty of a crime punishable by having their throats slit with a switchblade.

THE VALLEY

north

SALT FLATS

foothills

RAILROAD TRACKS

The

Desert
Center

Great

Ravine

Camp
Wonderful
gravel road

west

oasis

gullies and arroyos

Rattlers
Parish

foothills

10 kilometers

south

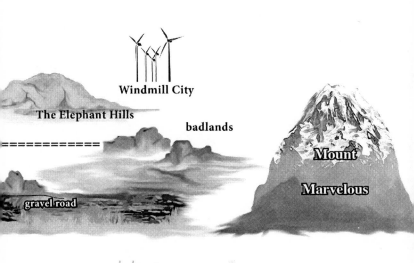

Windmill City

The Elephant Hills

badlands

Mount

Marvelous

gravel road

Cactus
Vale

Teepee
Village

east

foothills

The Chicanery

gullies and arroyos

golf course

SALT FLATS

THURSDAY

From afar Boyd could see it like the patched gray quilt his grandmother used to cover him with, saying, *Good night, sleep tight, wake up bright in the morning light, and do what's right.* She must have learned those rhymes before the Wars of Excision, back when doing what was *right* was a credible notion. Now, as the gray cloud swallowed hills and palm groves many kilometers east, he didn't need to remind himself that there was neither right nor wrong anymore. As he triggered his camera's shutter, hearing it snap over and over, he tried to recall an old proverb, something to the effect that *There is nothing either good or bad but Guv'na Brush makes it so*—but he soon gave up. The railroad tracks, black lines that covered The Valley's belly like surgical sutures, were beginning to recede. Whether the cloud had begun with the prevailing westerlies slamming into a cold front east of Mount Marvelous, or whether it had gathered force thanks to some unimaginably humongous fans constructed by the Looters on the shadowy northern slopes of the mountain, it was no still life. Its gusts were fast approaching. There wasn't much time to photograph dunes and rocky outcrops being obliterated, time to focus on sand dervishes reconnoitering, scouting out ever-widening swatches of ground. Although he couldn't hear it, soon, he knew, the deafening whoosh of a prewar freight train highballing directly overhead would block out every sound. Too soon there would be nothing to shoot, nothing breathable, even with a bandana pressed over his mouth.

For now the click of his Leica echoed his heart ticking, *tock tock.* Teepee Village vanished, but not before his telephoto lens zoomed in on a line of huts devoured in the twinkling of grit. Outside a row of attached condos west of Cactus Vale a speck that looked like one of Guv'na Brush's Sandstorm Troopers riding a moped disappeared once the camera captured his bumblebee-striped uniform; from epaulets to boots he faded, along with the condos, like a digital mini-cam scene in one of those home movies that became obsolete long before the First War of Excision.

If the storm continued its course, Rattlers Parish would take a direct hit. Not that sand had been a stranger in his town. With a desert full of it, Sonny still liked to play with his pail and shovel inside the black circumference of a dune-buggy tire filled with the grainy stuff. Maybe he was too old for that, his mother said, but Dolly, too, enjoyed weeding her small garden of cactus and yucca plants. Last winter she'd made a series of sand sculptures in the yard by their sun deck.

Look, she'd said, pointing to three life-sized figures: There's Sonny, there I am, and there you are, Boyd. And if he looked hard enough he could see his likeness, right down to the mole on his left cheek, sculpted and kilned, standing by his wife and son.

Unless the storm veered, nothing would be left of her handiwork—and precious little of their mortgaged condo. Its prewar kitchen, its timeworn bedrooms and bathroom, would once again be inundated, that is, if sand could be said to *inundate* anything. The last time the desert floor had poured all over their carpets and curtains, saturating everything, Sonny had been an infant. No matter that they'd stuffed chinks under their doors and window frames with damp rags; there was so much junk in the air that they had coughed and sneezed for days—while Sonny had developed bronchitis that nearly killed him. For a week they'd swept and vacuumed, dusted and mopped, but they could taste grit for breakfast, granules for lunch, and grime in every TV dinner they choked down.

Hunched over their black-and-white TV, they watched *The Evening Star Wrap-up* with the grim satisfaction of contestants who'd won a handful of dust. Between commercials for Mick's Comestibles and Miramar Mopeds, they gazed at cleanup crews scouring The Valley with Monster Vacs. They listened to a voice-over of Guv'na Brush declare the region a disaster area and say,

Call me Sage, call me Brush,
I'm your leader in a rush!

Once, Dolly tried to nurse Sonny in front of the TV, but the news about Looters invading the eastern reaches of The Valley scared her so badly that her milk went dry. By then Sonny was coughing up his formula. Guv'na Brush dispatched every doctor and nurse in The Valley to Teepee Village, where the storm and its attendant Looters wreaked the worst havoc. Dolly rigged up her own steam tent out of an old horse blanket under which Sonny inhaled vapors from a teakettle for two days—until his fever of forty degrees Celsius dropped to normal.

He'd never really recovered. Sonny still referred to The Great Storm of Brushwinters Ago as *The Late Swarm of Lushsplinters Aglow*, even if by now he was old enough to ride a moped and flirt with girls at school. Dolly and Boyd had no clue whether the sand blast had traumatized him or his occasional baby talk and spoonerisms were a put-on. Sonny had grown into a wiry, diminutive kid, which was all that mattered, given the statistics that one of every six infants perished in the wake of The Great Storm. The fact that Boyd had a swarthy complexion and black hair—as a child his classmates had called him a *darky Looter*—suggested that Sonny's white hair, his pink irises, had been the result of genetic mutation while Dolly was pregnant during the Latter-day Wars That Have No Name, which continued to drag on the winter Sonny was born.

The boy had coped with the taunts of his classmates. Nights, he'd sat over his tin plate of microwaved chicken croquettes and quietly shared the news that in school that day Donny called him a milk head and Bunny called him a paleface. In the schoolyard during recess the rest of the kids may have been light-skinned and blue-eyed, but that didn't prevent them from teasing Sonny, who tried to ignore their name-calling but couldn't.

They say I've been out in the sun too long, and that's why my name's Sonny, he said. They have no idea how the sun makes my skin blister and turn red. But I don't mind, I deally rohn't. I feel like one of those people Buv'na Grush is always talking about, a *leader.* I mean, that statue you did of me in the yard, Mom; that picture you took of me standing on a rock, Dad: I'm someone special.

Boyd had turned off the volume, but while the TV broadcast images of men on mopeds headed toward a wildfire—it looked like arson—Dolly said, That's the way to go, Sonny, don't let the creepy crawlies get to you—

Illegitimi non carborundum, Boyd had interrupted without fully understanding the words he'd learned by rote from his grandmother many winters ago.

—you just hang in there, Dolly continued, and one day that whole dumb class of name-callers will learn the old saying about sticks and stones; they'll learn it when you teach them.

That's right, Boyd added. You can be anything you want if you want it hard enough—

—and work for it, Sonny said before crumpling his tin plate in the trash and going over to his desk in the corner to do homework.

As far as Boyd was concerned, work consisted of rising early, skipping breakfast, which he had never really liked, and mopeding toward the hills with his camera strapped to his back. He would study a rocky gulch for a while. Then he would peer through his viewfinder at a single palm frond or focus on the streaked brown plumage and long tail of a crested roadrunner motionless between a cholla bush and a boulder whose mica bits glinted in the morning sun. Later that day, after a microwaved lunch of chicken broth and gizzards, he would set out in another direction to shoot some wind- and water-eroded formations he referred to as The Badlands. Or else he would plant himself in front of the statue of Guv'na Brush in Ye Olde Towne Square. Towering a good five meters over its pedestal, the stone likeness of the good Guv'na featured him in his ten-gallon hat and leather chaps, with a bullwhip in one hand and a large black Bible in the other. His clean-shaven, ageless face seemed to be caught in the middle of a smile or a sneer—no one could tell—and his bronze pedestal spelled out the words, *Ye Shall Not Loot Nor Lose!* No matter how many times Boyd had photographed him, the Guv'na's stone-carved expression appeared to change, depending on the hour of the day. Dolly had likened him to a cloudbank whose shadowy lines were as mercurial as the weather.

It was a good thing that Dolly wasn't jealous that someone other than herself had sculpted the leader. In fact, an anonymous team of artists from Desert Center had collaborated on his statue. It was said that the finest master craftsmen on the Guv'na's *A-1 B-List* handled his face, which accounted for its uncanny ambiguity—while lesser known sculptors oversaw everything from his granite hat and cowboy boots to his sandstone bullwhip, which he brandished, ready to snap, and his Bible with make-believe black leather fashioned out of obsidian. Dolly, who had an artistic temperament and who cried when one of her works was rejected from a local exhibition, had a hard time bearing the loss of a lucrative commission when the news from Rattlers Parish hit *The Evening Star Wrap-up* one night.

Oh well, she'd said, there're lots of good statues in the desert.

Boyd laughed, Yeah, look at The Elephant Hills. Think of how the wind shaped the ridges of *their* skin!

She barely tittered. She turned away from the TV's snowy pixels, the announcer's wagging chin, and addressed both Boyd and Sonny: I have no idea why the Brush administration in its consummate wisdom chose a group of unknown outsiders to do work for Ye Olde Towne Square. I can see why the Guv'na's gold-leaf colossus in Desert Center was done by local sculptors up there, but why here in Rattlers Parish? I haven't a clue. Still, if my father taught me anything, he said I should remember the words, *Trust Guv'na Brush; every heart vibrates to that iron string.* I love the image of a heart thwacking away like an iron string, don't you? It's so—I don't know—musical!

Boyd had gazed at his wife with pride. Amen! he'd said.

Now, as the toxic cloud of dust and debris approached the rock where he perched, ready for the blast, he could hear it. From perhaps five kilometers east it gave out a low bass rumble that sounded like *Amen!* The *ah*, supposedly associated with a kind of antediluvian Romantic awe, blended perfectly with the *men,* a growl Boyd thought of as coming from a mountain lion. With the railroad tracks soon to be shrouded, it would be a matter of minutes before that purring *Amen* turned into the roar of a ghost train bursting eardrums and echoing over mopeds and windmills, smoke trees and sandstone escarpments. Rattlers Parish and environs would enter into the storm's gates, and Desert Center would follow, sure as the east-wind devils.

Nonetheless, he continued to focus his camera on the whirlwind. He snapped a mule deer outracing the gray cloud, with her dappled fawn caught up in a gust. He snapped a murder of crows and dozens of smaller birds flapping desperately; the crows—or were they ravens?—were too slow to escape being enveloped. He remembered going on hikes with Sonny, bird watching for magpies, hawks. Sonny had built a birdhouse from some scrap lumber he'd found in an arroyo. He'd rummaged for rusty nails and borrowed a hammer and a crosscut saw from Grandpa A. After a few days of botched carpentry, he'd hung his creation on the arm of one of his mother's sculptures. Dolly didn't mind this, but apparently the birds did. During the half-week he sat by the kitchen window, Sonny spied nary a wing or feather—until he gave up and turned to his newly acquired stamp collection, while his bird house remained clinging to its statue like a letterbox from another era.

His fascination with stamps had started when Grandpa A showed him some letters he'd received long ago, or so Sonny told his dad. Sonny had loved the bold red, blue, and yellow stamps his grandpa said depended on a post office.

But *regard bien, mon petit-fils,* Grandpa A had said—removing a letter from a locked metal box— see, this stamp was issued later, right before the Wars. Back then there was ValeMail. Look at how carefully this stamp was printed.

When Grandpa A let Sonny examine it with tweezers, a woman's face glowed, embossed on a purple background. Stately, magnanimous, she appeared to be smiling ever so subtly, yet there was what seemed to be a single droplet, a tear, on her left cheek. Considering her snub nose and her full lips, which stretched into what looked like a smile, Sonny thought she resembled his schoolteacher, Mrs. Kissman.

Then, Grandpa A had tweezed open the envelope as meticulously as one would handle a pinned butterfly. Sonny had been too young to read the minuscule typeface, which seemed to dance up and down in single-spaced lines. The paper was thin, translucent; his grandpa called it onionskin. At the top of the page there was a faded, illegible insignia.

Would you like me to read this letter to you?

Oh, yes please!

Well, then:

Dear Dr. Stone:

This is to inform you that you are to report to Camp Wonderful on Friday. Please bring your personal belongings and medical kit. Please remember that the life you save, as well as other lives, may be you own. If active duty means anything, it means that alone we fail; togeth-er we hope to prevail. Here's to the enemy we soon will crush! I remain

Yours sincerely,

Guv'na Brush

Is that all, Grandpa? I see you have some other letters in there.

That's right, but you don't want to hear them.

Oh, yes I do. Won't you please read one to me—please, Grandpa!

Do you promise you won't tell anyone—not even your parents—if I read one to you?

Scout's honor! Sonny had said, using an expression he'd heard his grandfather use.

Well, then:

Arthur dear,

With the wildflowers in bloom and the yucca's sprouting white blossoms signaling winter's end, I should be taking long walks. I should be hitching Dorothy to my back and taking our annual hike up Waste-Not-Want-Not Canyon, sketching the chaparral, smelling the pine tar at higher elevations. I should be standing on Our Rock, that boulder where we used to view The Valley, singing Our Song, and doing Our Thing without being seen or heard by anyone but birds. I should be counting new leaves on the trees and imitating your wretched French, you dear man—think of it, before you met me, you didn't speak a word of the language!

It's true, since you left I can't bear leaving the house. Except for food shopping, I've become quite agoraphobic. The TV news keeps me abreast of the latest kill ratios and collateral damage. I think of you at the front, in the trenches with your morphine and scalpels, and I can't go outside. I can't bear to set up my easel. I can't face Bunny Olson or the other members of our reading group. They've been discussing War and Peace *for the past two weeks, and I can't bring myself to read it.*

The old man had turned to his grandchild and said, Can you understand this, Sonny?

Oh, yes, Grandpa. Please go on.

Well, then:

I keep thinking of how Dorothy felt inside me the day you were called up. The morning you read me that letter, I could literally feel her tiny heartbeat stop. The next day when you left for Camp Wonderful I thought it might be indigestion or the flicker of her heart beating again. It's been nearly two winters, and you may have forgotten this, which you dismissed as hysteria. You were obviously right; Dorothy is gooing and crawling around my desk like a little doll baby even as I write these words. But a part of me feels strange, and I'm not sure I'll ever get better, even when you return—which I hope will be bientôt, mon cher amour.

Better burn this.

Ever your own,
Marie Claire

12

Sonny had run home and immediately told his father about the letters. Boyd had glared at the stained wall-to-wall carpet and said, That's very interesting, Sonny. Thank you for telling me this. But you must promise not to tell your mother what Grandpa told you.

Scout's honor! Sonny said.

No, Sonny, you need to give me your hand and swear from the depth of your soul that you will not—absolutely *not*—mention a single word of what your grandfather told you in confidence. You've already broken your word with Grandpa; I won't tell him that. You ratted on him, but that will be our secret, yours and mine.

Boyd offered his hand to Sonny, who shook it. His son's grip was firm but warm, and Boyd could feel an electric charge between himself and the boy when Sonny scowled at the carpet as if he'd never seen a stain and said, I swear, Dad. I promise this will be our secret.

Which it had been. As far as Boyd knew, Dolly had never gotten wind of the letter. Grandpa A had never been the wiser, and the boy and his father had developed a bond made out of winks and handshakes, that had lasted over the Brushwinters; the other seasons were too hot and evil to be mentioned per se in Guv'na Brush's calendar. Sonny had begun mopeding to flea markets and swap meets—from Cactus Vale to the east they were called flea markets; from Rattlers Parish to the west they were called swap meets—where he hung out with dealers eager to sell their cancelled postcards and colorful stick-on antiquities to philatelists.

The postal system had gone the way of airplanes and automobiles, of course, not to speak of railroads. The double set of tracks that traversed The Valley had long been an eyesore. With shrubs and small trees sprouting between the half-buried creosote ties, those rails weren't carrying anything but rust. Things had been this way since Boyd was a child.

He rammed in a precious new roll of film and caught an image of the tracks at the instant just before they completely disappeared under the swirling dust-and-sand cloud. The noise of countless vacuum cleaners grew louder, if that were possible, and the storm's *Amen* turned into a lower, deeper roar than he'd ever imagined could come from any train, combined with the high-pitched squeal of innumerable pieces of chalk scraping on a blackboard as huge as the night sky.

Some rodents—or were they lizards?—scurried past him, and an animal that looked like a bobcat nearly bounded into him. He pointed his viewfinder at a spotted horse, undoubtedly one of the lost Wild Valley Nags. As it galloped toward him, he thought he might be trampled. But he continued to snap, snap, snap until, at the last minute, it shied and loped past him, nickering all but inaudibly in the tumult. Then sand must have fouled the mechanism of his Leica, because it jammed, jammed, jammed, dammit, he shouted alone where no one could hear him curse from his vantage point in the foothills as he used a bandana to cover his mouth but felt it sting while his eyes burned, though he narrowed them to slitted apertures, f-stopped at forty-eight, and saw that the cyclopean turmoil, the Holocaust shambles of sand, shale, and tumbleweed veered north in a flash and spared him.

He mounted his moped, miraculously undamaged, and coasted down to the road connecting his enclave of condos with the rest of The Valley. Southeast of where he'd perched with his camera, nothing had been touched. In the distance the golf course and driving range looked as pristine as ever, with BrushtroTurf as *green as real grass*—a lone billboard advertised this. The empty swap-meet lot looked unscathed, except for the flagpole whose banner sporting Guv'na Brush's ten-gallon hat had taken a drubbing; unflapping in the dead-still air, it had sprouted holes.

Boyd fingered the mole on his left cheek; he wished he could photograph that flag. Although it would be illegal to do so, the framed photo might be sold on the black market and earn some much-needed Valley Scrip. If the price of petrol had remained at one Bee per liter since last winter, making mopeds more popular than ever, TV dinners had doubled for a week, before the Brush administration put down a wildcat strike among Mick's workers. If Boyd could afford hypo and developing fluid, the price of Dolly's sculpting clay had skyrocketed so spectacularly that she had taken to using desert sand in her recent work.

Cutbacks in the budget at Sonny's school had resulted in fewer books—computers had been banned since the Wars of Excision—and more time for recess. While Mrs. Kissman looked on—so Sonny told his father—the boys banded together for games. Whoever could balance the heaviest stone on his forefinger was called King of the Yard. When they tired of these contests, lately they had taken to hurling rocks at a smoke tree they said looked like a Looter. After a week of stoning, the Looter Tree appeared bedraggled, and Mrs. Kissman delivered a rebuke to the boys. She hadn't lost her temper or threatened them with expulsion. Sonny told his dad Mrs. Kissman wasn't mean at all; she was bothered by the boys, but she seemed to sense their boredom as she stood by a flagpole near the schoolyard's barbed wire fence, reading one of the few books still available.

Meanwhile, the girls clustered alongside several broken-down picnic tables, tittering, playing House under the tables, and laughing at the boys. Sonny told his father that Jilly had once pointed at him and called out, Hey, Pink Eyes, why don't you come over here and play Kitchy-Koo?

Well, Boyd said, did you take her up on her offer?

Are you didding, Kad? Maybe one of these days I'll let her beat me in miniature golf. But if I did anything at school, Randy and Billy would never speak to me again. They'd bean me with a chunk of magma.

Wouldn't Mrs. Kissman object to that? Doesn't she encourage you students to play together?

Oh, sure, she says it's all right if we play with the girls. Once she even asked us in class if we knew how babies were made.

Boyd scratched his cowlick. Hmm, he said, she sounds OK to me.

Yeah, Dad, but if the principal heard her saying something like that in class, or if he saw she was getting the kids to play together, he'd report it to Desert Center—

And Mrs. Kissman would be fired. I know, Boyd said, I've seen that happen.

Yeah, but old Mr. Heetclit's got a big red scar on his face, and when he yells smoke comes out of his ears.

Ha! That's a good one, Sonny. I know he got wounded in some war or other, but that wouldn't explain smoke coming out of his ears.

No kidding, he really fumes. And you should see how scared Mrs. Kissman gets. When he shouts, she shrinks; she actually seems to get smaller.

The day Boyd scheduled his parent-teacher visit with Mrs. Kissman, Dolly could not attend; she was executing a commission from Windmill City north of Teepee Village. Boyd had parked his moped in the deserted visitor's lot, unslung the camera from his back, and photographed the schoolhouse. Its broken windows, its rickety doorway, its tatterdemalion teachers' lounge where Mrs. Kissman soon appeared, exchanged customary greetings, and offered him tea—all seemed to jump out of a prewar photography textbook. He declined the tea and watched Mrs. Kissman pour a cup for herself. Her olive-drab ankle-length dress highlighted her wasp waist and her red hair in a pageboy. He knew she didn't own a moped and used a pedal bike, which might have accounted for an athletic appearance he found unusual in one who apparently cowered when the principal yelled.

The florescent lights flickered as she took a seat in a folding chair. Well, do you have any questions about Sonny, Mr. Boyd?

Not really. From what he says you seem to be doing a good job.

Why, thank you.

From what he says recess seems to be his main subject.

Mrs. Kissman put down her teacup and crossed her legs. It's true, we haven't many books.

I understand you were forced to sell off your library.

Yes, budget cuts have stripped us.

Stripped you?

Well, she said—smoothing her dress—not exactly. We're supposed to have one or two of the best, most coveted charts in The Valley.

That's odd, Sonny never mentioned them.

Come to think of it, Mr. Boyd, I'm a bit concerned that Sonny's a loner. Sometimes he talks strangely when he plays by himself in the schoolyard, but I've noticed something else about him.

Boyd glanced out the window at a woebegone smoke tree. Something else about him? he echoed.

Oh, it's nothing major, nothing I need to report to Mr. Heetclit. But you know how boys Sonny's age sometimes mature early.

Boyd had a sudden urge to whip out his Leica and photograph Mrs. Kissman as she reached for her teacup.

As a matter of fact, she continued, it's not just Jilly he's got his eyes on. I think I need to tell you that I've caught him peeking up my skirt—which isn't easy, given my uniform!

Boyd felt himself blushing.

Mrs. Kissman went on: To top everything, the other day he wrote me a little note. You know how precious paper is, and, well, I was a bit nonplussed when I read it.

She handed a crumpled piece of paper to Boyd. It read:

> *It might seem silly,*
> *But I like Jilly.*
> *I'm also missin'*
> *You, Mrs. Kissman.*

Boyd felt faint. He thought he might fall off his battered settee.

I'm *so* sorry, he said. Thank you *so* much for not bringing this to Mr. Heetclit's attention. According to Article Seventeen, this would be cause for a severe reprimand.

As set forth in our Board of Education's Behavior Code, this would be cause for expulsion. It would mean Sonny and you would need to schedule a hearing in Desert Center, Mr. Boyd.

As if by reflex, he unslung the camera case from his shoulder, placed it on his lap, and began nervously polishing it with his left hand. How can I thank you? he said. Has Sonny told you—I don't know how else you could know—that I was once a teacher in Teepee Village? I taught photography and coached badminton back before the budget cuts. I was let go when Guv'na Brush's restrictions on photography went into effect. I'm sure you recall his words about badminton being *bad for the mind, as well as the mint.*

Yes, she'd said, uncrossing her legs, I remember

that, but I had no idea you used to teach in Teepee Village. My husband and I lived there for a few winters when he worked as a jeweler.

Boyd had stood up to leave. If I could only take your picture, he thought.

After they'd exchanged customary goodbyes, she said, I hope we meet again.

It was mid-afternoon when Boyd pulled over to a Broil Station and filled his moped with petrol. By now he—and, he assumed, the entire Valley—was used to Brush Oil stations offering fuel made out of chicken excrement; although it was still called petrol, it was really chickrol. *It didn't stink, it didn't blink, and it sure didn't shrink the economy,* Boyd thought, reciting Guv'na Brush's maxim. While a bell dinged with every deciliter he fed into his moped's tank, he thought of how Mick's and Broil Stations worked in tandem. The gigantic chicken farms surrounding Rattlers Parish had provided fuel for the innards of mopeds and Homo sapiens for as long as Boyd remembered. Ever since the Wars of Excision cut The Valley off from oil-rich regions rumored to be east of Mount Marvelous, mopedders had accustomed themselves to the *puck-puck-puck* of hens; to feed them, Guv'na Brush had long ago taken advantage of sprawling grain fields to the North, as well as garbage dumps throughout The Valley. But had the hens' byproducts, their very existence, been compromised by this morning's sand-storm? The blast had spared Ye Olde Towne Square, but had it missed the biggest farm, The Chicanery, to the east? So far the cost of chicken had remained stable, compared with the price of electricity. For sure, the Boyds no longer had the TV turned on at all hours. Neither did they let lamps burn in empty rooms or keep the heat higher than sixteen degrees Celsius in winter—there hadn't been air-condition-ing for eons.

Boyd emerged from the station's pay booth when a bearded, scruffy man pulled up. Although he carried himself with a stooped élan, he looked like every-body's sidekick. He was chewing a wad of tobacco.

Ho, Hayes.

Ho, Boyd.

How's Willy?

How's Sonny?

Never fear—

—Guv'na Brush is here!

Now that they'd exchanged customary greetings with high-fives, Hayes began filling his moped with petrol. Boyd sat on his moped's banana seat and no-ticed how much dirtier Hayes's bike was than his own. As the deciliter bell dinged, Boyd said, So how are things up at Windmill City?

That sandstorm was a humdinger. Lucky most of the mills did OK. Boss said we pulled in a mega-watt. Said he hadn't seen an upsurge like this since the last one blew through in The Great Storm of Brushwinters Ago. Five of our biggest took a hit. Went down like metal monsters. Boss says they'll be up and running again quick. No cutback in output. That big wind must've turned them mills like pinwheels.

Could you see anything? Boyd said.

Naw, we boarded up windows and hung in. Sure's a lot of sand everywhere, though. Can't keep them granules out.

From this particular Broil Station, Boyd couldn't see Windmill City, but he vowed to drive out there one day with his camera.

Yer durn tootin', Hayes grunted, last week Dolly paid us a visit, you know, for her commission. Boss said something about her making a thingamajig, doing a whatsis of Old Forty-nine, our first mill. Said she was as excited about doing this commission as Don Coyote tilting at windmills. Thing is, Boss noticed her and Suzy our receptionist. They were having a whispering contest, hissing like hens about to lay an egg. Boss finally goes over to Suzy and gives her the evil eye. Dolly gets busy molding clay after that. But I wanna tell you, Boss was—how can I put it?—pissed.

Hayes had whirled around to see if anyone was within hearing range before he said it. When he saw no one was listening—the gas pumps were deserted except for Boyd and himself—he said it again with conviction: Boss was *pissed*.

Just as a monster Moped Vac pulled up to the pump, Hayes muttered, Tell you what, my friend, what say I get in a good word about you with Boss. He can pull strings with some guys in Desert Center. If they see fit to let Dolly do a thingamabob of Old Forty-nine, I don't see why they wouldn't give the nod to your taking a picture of it with your doohickey.

Two burly drivers in dusty ocher uniforms heaved themselves from their moped. One of them glanced back at their vehicle's round canvas bag stuffed with storm debris, large as a boulder. The other rammed a petrol pump into his vehicle's tank and hawked up a wad of phlegm and saliva, which glistened on the Broil Station's tarmac like quicksilver.

Boyd pedaled. Then he let his engine do the work. As his moped putt-putted toward Ye Olde Towne Square, he thought how sheer acceleration had always been thrilling. What fun it had been to let a moped take you wherever you wanted. Mindy had shown him how to do it. It's just like anything else, she'd said; it takes time.

She had taught him to pedal and steer with the engine turned off. In the spider web of dirt-and-macadam lanes near their old condo, she explained that balance was the crucial thing, but fear of falling could lead to a crash. What was important was to relax into a rhythm, and balance would come naturally.

As naturally as birds learning to use their wings,

Little Bro, she had said. She liked to call him that:
Little Bro, would you please pour me more tea; Little
Bro, won't you help yourself to some boiled chicken.
But one day when he tried to reciprocate by saying,
Thanks a lot, Big Sis, she frowned and asked him to
refer to her given name. From that day, it had been
Mindy-this, Mindy-that. He'd felt the dry desert air
whip past him when he used his right hand to pour
on the petrol. With a flick of his wrist his moped had
lurched to life on lonely roads, transporting him as
far as Cactus Vale.

He'd returned and couldn't stop yammering to
Mindy about how the buckthorn clusters south of
Cactus Vale were more beautiful than anything he'd
ever seen.

More beautiful than the organ cacti northwest of
Rattlers Parish? she'd asked him.

Yes, and even more beautiful than the Joshua
trees shimmering at sundown near the lower slopes
of Mount Marvelous, he'd answered. There has to be a
way of telling you this, Mindy. There has to be a way
of showing how beautiful stuff can be.

The next day after school they'd driven their mopeds to Ye Olde Towne Square and gazed at a shop
window on a side street. The store had a sign on its
door: *Going Out Of Business.* One item caught Boyd's
eye. Oh, but that's so expensive, he'd said.

When they stepped inside the shop, a recorded
message barked its customary, *Who goes there?*

Mindy Boyd, his sister had said.

Ho, Mindy, the shopkeeper had said, my name is Jersey.

Ho, Jersey. Never fear—

—Guv'na Brush is here.

After exchanging high-fives, Mindy had said, That's a very expensive piece of equipment—pointing to it in the window.

Yes, one of the last of its kind, Jersey had said. They stopped making it eighty winters ago.

Maybe Little Bro and I can save up.

Well, you'd better save up quick because we're shutting down next week. Guv'na's orders, you know. She recited the newly mandated Article Thirty-nine:

> *No means of reproduction,*
> *Other than natural birth,*
> *Or else your deconstruction*
> *Will blur real things on earth.*

Boyd and Mindy had missed hearing about Article Thirty-nine on *The Evening Star Wrap-up*. According to the Brush administration, TV was OK, but nothing else that attempted to depict what Desert Center said was *too unimbibable to be describable* could be bought or sold in The Valley. The Internet had long been dismantled, and the use of all radios, DVDs, and cell phones had recently been discouraged and would soon be forbidden by Article Forty, currently being scripted.

Despite the danger of trafficking in contraband, Boyd had been able to put together three winters' worth of allowances, as well as his grandmother's loan. When he and Mindy returned to greet the shopkeeper, her shelves had been empty, and only three cameras remained in her storefront window.

He'd jumped up and down. It's here, it's here! I'm so glad it's still here! He handed Jersey five hundred Bees in banknotes.

She'd reached into the store window while Boyd began jumping up and down again. Tell you what, she said, I'll throw in this leather case and five rolls of film for good measure. From now on you'll have to buy rationed film at mini-marts.

He was acting too much like a pogo stick to do more than glance at his sister, grinning, showing her teeth. She thanked the shopkeeper: My grandmother blesses you, I bless you, and my Little Bro blesses you.

He'd fondled his gift like an infant; he caressed its lens cap, he kissed its viewfinder and the top of its black rectangular hood cap—before Jersey placed it in its case, along with five yellow boxes of Brusha-chrome film.

There's one thing I've been meaning to ask you, Mindy said to the shopkeeper. You have a funny name. I've never heard of anyone in The Valley with a name like yours.

I'm glad you asked, the woman said. I was born thousands of kilometers east of here, where it rained a lot. There were maples and lakes, not just the artificial ponds we have on our golf course. My parents and I came out to The Valley when I was a little girl fifty winters ago, so I can hardly remember. But one day at Brush Library, before it was torn down, I read about my name. I guess I was named for a place on what they used to call the eastern seaboard, where there were garden plots and sand beaches. Gambling casinos and oil refineries, too, I once read.

Neither Mindy nor Boyd knew about anything like this, so they remained silent.

Jersey ran her fingers through her long gray hair—it reminded Boyd of the silvery windmill blades north of the railroad tracks—and she said, Well, folks, take good pictures. As they went through their customary parting exchanges and stepped through the shop door, Boyd could hear the recording which would be silenced when the shop closed in a few days: *Who goes there?*

In fact, Boyd had gone and done what he had dreamed of doing, snapping wildflowers, mopeding up as far as his bike took him on Mount Marvelous to photograph The Valley. But he'd been careful not to show off his new possession in public or take pictures of official sites. In due time, after he graduated from Rattlers Parish Tech, he was given a special dispensation to teach a class in landscape and still-life photography at Teepee Village; portraiture was disallowed after Article Fourteen, but it was still permissible to shoot flora and fauna. For a while Guv'na Brush's administration saw the value of promoting The Valley to tourists north of Desert Center by printing posters of luxury condos with swimming pools. Even back then, however, Looters from the East had made off with many of the photographed objects—deck chairs and tables—which made Boyd's choice of a profession dubious. On one hand, the Guv'na needed cash from day-tripping northerners; on the other hand, he needed to use Mount Marvelous as more than a tourist lure; it was a restricted water source and a snow-capped, unclimbable fence between The Valley and the vast, looted wasteland east of its slopes.

During the single term that he'd taught at Bee Rush Academy in Teepee Village, Boyd spent many hours aiming his Leica at Mount Marvelous. Pitched in its foothills, the tents and wickiups of Teepee Village lay in morning shadow, allowing Boyd to shoot the lower mountain slopes, as well as the Great Ravine, which turned into a plateau between two mountains surrounding Desert Center more than fifty kilometers away. The low-lying hills, a good twenty kilometers northwest of Teepee Village, had no name. But these wrinkled, umber rock piles reminded him of a picture of an animal herd he saw in a book long ago. Accordingly, his own private name for them was The Elephant Hills.

The faculty and students at Bee Rush Academy had been nice enough. The drama coach, who was about his age and lived nearby, was particularly friendly. One day she'd invited Boyd to tea and told him that he looked like Rudolph Valentino.

Who's Rudolph Valentino? he'd asked.

She sneezed demurely, then poured another cup of tea. Someday you'll have to come over to my tent, she said. My great-grandparents left me a photograph album. You can't believe how old and musty it is. When you take a sniff, it's as if you go back a hundred and fifty winters. Anyway, my great-grandmother must've been fond of him, because she pasted a picture of him in her album, with the name Rudolph Valentino as clear as if it were printed yesterday. You must come over to see him; you could be his brother—really!

The drama coach had been persistent. One afternoon after mopeding back from Cactus Vale, where he'd taught his students how to use f-numbers while working the rangefinder and shooting chicory and prickly pears with the sun over their shoulders, Boyd decided to pay her a visit. He lowered his kickstand and parked his bike outside her modest abode not far from Teepee Village Center. At her tent flap he smoothed his cowlick and tried to sound dramatic when he called out, Ho, anybody home?

As soon as she appeared and they exchanged their customary greetings with high-fives, she waved him inside with a flourish. Later, he admitted to himself that he'd never been so impressed. Next to a shelf brimming with books, a windup gramophone was cranking out a cracked, metallic tune that sounded like *Mine Talks Like You Talk*, but he soon realized it was something called *Sidewalks of New York*. The smell of incense filled the air—he had often savored this odor in church—though he couldn't detect its source. While she boiled water for tea on her propane stove, he let his eyes wander to a cranny in the tent, where a caged rodent—probably a pet—ran a treadmill. A genuine antique guitar stood propped against an armchair. The way it leaned, the guitar's shape gave him pause; it reminded him of a woman with a long neck, a curved waist, and a big bottom. He wanted to pluck its strings, but that would be rude.

She returned with a teapot and two cups. Let's sit over here, she said, nodding toward a couch with a raggedy green blanket thrown over it. She opened an album flecked with rust spots. Right away he could smell it: the dank aroma of what he thought was mildew the morning he had once poked his head inside an alcove off the main reading room in Brush Library to find cloth and paperback editions piled at least a meter high, waiting to be carted away. In the desert mildew was a stranger, but this album led him by the nose like an old friend from the library to his grandmother's clothes closet. One day eons ago he had been playing with his yoyo, skipping around her condo, when he found himself in her bedroom and opened a windowless walk-in chamber. Fingering her blouses made of crêpe de Chine, her flannel nightgown, and some mohair sweaters, as well as a blue woolen skirt and a yellow strapless dress he later learned was organdy, he'd been overcome with the odor of perfume and something else: it was the same musty odor that came from the drama coach's photo album.

Now, here *you* are, she said, pointing to a snapshot of a man wearing a checkered cloth headpiece, a vest with fancy tassels, and a pinkie ring; he looked as though he could ride a Wild Valley Nag and hunt Looters with ease. Below the name Rudolph Valentino, someone had handwritten the words: *My dearest Ahmed, let me forever be your Lady Diana.*

I love this picture, she said. Not just because it reminds me of you.

Boyd felt himself blushing. I'm afraid I don't see the resemblance, he said.

It's your dark complexion and pouting lower lip, your brows and intense eyes, she said. Her own butched strawberry-blond hair, which gave way to facial freckles, seemed pleasant enough to him. He wouldn't call her beautiful, but she had something, an energy he hadn't noticed in any other woman.

This, she said, is a studio portrait of Rudolph Valentino in a production called a movie, *The Sheik*, which was very popular a hundred and fifty winters ago. I don't know anything else about him. My great-grandmother must've been a fan, though, because she glued his picture here and wrote words in her own hand. Strange that there's only one picture of him. I mean, he probably lived a long life and starred in many movies. Why she kept this one picture I can only guess. Maybe she did it because she foresaw that I would meet you at about the same age. He looks to be, I'd say, around twenty-five. How old are you?

I'm sixteen.

I'm eighteen, she said.

You live alone, right?

Right. My parents were killed during the Fourth War of Excision.

Uh-huh, my parents are gone, too.

My parents tried to ward off some Looters.

Uh-huh, my sister was kidnapped three winters ago. I don't know where she is.

So it is with war, she said.

So it is with war!

Now that they had expressed customary condolences, she paged through the album. We've had enough sadness, she said. Look at this! She pointed to a thicket of tall buildings. Those are skyscrapers, she said. Another photo showed a cloverleaf of roadways filled with automobiles. Those are eucalyptus trees, she said, but I'm not sure what to make of this.

She turned to a page where a solitary photograph had been pasted—again he was overcome with the musty smell. Atop a scrubby hill a giant sign had been constructed; he had seen billboards like this with Guv'na Brush's smiling, sneering face on roadside posters spelling out slogans like POOT ON LOOTERS! But he had no idea what to make of a sign that spelled out a word with one of its huge white letters smashed, knocked to the ground: HLLYWOOD.

Hey, she said, what's your first name? I only know you as Boyd.

It's Bill, he said.

Bill Boyd, that has a nice sound, she said.

Oh, I don't know, he said. Most of my friends just call me Boyd. What's your name? He realized he knew her only as Loy.

She puckered her lips. Myrna, she said.

As he mopeded past the Broil stations and mini-marts on the outskirts of Rattlers Parish, Boyd realized that it had been exactly fourteen winters since he'd been dismissed from Bee Rush Academy. He could hardly remember Myrna's face. For all that she tried to get him to photograph her, with and without her clothes, he'd been too shy or scared to do so. They'd sipped tea, they'd heated chicken potpies in her microwave, and dined by candlelight—she owned boxes of candles that gave off incense. They'd made love on her couch every day after teaching. For weeks he'd felt himself enter her and tried in his mind to describe the sensation. Was it like taking a dip in a hot spring? Was it like plunging your hand under warm sand and letting its granules tickle your fingers until you could feel an aura resonate up your spine? Was it like wanting to sneeze but not being able to, holding your breath when you inhaled with a shudder, only to exhale in futility until the irritation or whatever it was triggered a reflex you knew you couldn't resist, a reaction wholly beyond your ability to do anything about it—like a person on a moped who's headed for a cottonwood tree, and all he can do is wait micro-seconds for the crash, the explosion, the bursting outward into blackness?

Those afternoons, he realized now, had been foredoomed. No one who played vinyl records on a gramophone, no one who owned a guitar or who kept a rodent as a pet could be exempt in The Valley. The day he found her place ransacked, he cursed himself and stumbled through the empty tent. Nothing remained: not the microwave, not the beat-up remnant of a rug passed down from her great-grandmother— only the faintest scent of incense hung in the air like a question.

When he made inquiries at Bee Rush Academy, nobody seemed to know where she was. Her students deflected his questions with smirks and questions of their own, like, Why do you want to know? What's she to you? and—worst of all—Were you two flouting Article Three about concupiscence and Article Six about fornication outside of wedlock?

Needless to say, the next day the headmaster of Bee Rush Academy had dismissed him. *Loose lips lead to pink slips*, he had said, and shaken Boyd's hand. It's unavoidable, I'm afraid. But I predict you'll have better luck as a freelancer. We've been told to phase out photography at the Academy—and drama, too. I suspect we'll be sticking to Bible recitation and chicken farming from now on.

Now he slowed outside of Ye Olde Towne Square Mini-Mart as Dolly said goodbye to a friend—was it Annie? Franny?—and made her way over to her own moped. With her backpack full of groceries, she hunched a bit, but she was still fairly good-looking, Boyd thought. Taller and blonder than Myrna, Dolly certainly did not have the figure of someone in her eighteenth winter. But she reminded him of a slightly worn, homey cushion, a pillowy quilt to lose himself in at the end of a day.

Ho, Dolly.

Ho, Boyd.

How's Sonny?

How's your Leica?

Never fear—

—Guv'na Brush is here!

They gave one another high-fives. That was some sandstorm, she said.

It sure was, he said. I got some pictures.

They mopeded past the squalid section of town known as Rattlesnake Alley.

Ugh! she said. Can you smell it?

I know what you mean, he said. It was illegal to use four-letter words in public.

Dolly sped up. Ugh! I'm tired of the stink of ordure.

I know what you mean.

No you don't. I've seen how you photograph these hovels. I know you care about these people—don't deny it! I think you'd actually weep if Guv'na Brush's Sandstorm Troopers burned down these wretched dwellings.

Boyd thought of his photo portrait of beggars in Cactus Vale, *Blessed Are the People in Huts*. But where would all these poor folk go, Dolly? he said.

There's plenty of land north of Cactus Vale, she said. They could squat there for free, and who would know the difference?

Sonny met them at the door. He was bouncing a golf ball on the driveway, trying to avoid clumps of crab grass. The ball's bounce had a *pock-pock* sound that Boyd found pleasant.

After they exchanged customary greetings with high-fives, they entered the condo.

Doesn't look to be any damage at all from the storm, Boyd said. He turned on the TV. On *The Evening Star Wrap-up* a chicken-faced reporter spoke to the camera:

—after which, as we all know, it was a grab bag of horrors. It's too early for definitive body counts, but three inhabitants from Teepee Village appear to have perished so far. And Cactus Vale suffered two deaths due to storm-related injuries. Thanks to Guv'na Brush's Bureau of Protection and his Sandstorm Troopers, no Looters have been sighted today, unlike The Great Storm of Brushwinters Ago, when eighteen of the bandits were taken into custody.

The camera panned to at least a dozen downed tents, with people digging their belongings out of sand or just standing around moaning and crying. Closing in on a person so bandaged and grimy Boyd could barely recognize him as a middle-aged man, the reporter quipped, What was it like, sir?

What was it like, you want you know, he answered in a voice Boyd thought sounded familiar. Thank Guv'na Brush, I missed The Great Storm of Brushwinters Ago. I have no storm to compare it with. But if I had to compare it with anything, I'd say that it was like being whirled inside a giant trash barrel, being smacked and slashed with ten thousand sledge hammers and cactus needles.

As the camera backed off, Boyd recognized the sandstone arch and redwood portal of Bee Rush

Academy, half-buried in heaps of debris.

The reporter was in the midst of interviewing another survivor when Boyd realized that the grimy,
middle-aged spokesman just interviewed had been
the headmaster of Bee Rush Academy.

At sunset after a dinner of chicken stew, Boyd felt
too tired to work in his darkroom. He and Sonny
went out on the deck while Dolly compacted the re-
cycles. She said she had a headache and would stay
indoors watching *The Ancient History Channel*, which
was about to feature the life story of a man named
Alfred C. Fuller who began a door-to-door salesman
entrepreneurship more than a hundred and fifty winters ago. Then she would sweep up and go to bed.

Is Mom OK? Sonny asked.

She'll be OK. It's probably all the junk in the air,
Boyd said.

Oh, look, Dad, there it is again!

Uh-huh. The sandstorm hasn't blocked it out.

I wonder if the people in Veepee Tillage and Vac-
tus Cale can see it.

I doubt they'd be interested in sky-gazing tonight,
Sonny.

Yeah, I guess they're too busy with their pails and
shovels.

Uh-huh, but at least we can see it. And I'll bet Desert Center can see it.

There's one question I keep meaning to ask you,
Dad. Who put it there?

Boyd stared at the redwood deck, which had long been in need of repairs. That's a good question, Sonny, he said. A book my Grandma B read, the Bible, says one thing, but ever since your Aunt Mindy went away, I've come around to believing that it was put there by Guv'na Brush.

Yeah, I heard that, too, at school, but Mrs. Kissman isn't sure. But anyway if Buv'na Grush put it there, why would he do that?

Well, according to the *Guv'na's Good Book*, he put it up there to remind us that all Valleyites can be like it.

How's that, Dad?

Well, if I remember right, there's a passage in the *Guv'na's Good Book* that mentions a ruined observatory:

Who needs old Mount Palomar?
You can be an evening star.

Yeah, I see what he means. I can be famous. But what about all those other bright dots in the sky?

Long ago my grandma told your Aunt Mindy and me that some scientists named Gally Leo and Ein Stine explained those dots. The fact is, the *Guv'na's Good Book* explains them better than anybody, although here, too, as in the case of the evening star, there's a discrepancy. Do you know what the word *discrepancy* means, Sonny?

Yeah, it means that when there's a difference of opinion, whatever Buv'na Grush says is right.

Uh-huh. And he wrote a passage about those bright dots being the dead eyes of his followers. They'll always be looking down on us from the sky, so in a sense they're not really dead.

Mrs. Kissman never said anything about that in school.

Sonny, Rattlers Parish has big problems with its school system. Mrs. Kissman probably never told you about the white thingamajig up there that changes from being a sliver to a round egg. We're not supposed to talk about it because it's too changeable. It's unfaithful; some people used to call it *Romantic*; it's everything Desert Center opposes. Mrs. Kissman probably hasn't mentioned the Guv'na's special injunction, in Article Seven—subtitled *What's Up There*—which goes,

> *Ask not about the treacherous cartoon*
> *that's pasted in the sky! Forget the* _____ *!*

Well, I'll bet tomorrow Mrs. Kissman will have plenty to say about Buv'na Grush's Bureau of Protection and Sandstorm Troopers. She'll wheel in the TV and show us reruns of tonight's *Evening Star Wrap-up*. But will she say a word about the actual evening star and the bright dots?

As I say, there are problems with education in The

Valley. Your mother and I sometimes talk about complaining to Desert Center, suggesting they hire another teacher.

I wonder if the evening star had something to do with today's sandstorm.

Ha! I doubt that, Sonny. Still, Boyd recalled a line from that same ancient play that had been on his mind lately: *There are more things in heaven and earth, Valley Dwellers, than are dreamt of in your philosophy.* Actually, these words may've come from the *Guv'na's Good Book*—Boyd wasn't certain. But, he said to himself, if the evening star caused today's sandstorm, that would mean the Guv'na didn't put it up there—because why would he want to heap destruction on his subjects? The only answer to this would be if the sandstorm victims in Teepee Village and Cactus Vale were Looters.

Sonny interrupted his father's thoughts. Look, Dad, he said, look at that bright light flashing across the sky!

Before Boyd could blink, it was gone. But he knew what it was. Sonny had never seen one, but Boyd had witnessed dozens of them over the Brushwinters. He knelt down and whispered into the boy's ear: I'm not supposed to tell you this until you turn thirteen, but that trail of light flashing up there is what will happen to you if you disobey the law, *Ye Shall Not Loot Nor Lose!* What you just saw was the dead eye of someone who disobeyed that law. His or her eye never makes it into the sky to stare down at the rest of us. Instead, the eye is burned into ashes and fades from memory for all eternity.

FRIDAY

Boyd woke to the shrillness of a midnight all-clear siren and couldn't fall back to sleep. In the aftermath of the siren, the silence felt oppressive. He wasn't sure what he could compare it to. Perhaps it was like a low-pressure weather front ringing in his ears. No, it felt like the dentist's drill bearing down on his poor decayed back tooth winters ago. With a painkiller—the dentist had used some Brush's Feelgreat Gas—Boyd had only been aware of a heavy pressure grinding at him. The wooziness from the gas blocked out all noises, but the dead weight on his jaw was unpleasant; it kept interfering with images of Mindy's yellow school uniform and her advice to him to sit tight in the dentist's chair, it would all be over soon—

Soon he put on his robe and heated water for tea before wandering outside on the deck. Clouds had thickened, and it was too cold to stay out for more than a minute. But he allowed himself time to think of Mindy, as he had quite a bit lately. Today was her thirty-fifth winterday, but where was she? Ever since she'd been kidnapped seventeen winters ago, he hadn't heard from her. He'd give a hundred Bees to know what she was doing—if she was still alive. Without phones and a postal system, it was hard to keep track of anyone. People like Jersey retired into obscurity. Not that he cared much about a camera shopkeeper. But Mindy—and Myrna—well, he had no words to describe the ache he felt for them.

The tea had steeped long enough. He poured himself a cup and savored its bittersweet aroma. The first time his grandmother had let him sip tea, he'd come in after biking all over Rattlers Parish with Hayes. They'd pedaled through Ye Olde Towne Square as though they owned the place. They'd humped it through Rattlesnake Alley, warding off stray dogs by kicking at their snarling teeth. And they'd coasted through Boyd's neighborhood of condos, more upscale back then than now, challenging one another to a race, calling one another *stinkbug* and *woodrat*.

It was getting on toward dinnertime when Hayes had said he needed to go home; he lived in an over-sized umbrella tent with his aunt. It was hot out, and Boyd was sweating hard as he entered his condo, shouting, *Grandma, what's for supper?* This was silly—Boyd had known it at the time—because even then supper consisted of Mick's frozen chicken dinners; whether you had defrosted chicken a la king or chicken cordon bleu, it was all the same, despite the difference of a few Bees at the mini-mart.

That afternoon Grandma had offered the overheated boy his very first cup of tea.

Can I really, Grandma? he'd said. Won't it make me hotter?

O taste and see, she had said.

His first sip wasn't what he expected, which was something treachly like Mick's Juicywoosie Brushy-crushy that had made his teeth ache. Instead, the tea's fragrant bittersweetness, an almost viscous liquidy something-or-other, made his tongue tingle.

Yum, he said. It makes my tonsils feel like singing.

That's your larynx, she said.

Yeah, my larynx wants to say something.

You don't sound like the man whose pharynx was bad.

No, my pharynx is happy. Where's Mindy?

In school, dear. She'll be back soon.

I can't wait to tell her, Grandma. I can't wait to pour her some of this stuff. It doesn't make me hot at all.

No, it's sort of cooling, isn't it?

Yeah, I feel like I'm smiling on a sunny winter day. What's in this tea, Grandma?

I'm not really sure, dear. It's Mick's. That's all I know; that's all I need to know.

Hey, Grandma, why do you sometimes talk funny? Like what you just said, *That's all I know; that's all I need to know?*

I'm not sure, dear; they're phrases that pop into my head.

Sometimes you sound as if you're talking like some old book.

No, dear, I've stopped reading books. They're not supposed to be good for your eyes.

Suddenly, Mindy burst through the door. Her nose was bloody, and tears streaked down her cheeks. When she saw Boyd, she stopped crying.

Ho, Little Bro. Ho, Grandma. She had not exchanged greetings with high-fives.

What's the matter, dear? Grandma said.

Oh, it's nothing really, just those kids from Rattlesnake Alley. They got together after school in a group. They surrounded me in the schoolyard; I don't know where Mr. Heetclit was. They made a tight circle, and they called me a Looter. Looter, they screamed, you're just a *darky Looter*! I did some biting and scratching after that, I'll tell you—but there were five of them. I don't know their names or anything. And if I report them to Mr. Heetclit, the word'll get back to the other kids, and it'll be worse.

Grandma had wiped Mindy's nose with a wet towel and had held Mindy in her arms until the girl calmed down.

Boyd hadn't known what to say. He'd been too young to say he'd beat them all to smithereens. He'd wanted to pour Mindy some tea and say, There now, Sis. He'd wanted the smiley feeling that reached his stomach, his spine, and the tips of his toes, to return. Above all, he'd wanted to kiss Mindy, to make her smile, to quit his own sniveling.

Now, caressing the empty teacup by his propane stove, he felt better. At least Sonny wouldn't suffer as his Aunt Mindy had. If his schoolmates called him a milk head, that was better than being called a *darky Looter*, which Boyd and his sister had both been called. From the start Dolly's sand-colored hair had cast a net over young Bill: the lure of opposites, an attraction he found as deadly in its pleasure as his temptation to use foul language in public, specifically prohibited by Article Four. During their courting days Boyd had relished Dolly's blond pubic hair to the extent that he violated at least three Articles respecting hygiene. For that matter, Dolly had enjoyed what she called Down-in-the-Mouthing so much that he once had to push her off him, only to see her fall from their bed and wrench her wrist. Once upon a time they Down-in-the-Mouthed and Rear-Doored several nights a week. They went at each other like jackrabbits—Dolly had said they were desert foxes—except on weekends, when Boyd would repair to his darkroom while Dolly sculpted clay into sidewinders and long, sinuous blacksnakes. Her so-called Serpent Phase lasted for two winters, during which she sold a diamondback, a king snake, and what she titled a *Hissing Red Cobra* to the Desert Center Natural Brushtory Museum. For his part Boyd did what he'd only dreamed of doing with Myrna; he'd surreptitiously taken twenty-four snapshots of his wife in the nude.

This, he knew, was illegal—there could be no sales of these photos to local collectors—but he executed his project with the impatience of a roadrunner outracing a moped to sink its talons into a kangaroo rat. He ended up having to bury most of his stash somewhere in the foothills east of Teepee Village, but in his heyday he reveled in ogling *Pillow Chaser, Warm Woman in Her Skin*, and his favorite, *Doll Baby with Her Eyes Closed in Mid-winter*, which portrayed Dolly lying supine in the buff. She had used rouge, heavy lipstick, and mascara; in dishabille, her long lashes resembled an antique doll's glass eyes that clicked shut when you set it on its back.

Naturally, things changed when she became pregnant. After Sonny's birth, Boyd was eager to take up where he'd left off with Dolly. Despite some difficulties during Sonny's birth—Grandpa A had been in attendance as a physician, but the good doctor couldn't avoid his daughter's prolonged labor and the eventual C-section—despite Dolly's having put on weight and having spent most of her time caring for the baby, Boyd had longed to make love with her again. But it was as if something had suddenly died. Their sex grew to be routine, a common story, Boyd guessed. Ironically, it was precisely a *routine milking of the glands*, which the Brush administration endorsed when it came to procreation. Gone were the nights when Down-in-the-Mouthing and Rear-Dooring were delicious variations on the Brushary Position. Gone were the endearments and love bites, the heaven-bent soulful kisses and *snuggle-huggles*, the bouts of mutual jerking and squeezing.

Before Boyd got back into bed, he studied his wife. The pilled blanket that covered her up to the neck didn't prevent him from visualizing her breasts and torso. He still found her bellybutton exciting; he had once told her it was a *delectable portal*, though of course the real door lay somewhat to the south. He visualized the tender second mouth he had licked and lipped—and felt himself harden—

whereupon she turned over on her stomach with a grunt and proceeded to snore even more loudly than she had when she lay on her back.

In the morning he woke to find the imprint of her head on the pillow next to his own. She had left early, undoubtedly to work on her commission up at Windmill City. Sonny had also left for school, and the condo made a hollow sound when he called their names. *The Morning Star Wrap-up* showed men with Monster Vacs on mopeds cleaning up yesterday's debris. Guv'na Brush's ballyhooed *Wizened Words* for this Friday were

> *Talk nice, stay clean,*
> *Don't be obscene.*

Hmm, Boyd wondered while sipping his tea, it's redundant to say *talk nice* and *don't be obscene*. What if today's *Wizened Words* rhymed *clean* with the *Brushtro Turf's pure green*?

Suddenly, Boyd realized he was late for an appointment.

He rinsed his cup and headed outside. He jump-started his moped, poured on the petrol, and the bike zoomed to thirty kph. Flying through Rattlesnake Alley, he was aware that the noisy putt-putt of his engine could be a problem. Luckily, as he sped south of town into the open desert, no one in yellow-jacket uniforms from the Brush Patrol pulled him over for speeding—which would have meant a ticket for fifty Bees. The barrel cacti and cholla bushes looked unscathed by yesterday's storm, and he remembered that Desert Center Weather had forecasted sunshine, perfect for his plans.

He approached the flagpole by the gate with some trepidation. What if Grandpa A had already arrived and had been waiting for Boyd for—what?—ten minutes? No, Boyd was only eight minutes late, but he knew how punctual Grandpa A was, how he tapped his wristwatch and said things like *It's not a crime to be on time*. As a matter of fact, Grandpa A had plagiarized that one from Guv'na Brush.

Ho, sir.

Ho, Boyd.

How's your arthritis?

How're Sonny and Dorothy?

Never fear—

—Guv'na Brush is here.

After exchanging customary high-fives, Grandpa A unhitched the golf clubs from his Miramar Maxi-Bike, much larger and flashier than Boyd's moped. Despite Boyd's tardiness, the old man appeared jovial.

Are you ready to be whipped? he said.

As ready as I was last week, said Boyd.

They parked their bikes at the clubhouse by the driving range and walked over to the first hole. Boyd had relieved his father-in-law of the weight of the golf bag. While he followed the old man to the tee, Boyd wanted to imitate the *queh-queh-queh* of a short-tailed pinyon jay he heard calling somewhere, but he couldn't get up the courage.

So how're things, Son? That sandstorm was sure something, *n'est pas?*

Boyd clutched his driver and, without looking up from the ball, took a few practice swings. It sure was, sir, he said. I nearly got knocked off my feet. My Leica froze up finally, but I was able to clean it last night.

I notice you're not carrying it today. That's odd for you.

I forgot to bring it. Too rushed, I guess.

Boyd swung and sliced the ball into a sand trap.

That's good, said Grandpa A, who took the driver

from Boyd and began taking practice swings himself. You know, Boyd, photography is a way of looking in on life, rather than participating in it. It prevents you from seeing things as they are, facing reality.

The old man took a swing, and the ball sailed straight toward the green, landing about twenty meters short of it on the fairway.

You know, Son, he said while they strode over the BrushtroTurf toward the sand trap, the only reason you can still use your camera is that I've had words with Desert Center.

Dolly had mentioned something like this to Boyd, but he hadn't been clear on the details.

What do you mean when you say you've *had words with Desert Center*, sir?

I mean that I personally have had a conversation with Guv'na Brush's spokesman about you, Boyd. You certainly must know that the Guv'na and I fought alongside one another during the Wars of Excision. I tended the Guv'na's wounds; I saved his life in the First War during the Battle of Honor and Hope.

Again, Dolly had mentioned something like this to Boyd, but he hadn't been clear about the details. He swung at the ball with his wedge. It flopped out of the sand trap and rolled down the fairway a few meters.

Damn! he said. Oh, excuse me, sir!

The old man used his three-wood to slap the ball onto the green. That's OK, he said. You know I care about Sonny and Dorothy more than anything. I call you three *My Little Family*. I'm not going to report you to the authorities about cursing in public. What good would it do me to see you in Desert Center Penitentiary, with Dolly and Sonny weeping like Looters?

Wondering whether Looters wept, Boyd took a swing with his seven-iron and hooked the ball into a shallow pond where mud hens paddled. The ball splashed, but they swam on, aloof.

Drat! he said.

That's better, Son. I'm sure you know that I've had considerable influence with the authorities. Over the winters Guv'na Brush and I have had tea on several occasions.

Yes, sir, I've heard this, but I'm not clear about the details.

That's just it, Boyd. You're too interested in details, the spines on the cactus, rather than *tout*. You need to come out from behind the camera lens and smell the Mick's.

Boyd stepped into warm pond water up to his ankles, soaking his desert boots, while he retrieved the ball. I'm trying to understand things, sir, he said and positioned himself on the fairway before taking another swing. This time the ball lofted high over the green and landed in another sand trap.

Gosh! he said. Gosh gosh gosh!

Easy there! Just remember to keep your eye on the big picture, *mon gendre*.

While trudging toward the old man's ball that looked like a pocked hard-boiled egg, Boyd wondered aloud about why Grandpa A spoke in a foreign language. It sounded familiar, but it wasn't normal.

Mais oui, the older man said, as a native Valleyite, I know I should speak normally. But I had a wife once, you know, and she spoke this way, not normal speech. She grew up in a country many thousands of kilometers east of The Valley.

Dolly told me about her mother, Mary Ann.

Not quite right, *Monsieur*. Her name was Marie Claire. I loved her more than anyone.

Yes, Dolly told me, but I've never asked you about the foreign language; I happen to have caught a bit of it from you, but—

Grandpa A stood over his ball with a putter and tapped it straight into the hole. Right, and when she died shortly after I was called up in the Third War of Excision, I vowed that I would keep her alive in my mind and on my tongue.

Uh-huh, said Boyd. He wondered whether he'd feel that way if Dolly died; would he want to take up sculpture and use her favorite expressions, like *Ugh!* and *I'm tired of the stink of ordure*. He studied his father-in-law for a clue; then he glared at his golf ball about ten meters beyond the hole.

Bonne chance!

Brandishing his club with all the confidence of a titmouse, Boyd swung—and missed the ball entirely.

Before he could utter a *by golly*, Grandpa A cried, Do you see them? Look over there by those palm trees. Or am I imagining things?

Saved by whoever had distracted the older man's attention, Boyd thought he caught the image of two dark figures stooping next to a stand of palmettos about a hundred meters away. Yet it was as if he couldn't see them, as if they were invisible or had blended into the background. He couldn't tell; they appeared to be dressed in rags. As soon as they knew they'd been seen, they bolted to their feet and began running toward the open desert.

Boyd broke into a sprint and followed the two mirages, ducking and dodging past chaparral and smoke trees. The two pixilated ragamuffins had reached an arroyo and appeared to be clambering up the sandy face of a hill, glancing back at him as he gained purchase on the loose ground. In his desert boots, still wet from their plunge in the pond, he was narrowing the space between them, yelling, *Stop!* He couldn't make out their response—did it sound like a low growl, a little like the bass rumble of yesterday's whirlwind, though on a much smaller scale? Or was he imagining things?

By now he was maybe a kilometer from Grandpa A, and the sandy slope turned into pebbles and then scree. Up ahead a rocky gulch loomed, and the shabby duo darted that way, disappearing around a bend, their lank hair whipping behind them. Boyd followed, panting, stepping out of sunlight into the shade of the gulch. He slipped and slid over rocks, made his way around a prickly cactus, and saw that the small ravine branched out in two directions. He picked up a chunk that glittered with rose quartz, aimed it at the cleft in the rocks, which seemed to be headed in the direction of Mount Marvelous, and hurled it far up the gorge, so that it hit what sounded like a boulder. *Who are you?* he shouted. *Come out, I won't hurt you!*

Like hell, he said under his breath, aware of the prohibitions against cursing. *Like hell I won't hurt you! I'll rip out your tongues, that is, if you're real and not just figments.*

As if in answer, a low growl seemed to emerge from the other fork in the trail. Did it sound like a mountain lion trapped, with its cub? Surly, unbudgeable, it gave Boyd fair warning with the unmistakable pent fury of a Looter.

Back on the golf course, the old man was wielding his putting iron like a horsewhip. That's the way, Son. You gave them a run for their Bees, he said and threw down his putter to give Boyd a bear hug.

Boyd was still breathing hard when he heard something entirely different from a growl that might have been imaginary. At first he thought Grandpa A was whining, or whinnying like a Wild Valley Nag. But that would be ridiculous, and anyway his father-in-law had obviously heard it, too. He had pushed Boyd away and was scowling at the BrushtroTurf, as though it held the answer to a question Boyd had barely formulated in his mind, much less translated into words.

All at once he felt it, from the bottom of his desert boots to the tuft of his cowlick and then back down again to settle somewhere between his cheeks and his forehead—his face which Myrna had compared to Rudolph Valentino's. He saw that Grandpa A had also felt it; the old man's face was twisted into a question mark, and he made no attempt to retrieve his gold club.

In fact, the putter had begun rolling back and forth, penduluming on the ground that also appeared to be rolling. Like a giant green teakettle, the Brush-troTurf came to a slow boil; then, abruptly, someone turned on the heat—upped the propane—because things started to bubble and bounce. The old man fell to his knees and began a prayer that included Guv'na Brush's name, though Boyd could barely hear it. Amid the grinding and scraping—as if the earth were fulminating, issuing a proclamation which would defy all Seventy-seven Articles in the Brush administration—Boyd could barely hear himself think, What is this? I think I know what this is.

He threw himself to the ground just as—accompanied by a noise halfway between a thump and a bang, something like the *thwank* of a thousand hors-es' hooves becoming unstuck from mud—the fairway and putting green were split by a black line, a fissure that began somewhere south of where they huddled, zigzagged around them, and traveled toward the foothills of Mount Marvelous. Later Boyd would ask Grandpa A what it felt like to him.

What it felt like, he would say. You want me to tell you what it felt like? *Eh, bien,* I'd say it felt like the day Guv'na Brush's forces and I were ambushed during the Third War when an army of Looters pinned us down in a ravine by hurling stones and causing a rock slide that buried three hundred and ninety-six of our troops.

By afternoon reporters from *The Evening Star Wrap-up* had interviewed Boyd and his father-in-law. Grandpa A had told them he hadn't feared for his life as much as that of his *gendre.* After all, the seismic event had been listed as a mere eight on a scale of thirteen, so there was *little to fear except fear itself*—an adage coined by Guv'na Brush before the First War of Excision.

Boyd had pointed at the fissure, calculated to be fifteen kilometers long, and had quipped, I guess it was more than a tempest in a teapot!

Seriously—while Boyd had mopeded alongside the old man, before he turned off towards his spa-cious condo—Grandpa A had wondered aloud whether there was a relationship between the Looters and what occurred next on the fairway. Before they'd exchanged customary goodbyes, Grandpa A had said, *Écoutez,* those tricksters have always caused havoc. I don't need to tell you that they'll return to put us in harm's way. Today's events are a premonition, believe me, Son. What happened on the golf course will happen again in four twinklings of the evening star.

Farewell, Grandpa A.

Au revoir, Boyd.

Never hush—

—Guv'na Brush.

Now, standing outside his booth at the swap meet, Boyd thought about his father-in-law's words. Maybe the Looters had been responsible for The Valley Quickshake, which was what reporters had dubbed the event. But did it follow that the Looters would return to spread more destruction? Would they cause a Valley Longshake, or something worse—another sandstorm or some flood or fire—*in four twinklings of the evening star?* Brush forbid, would they bring about the very obliteration of the evening star?

A throng of Valley Dwellers strolled between the booths of dealers hawking hairbrushes, toothbrushes, paintbrushes. Boyd could tell that most of his clients were locals. Many of them had Rattlers Parish accents; they stressed the second syllable in Joshua when they asked, How much is that picture of a JoshUa tree—so that *Joshua* sounded like a sneeze. Or else they used quaint South Valley expressions in describing Boyd's still lifes of bottle brushes and oleanders, such as, *I sure do cotton to those pictures of flars.*

Unfortunately, many of his fellow townspeople stared at his landscapes dumbly, as if they'd never seen Mount Marvelous or an ocotillo plant. One of them might ask, Is that really a lizard? But most of them said nothing while they ambled past his pièce de résistance, a moody telephotograph of the Great Ravine separating The Valley from Desert Center and areas to the west. He'd titled that photo *Who Goes There?* and had paid special attention to the way the sun hit the gravel road and railroad tracks that split the huge mountain pass. He'd spent hours waiting for the sun to cast precisely the shadows he'd wanted to highlight those tracks. But whether *Who Goes There?* puzzled or affronted passersby, no one said a word about it— or reached into their pockets for sixty Bees. During the course of the afternoon, the winter wind died and then blew down from the north, a remnant of yesterday's sandstorm. One man in a deerskin jacket slapped twenty-five Bees into Boyd's hand and walked away with *Arroyo at Sunrise.* Another man wearing a buckskin vest got into an argument with Boyd about The Valley Quickshake. He planted himself under Boyd's nose and contended that the event was a ruse cooked up by reporters, that nothing bad like this could happen with Guv'na Brush at the helm. Boyd nodded compliantly—no sense starting a ruckus with a hot-head when there were no doubt government agents plying the crowd, eager to arrest dissidents.

It was late in the afternoon when a woman who'd been shopping for nailbrushes turned to greet Boyd. Without exchanging greetings, he recognized her ol-ive-drab uniform. They didn't exchange courtesies at all; they simply stared at one another until she let out a laugh and said, Lovely to see you again, Mr. Boyd.

Speechless, Boyd spread both arms as though he were about to embrace her. Instead, he stood spread-eagled dumbly, then began pointing out his framed work laid carefully on the ground or hooked to the wooden boards of his booth.

Finally, he stopped blushing and said, Oh yes, I have whatever you want here. Just tell me, and it's all yours for free.

Mrs. Kissman laughed again, a throaty *ha ha* that he somehow thought of as a tiny silver gong. What, she said, do you mean by that? Are you offering me your life's work gratis?

The tickle in his throat spread to his spine when he said, Gosh no, Mrs. Kissman, I have more to give you than that?

She stood in a gust of north wind, apparently try-ing to decide what to say. She moistened her lips; they glowed in the sunlight, which just then came out from behind a cloud and dappled the ground. She used her tongue to clean her teeth. Right then, in her ankle-length dress with her red hair she reminded him of someone he'd seen in a book long ago. It was a famous painting, his grandmother had told him, called *Spring*, by an artist who lived many thousands of kilometers east of The Valley, on the other side of the eastern ocean. Beautiful as she was, the woman in the painting did not have a wasp waist like Mrs. Kissman. Mrs. Kissman's wasp waist made him want to whip out his Leica and shoot her just as she was, in everyday garments, nothing diaphanous or lewd. Mrs. Kissman's moistened lips made him want to—

Are you OK, Mr. Boyd? You look ill.

Ill? he said.

Sonny did well in school today. He didn't hide or cry when the Valley Quick Shake hit.

Really? Boyd said.

No, when it hit, I was right there by the fence while they were pitching rocks at their smoke tree. I tell you, Sonny stood there and locked eyes with me; then he yelled, *Students, line up!* I don't think Guv'na Brush could've been more authoritative. The ground shook for a while, but the others listened to him and didn't run inside, which would've been dangerous. I was there to answer questions and hold peoples' hands, but it was Sonny who held down the fort. Where were you, by the way?

It took a lot of control for him to answer her question. After he described this morning's events, she quipped, What nonsense! Those Looters had nothing to do with The Shake. One day I'd like to tell you a story about some other wars, Mr. Boyd. I guarantee it will shake you.

Why not tell me now? he said.

I can't. Not in front of all these people.

Tomorrow, then? Maybe I could meet you at school.

Tomorrow's Saturday, no school.

Maybe we could have tea.

Yes, that might be a good idea. Why don't we meet in the school lounge; I've got a key, and I'll leave the front door open for you at about three in the afternoon. My husband will be away at work for Mick's in Desert Center.

Uh-huh. Sonny will want me to take him to the railroad tracks beforehand. He's been wanting me to take him there for weeks, and I promised him we'd go tomorrow.

Right, and my book club meets tomorrow to recite The Book of Ruth in the Bible.

My wife will probably be working all day on her commission at Windmill City.

Right. And if you really want to know, Mr. Boyd, I haven't read The Book of Ruth, and I'm not sure I want to.

Amen, he said, stressing the *ah*.

***

By the time Boyd dismantled his booth, the wind had picked up again. The deserted swap-meet grounds, a sandy stretch with bare blankets and crates strewn among flimsy wooden structures, reminded Boyd of a bazaar. Long ago his grandma had described sizable gatherings at merchants' markets. There was no great canvas overhang to protect a swap meet from the elements, but the idea of tents with sellers and buyers doing business in far-off deserts fascinated him.

When he was a boy, his school had sponsored annual bazaars to raise money. Huddled in stalls in the schoolyard, his teachers had sold candies and homemade cakes to Rattlers Parishioners. Grandma B had bought some macaroons and nougats—which she divvied up among Mindy, Sonny, and herself. Thanks to these events, the school library flourished. But when his teachers dismantled their stalls, the next day the bare schoolyard looked strange.

It's odd, his grandma had said, that the words *b*a*z*a*a*r* and *b*i*z*a*r*r*e* sound the same—she'd spelled the words.

Boyd had faked a sneeze. Yeah, that's right, Grandma. Just like the word *p*e*a* sounds the same as the word *p*e*e*, like in Teepee Village!

That's gross, his grandma had said.

Well, I have to pee, he said.

Better to use the word *urinate*, dear.

One day Grandma B had described countries many thousands of kilometers east, on the other side of the eastern ocean, where bazaars were called *souks*. Men in heavy headdresses drank tea. They smoked water pipes and sold figs and dates.

Just like our date palms in The Valley? he'd asked.

Right, she'd said, but the deserts they lived in were much larger and drier than our Valley. Their deserts stretched for thousands of kilometers. The men rode camels, and the women cooked flat bread called *pita*. The women wore garments called burqas that covered them all up, including their faces, and they didn't get out much, except to shop.

Doesn't sound like fun, he'd said.

Right, she'd said. Think of a woman way back then. Let's call her Sandy. What would Sandy do for kicks?

Play in the sand, he'd quipped.

Sometimes I wonder about you, dear, she'd laughed.

The next day Grandma told him that, after Mindy had been born, her mother had been forced to go to work as a librarian in the redbrick building on Ye Olde Towne Square. She'd hated books, but she especially loathed one called *Riders of the Purple Sage*, which she considered exceedingly frivolous. Even then before Desert Center lay down the law, the Bible was the book of choice, and Mindy's mother chose to stick with it, as well as the *Guv'na's Good Book*.

Grandma fixed her gaze on Boyd. One day Mindy's

mother simply left. She said she just couldn't live under the same roof with a man who had literary interests. Here she was, my daughter-in-law—whose name
really happened to be Sandy—about to fly the coop.
Well, considering the laws back then, there was little
your father could do except sulk; back then Guv'na
Brush was allegedly in favor of women's rights and
was totally anti-literary. Mindy wept. I cursed Sandy and cried for a week, but she slammed out of the
house with a suitcase and two dog-eared Bibles, plus
a copy of the *Guv'na's Good Book*.

What happened to her, Grandma?

The last I heard she went to work as an army nurse
in Camp Wonderful. Once the Wars of Excision started, I lost touch with her. She may've been killed, like
so many others.

So it is with war, he'd said.

So it is with war!

But I don't understand, he said.

I never told you this because I knew you would
be too young to understand, dear. I told Mindy not to
tell you.

Boyd had begun to cry.

What I didn't tell you was that your father re-married the woman who ended up being your mother.
Maybe *ended up* isn't the right word.

Boyd had known what she meant. Both his parents had been killed in a skirmish near Teepee Village
during the early days of the Third War of Excision.

They had mopeded to Teepee Village, hoping to defend some property they owned there, but the Looters beat them to it and killed them outside of their teepee.

Then Mindy's not really my sister, Boyd had said.

No, dear, she's not really your full sister—Boyd thought she'd said *chill blister*. She's what we call your half-sister.

Boyd had stopped crying. Does that mean I can cut her in half?

Just then Mindy had walked through the door. Peugh! she said. It stinks in here.

She was right: it was hot, there was no air-conditioning, and the condo smelled of a dead mouse.

Hey, Mindy, he said, did you know I can cut you in half?

Ha ha! she said.

I'm sorry, dear, I told him, Grandma B said.

Yeah, she told me you're not really my sister.

Well, Little Bro, I guess you've learned what's what at last. But—she turned to Grandma B—did you tell him about our father?

Which art in Heaven, hallowed be Thy name, Grandma B chanted, according to Article Twelve's stipulation that Bible verses must be recited in full whenever their phrases were alluded to or uttered in fragments.

No, I didn't, dear. He's too young. Let's wait till next winter.

Let's tell him now. He's old enough to learn the

truth—

—*shall make you free!* her grandmother chanted.

Whereupon the old woman and Mindy had told Boyd about how their dad, a writer, had long ago dealt with Guv'na Brush's edicts to publish work about him only. Old Man Boyd, as they referred to him, wrote about the Guv'na all right. But *Thunderhead* was a scathing exposé of how the Brush administration had its finger in every chicken potpie made at Mick's Comestibles. Brush controlled Miramar Mopeds and Windmill City as well, and he was on his way to becoming what Old Man Boyd called *The Emperor of Chickenfeed*. North of Desert Center, the megalithic mountain of recyclable TV-dinner plates filled a no-man's land that Old Man Boyd had managed to visit and see for himself. He'd described an ever-shifting, shaky pile of compacted tin dishes that rumbled like a kind of thunder when the wind blew. Although recycling was supposed to be in effect, the tin mountain grew higher and higher as time passed.

Grandma B paused and looked at her propane stove. Neither of you kids knows the rest of the story, she said.

Young Bill and Mindy had cupped their ears with their hands so they could hear better while Grandma B described Old Man Boyd's small-press book, *Dobbins Forever.* A slender biography of about two hundred pages, it told the story of Guv'na Brush, AKA

Rudy Newhouse, who grew up about five thousand kilometers east of The Valley in an urban neighborhood known as Can Ah See. Somehow, Old Man Boyd had obtained an authentic copy of the Guv'na's birth certificate before it had been altered. He had left Can Ah See when the entire city of which it was a part burned down in the wake of uprisings and what became a full-blown insurrection. He was one of the lucky ones to escape, one of The Youthful Survivors, as they became known. But whereas the other Survivors had forded rivers, hitched mules to wagon trains, and settled on farms and ranches in the hinterland, Newhouse had continued west until he came to The Valley, already sparsely populated with wandering families who'd fled from insurrectionary conflagrations to the west. Legend had it that when he reached a ridge on Mount Marvelous and gazed out over The Valley, he uttered the words,

> *Here will I set down my boot,*
> *Never to kick butt or loot.*

On the night of his arrival itinerant families welcomed him with venison stew. He was said to have politely asked for the mutton from native Big Horn Sheep, but declared his real culinary preference for poultry, the white meat of Leghorns. When his hosts demurred, saying it had been a bad hunting season and, as far as they were concerned, chicken meat was stringy and unpalatable, Newhouse stormed out of their teepee, declaring he would feed himself. A number of itinerants followed, and in coming weeks Newhouse and his band of no-count adherents pitched their tents on the high plateau between two mountains at the western edge of The Valley. Unfortunately, their craving for poultry came to naught. After they had depleted the local population of wild turkeys, pheasants, and quail, they were forced to raid their neighbors' tent farms and rustle their chickens, prized as egg layers, rather than oven stuffers. This did nothing to enamor them to their fellow Valley dwellers, but the size of Newhouse's cohort of chicken rustlers grew with every speech he delivered in Ravineville, which later came to be known as Desert Center. Because he was a short man, he would stand atop a pile of hefty hardbacks—but never the Bible—and decry the Valleyites' way of life. That grungy bunch of ex–hunters and gatherers, he said, was *responsible for the depletion of our water sources, the desecration of religion, and the prohibition of our best mode of transportation, the moped.* Thanks to such fiery oratory, Newhouse's followers began to track down horses and ponies in The Valley. His midnight raiders made their way into every Valleyite's tent-yard corral and slit the throat of at least one horse, only to leave its carcass rotting there so that its owner would come upon it in broad daylight. Eventually, the Valley dwellers feared these midnight massacres so much that they freed the few steeds that had been spared Newhouse's marauders. These liberated stallions and mares became known as Wild Valley Nags more or less at the same time as Newhouse decided upon a name change. Looking west at the rugged highlands which were to become Camp Wonderful, gazing east at the snowy summit of Mount Marvelous, he was said to have told his vast group of hangers-on that he loved to let his eyes wander over countless square kilometers of scrub and shrub; that it was time for him to move into a new home, his headquarters in Desert Center; and from that time forward he would adopt a new moniker based on a polite term of address used in a country called Ing Lund thousands of kilometers northeast of Can Ah See, along with a five-letter word which described The Valley flora.

And that, Grandma B said, was how *Dobbins Forever* dealt with the rise of Guv'na Brush. Old Man Boyd's biography sold out overnight, which might've been a cause for celebration. Instead, the next morning his condo was surrounded by troops. From then on he was kept under house arrest. He wasn't allowed to join the protest march when the teahouse where poets gave readings in Ye Olde Towne Square was torn down to make room for a parking lot for mopeds. He wasn't allowed to publish a sequel to *Dobbins Forever,* though it supposedly exists somewhere as a manuscript titled *Canyon Captives*. And neither he nor your mother, a sloe-eyed beauty from Teepee Village, was allowed to leave their condo unless they were accompanied by a squadron of elite bumblebee-striped uniformed Sandstorm Troopers from Guv'na Brush's Bureau of Protection.

Mindy and her Little Bro sat, mesmerized.

Grandma B continued: The rest of my tale came down to me by bits of news stories and local legend, the chitchat of well wishers and pals.

Several winters after The Fourth War of Excision, Old Man Boyd heard some sad news about his second wife—whose name was also, coincidentally, Sandy. Well, *The Evening Star Wrap-up* had a story about her elderly parents in Teepee Village. They'd been ambushed and killed while walking to church one fine Sunday morning. After the Boyds wept, wrote in their journals, and chanted for two days, they hatched a plan. The next night, during the wee hours, they left me in charge of you two kids and were able to slip out of their condo without being detected. They fled east through the desert without mopeds and with very little water. Hiding in arroyos and gullies, avoiding squads of the Guv'na's men on mopeds, they hiked overland. As the story goes, they entered Sandy's parents' blue and red teepee house and were revolted by the mess. The propane stove had been overturned.

The TV, fridge, and microwave had been painted with blood. And the rest of the furniture had been carted away. Word has it that the Boyds had no more than stepped outside of the teepee house when a band of Looters slit their throats, leaving their bodies to rot. If you want to know what I think, kids, I'm not sure that your father's murderers were Looters. Accounts get mixed up, and the true facts are hard to know.

Who else would it be if not the Looters? Boyd had asked.

Impossible to know for sure, Grandma B had answered. But give it a guess!

That evening Boyd let down his kickstand and hefted his portfolio of photos inside the condo. He'd been surprised not to see Dolly's moped parked in its usual spot, though Sonny's bike leaned on its stand like a landmark. The wind was blowing up again, rolling tumbleweeds into Boyd and his neighbor's front yards. Dusk hung over The Valley, but Boyd wasn't able to compare it to anything.

Inside, Sonny had made himself a TV dinner and was watching *The Evening Star Wrap-up*. Where's Mom? he said. Have you kept up with the news?

Boyd sat on the floor in front of the TV in lotus position. A military band was in the middle of oom-pahing a rendition of *Sunrise Gold*, accompanied by a soprano in a gold lame gown. She belted out the refrain:

Nothing bought and nothing sold
Can match The Valley's sunrise gold.

Boyd realized he should be standing at attention, but neither he nor Sonny rose to honor The Valley Anthem before it ended in a drum roll. The camera panned to a podium outside the arched portico of Sandstone Manse—commonly known as SM—originally The Valley's central post office, which had been converted into Guv'na Brush's living quarters.

The drum roll went on and on. Someone, probably a reporter, was heard in the background, saying, For the cry eye, where is he? Another voice, a woman's, mumbled, He had to go potty.

Finally, a pudgy mustached man who looked like a mortician, stepped up to the podium, surrounded by bumblebee-striped uniformed guards in mirrored sunglasses from the Guv'na's Bureau of Protection.

Ahem, said the mustached man, good evening. Fellow Valleyites, I regret to say that Guv'na Brush is unable to attend tonight's news conference. I've been asked to make an announcement and answer your questions.

Who's he? Sonny asked.

Clarence Crabbe, said Boyd. He's the Guv'na's spokesman.

I stand here before you tonight on the doorstep

of SM on the eve of auspicious events. I'm sure that, 'hem, everyone knows that yesterday's sandstorm was responsible for Yellow Alert Damage Assessments in Cactus Vale and Teepee Village. Twenty-nine moped-vac detachments of Sandstorm Troopers have been deployed and, thank Guv'na Brush, the situation is in control east of Rattlers Parish. But what you might not know is that two Looters were sighted at the golf course southeast of Rattlers Parish today. An eyewitness described them as *hateful, heckish snakes.* According to this, 'hem, witness, long a trusted confrère of the Guv'na's, the two Looters were—and I quote—*hanging around the fringes of the fairway near the first hole, looking for trouble.* The witness, a physician, said they looked as though they were suffering—quote, unquote—*mal de mer.* He sent his son-in-law, a strapping young Rattlers Parishioner, on a chase, hoping to capture—and again I quote—*the two scruffy bums.* Alas, the young man's pursuit was unsuccessful. But here is my main point: precisely at the moment that the young man returned to his father-in-law, our witness said that The Valley was wracked with tremors before being split by an earthquake of more than modest magnitude. Our witness says he himself then took off, brandishing his best putting iron, in pursuit of the *Bohémiens,* the *Pillards* who had caused the seismic events. Unfortunately, he had to give up after a few kilometers, foxed by some tricky ravines. On behalf of our leader, I declare the entire eastern reaches of The Valley to be in a state of Yellow Alert. As of tonight, I ask that citizens of Rattlers Parish, Cactus Vale, and Teepee Village stay home whenever possible. It may well be necessary to impose a curfew in upcoming days. For now, I ask your, 'hem, patience, fortitude, and your determination to—

never crush—

—Guv'na Brush!

These last words were delivered antiphonally by a raucous chorus of hundreds of spectators crowding the plaza outside of Sandstone Manse.

Wow, Sonny said, that sure was something! But who's the guy he keeps calling 'hem?

By now Clarence Crabbe was busy hemming and hawing with reporters, answering their questions.

No, not ill, just some, 'hem, momentary problem.

No, Mick's Comestibles has never been responsible for diarrhea.

No, I think I can categorically deny that the Guv'na is, as you say, suffering from hysteria. He is in perfect control of his bowels—'hem, I mean his duties. He knows what's going on, and

He's here to protect us from falling,
For that is his God-given calling.

Wow, Sonny said, Buv'na Grush is like God.

Before anyone could do anything about it, an unsightly drunk wobbled behind the podium where Clarence Crabbe was pontificating. Say, Buster, the drunk man slurred, who d'ya think you are?

He barely got these words out before a pack of uniformed guards in sunglasses from the Guv'na's Bureau of Protection wrestled him to the ground and dragged him away.

Boyd turned off the TV. He wasn't hungry.

Where do you think your mother is? he said.

Later that night he thought he heard Dolly in the kitchen; as a newlywed she had loved to whistle melodic bits from a prewar song they'd learned from Grandma B, *Dune Buggy*. Dolly had also been good at imitating the cry of birds. From the rasping hiss of a barn owl to the *cheh-cheh-cheh-cheh* of a cactus wren, she could translate what she heard into audible calls. Well, here she seemed to be peeping and trilling like a song sparrow again as she had that night long ago when they Down-in-the-Mouthed and Rear-Doored on a stretch of open desert under the evening star.

Too soon he realized the song sparrow was just the wind whistling through some chinks in the kitchen window frames. Sonny had done his homework, written out the First Ten *Articles of Deliberation* and recited the early history of Camp Wonderful to his father—until Boyd yawned, not, he said, because he was bored, but because it had been a hard day. His stomach ached with worry about Dolly, who had never been away this late. What if a Looter had ambushed her on the road back from Windmill City? What if a gang of *Pillards*, as Grandpa A called them, had slit her throat, stolen her moped, and left her to rot? He visualized her in a bloody heap alongside a road somewhere north of Teepee Village. By morning the vultures and ravens would have done their work.

He lay in bed, tossing, listening to the wind's whistle turn into a howl. One minute his eyes fixed on the shabby bedroom curtains, the next minute it was thirteen winters ago in Dolly's condo the day she introduced him to her father.

After their customary greetings, Boyd had said he was pleased to meet Grandpa A, whom he then referred to as *Dr. Stone.*

Enchanté, the old man had crooned. And what do you do for a living, young man?

W-well, sir, Boyd had stammered, I used to teach a class in photography at Bee Rush Academy in Teepee Village.

Dr. Stone's gaze shifted to his daughter. From then on, his eyes never returned to Boyd, which was uncanny. It was as though Dr. Stone were speaking to Dolly, yet he directed his questions to Boyd.

You're aware, I'm sure, that Guv'na Brush is gradually phasing out photography?

Y-yes, sir, but I thought I—

You understand, no doubt, that Desert Center has not been pleased with the way the arts have distorted reality?

Y-yes, sir, but—

Très bien, then what should a good papa like myself do when his daughter Dorothy decides she is in love with an artist?

But sir, Dolly has always enjoyed doing sculpture.

Oui, monsieur, despite the trepidations that my late wife and I always had about this.

As far as my teaching, it was just one class. Since then I've been able to freelance—

I understand there is still an interest in the arts. Although I personally can't see why anyone would trade a real sand dune for a photograph or a sculpture, I see that some people crave reproductions. To be frank with you, young man, I crave grandchildren. Now that you have declared your intentions, *peut-d'etre* Dorothy will oblige. Considering this, considering that you may grant me even so much as one grandchild, I'm willing to do whatever I may to advance your career, as well as my daughter's.

The old man, who really wasn't much more than middle-aged back then, continued to stare at his daughter. Boyd could hear him wheeze, as if he were stifling a sob, when he said, Well, what do you think of that, Doll Baby?

Just as the curtains in Dr. Stone's condo had

whooshed in the breeze—

—Now Boyd's eyes sprang open when Dolly tiptoed into their bedroom. After her customary ablutions, she turned off the bathroom light and crept under the covers. Much as he tried to feign sleep, breathing evenly, faking a snort, he couldn't mistake the faint aroma of perfume. Dolly's favorite scent, Cactus Flower, had long acted as an aphrodisiac on him. But this was something different. Despite her sitz bath, Dolly *emanated strange*—a phrase he had learned from his grandmother. Was it the odor of lemons? It made him think of an abandoned grove east of Cactus Vale on a freakish, humid day.

Mmmf, he said. W-welcome back, Dolly! What time is it?

I can't see the clock, she said.

I wondered where you were.

Nowhere. Just working late at Windmill City.

How's it going up there? Any earthquake damage?

Not much. We were fifty kilometers from the epicenter.

How's your clay work on Old Forty-nine coming?

It's coming, she said. I'll tell you one thing, your friend Hayes is a fusspot.

Really? He invited me up there. Said I could photograph the mills.

Make sure you let me know before you come, all right?

Sure, Boyd said.

Anyway, your friend has been gabbing.

About what, for Brush's sake?

He's been yakking to the Boss about I don't know what. And lately the Boss has given me the evil eye.

Hmmph, maybe I'll drive up, check things out.

Make sure you let me know beforehand, OK?

Sure, Boyd said.

All at once, as if someone said, *That's that!* Dolly rolled over onto her side away from Boyd.

Goodnight, he said.

She didn't respond. From the sound of things—authentic snorts—she was asleep.

Saturday

Rain fell during the night. He could hear it on the roof and in the drip-dropping inside a bucket he'd placed on the kitchen floor. The ceiling had leaked for winters, but rain wasn't a major problem in The Valley. Dolly and Boyd had used their Bees for other things than roof repair.

After his morning wash-up Boyd stumbled into the kitchen to find Sonny fiddling with a couple of his sand pails, looking up at the water-damaged ceiling panels, manipulating his pails so that they were directly underneath two leaks.

Dorning, Mad.

Where's your mother? Boyd said.

I don't know. Did she make it home last night? Maybe the rain kept her up at the mills.

I guess so. Well, what do you think of this weather?

It's pretty much stopped raining.

Boyd glanced out the window. The sky looked like a great gray bowl of chicken consommé.

Aw, Sonny said, I was hoping we'd drive up to see the tailroad racks today.

Well, what do you think?

Oh please, Dad, please! You promised we'd go up there today.

Uh-huh. You've been pestering me for weeks to see the tracks.

Yeah, I've never seen them up close, only in your pictures.

Boyd thought of *Rusted Rails in Sunlight* and *Hear the Train Blow*. He thought of his Leica wearing its lens cap in its timeworn leather case.

Yeah, Sonny said, it hardly ever rains like this. I mean, I know it's stopped raining, but this is great weather for my skin.

Boyd thought of photos he could take: *Rain on the Roadbed; Stop Look Listen: Rainfall.*

He winked at Sonny: But what about school? Didn't you study for Mrs. Kissman's test last night?

Aw, c'mon, Dad, you know it's a weekend. There's no school today. I was just studying to get a good grade on Mrs. Kissman's test on Monday.

Monday, Boyd thought. It sounded like *Mindy.*

Well, Sonny, why don't you have some Breakfast Chicken a la Brush before we hit our kickstands. I'll just stick with tea.

Soon they were outside, revving their mopeds. Boyd warmed his up with an impressive *vroom.* Sonny followed suit, shouting something about the winter cold. Bundled into lion skin sweaters and leg wear, they looked like overgrown cougars—with two legs and without fangs, of course.

It was still so early that the big dogs in Rattlesnake Alley must have been asleep when they mopeded past. Only one tiny chihuahua yapped at Sonny, who sent the dog flying with one of his desert boots.

Wow, Sonny said, listen to it shriek!

Boyd fingered his cowlick. He thought of Myrna, who probably shrieked *Ai ai* in pain the day Looters attacked her tent.

Easy does it, Sonny. You could've killed that pooch.

Naw, I just laught it a tesson. Poy, this blace sure smells!

It was true, the black smoke that wafted from the tops of broken-down wickiups stank. In private, Grandpa A might've referred to this smell as *merde*, but Boyd didn't know enough about language to describe what came over him. His travels north of town often took him through Rattlesnake Alley, and he'd never been able to dispel a certain feeling. In a combination of sadness and joy he'd risen above the stink and squalor of families who never emerged from their huts, except to beg in Ye Olde Towne Square—or pilfer during the wee hours. In all his winters he'd never seen a person tend a single cactus or walk a dog on a leash in Rattlesnake Alley. Ordinarily, there were canines aplenty, but this morning the place could have been a ghost town.

Wow! Sonny said, once they reached the outskirts. Already the stench gave way to the tang of sagebrush after the rain. The hardpan road lay before them, a straightaway that headed north in a steady incline. They twisted their handlebars to full throttle and whizzed past soaptree yuccas as tall as signposts and billboard photomurals of Guv'na Brush in his cowboy hat, with his combination smile-sneer.

After about five kilometers the billboards and signposts began to thin out. Even Guv'na Brush lacked the resources to fill hundreds of square kilometers with his image. Everything fell away: Boyd's worries about Dolly, Hayes's invitation to photograph the mills, his appointment with Mrs. Kissman later that afternoon—the whole Monster Vac of apprehension whirled up and away like a plague of sand flies as he and Sonny sped over the desert floor festooned with wildflowers that had sprouted overnight in the rain. When the steady incline steepened, Boyd thought he might have to pedal the final meters before the hill crested. But behold! Sonny and Boyd's engines barely coughed, managing to carry them to the hillcrest—

—where they pitched into a stiff north wind and let themselves coast down a slope as steady as the one they'd ascended, past chaparral from which a couple of long-tailed quails made a sharp, metallic *pit-pit* and burst upward with whirring wings. Boyd had sighted wild turkeys and partridges in this area, once a popular hunting ground for Guv'na Brush and his cronies. But neither Boyd nor Sonny was prepared for the family of collared lizards that scurried across the road in front of their mopeds.

Wow, Sonny yelled, we must jissed them!

After a while the road leveled, and they returned to full throttle.

Dad, I've never been, well, I've never been so happy.

Me, too, Sonny, Boyd lied. He was happy now, but he'd been happier. No need to be a fusspot and spoil the boy's illusion that his dad had never been happier. If only Boyd had been old enough to get to know his own father. If only Old Man Boyd and he had set out on an excursion like this. Maybe that would have been what Myrna had once called The Height of Happiness. She'd talked like this one afternoon late, after they'd made love. She'd said that, as far as she was concerned, what they'd just done had constituted The Height of Happiness. He'd nodded and said *Affirmative* like a military man. But in his heart he knew that moment was no pinnacle. He'd been happier the day his sister and he had purchased his camera from Jersey. He'd been happier in his darkroom, developing photos, finding one or two, out of dozens, that had been outstanding. Mopeding alongside Sonny, he couldn't remember the titles of his best photos. He felt a glow, though, a glittering in his veins.

During the long up-and-down straightaway not one moped passed them in the opposite lane. They had the road to themselves; when they putt-putted up a hill, Boyd remembered the word *highway*. When they coasted down past sand dunes and prickly pears, he thought of the word *freeway*. Not that these words had credibility in everyday parlance. Yet somehow they seemed as right as rain.

In fact, it had started to drizzle, and the gray clouds had begun to descend by the time they reached the train tracks. Boyd put down his kickstand, but Sonny was so excited that he let his moped fall to the ground before dashing to the rails.

Look at 'em, Dad! They're all rusty. I never thought there'd be mesquite and stuff growing up through the ties.

Sonny stared east at Mount Marvelous and west toward the Great Ravine and Desert Center beyond it, while Boyd busied himself with his light meter—it looked to be a four f-stop day. The snowline on Mount Marvelous seemed to be lower this morning, because of last night's rain. The gray stone cliffs at the mountain's base blended into evergreens a little more than halfway up; then the trees grew a sheepskin coat of snow that wrapped them snugly all the way to the domed summit. If he'd been five kilometers closer and used his telephoto lens, Boyd fancied that he'd have been able to catch the muted morning sunlight on the mountain's west side, turning the white slope into a kaleidoscope of sparkles. Like a boulder encrusted with mica, the mountain would gleam, despite the overcast—just as he hoped Dolly would look at herself in the mirror one day and brighten up.

While Boyd fiddled with his rangefinder, Sonny stooped and put his ear to one of the rails. Gee, Dad, I saw on a TV documentary that in the olden days people would listen like this, and they could hear a train rumbling far away.

That's right, Sonny. But that was long ago. Nothing comes this way anymore.

But listen! Come over here and listen! I think I hear something.

Boyd stooped alongside his son, who, Boyd noticed, had stopped using spoonerisms. Now Boyd could hear it, too, a thrum, more like the distant buzzing of bees than the hum of rolling stock. He'd been looking east, but now he stood and studied the two pairs of rails as they stretched westward in four straight lines to the base of the Great Ravine. He let his eyes rise with the tracks toward Desert Center. Then he followed them back down again into The Valley, and all he could see were sand dunes and salt flats. But no, there was something—

Have a look over there, Sonny. I've been using a camera too long. Are my eyes fooling me? He was pointing to the tail end of a moraine, a tidbit of scree west of where The Elephant Hills met The Valley floor.

Yeah, I see. What is it?

Looks like a tiny dust storm.

Funny to see dust in the rain.

But it's hardly raining, Boyd said. And you know how dry it's been until last night. The ground's still dry.

Who cared? The dust storm—or whatever—was no fewer than fifteen kilometers away. Boyd turned to Sonny and said, In the olden days huge trains hauled freight back and forth. Your Aunt Mindy once told me about a passenger train called the Super Chief; people could sleep on it in little Pullman rooms with lavatories. They could have meals in a dining car. Your great-grandmother once said her grandmother told her she and her husband had ridden something called the Twentieth Century Limited, and every man who was a passenger was given a carnation to wear in his buttonhole. Women were given tiny bottles of perfume.

Aw, c'mon, Dad, you're kidding!

Well, Grandma B might've been fibbing, but she told me her grandmother had said riding a train was like sitting as pretty as can be, presiding over the land that whipped past while you watched behind safety-glass windows and the wheels clickety-clacked over the rails like a desert birdsong that wouldn't stop until you reached a switch where one set of rails intersected with another. Then the clickety-clack would turn into a rumble-dee-dum. And whenever a train passed in the other direction, its whistle suddenly dropped from a high-pitched squeal to a low roar, and the rolling stock that rushed past glued you to your window for hardly any time at all because the other train was more than a kilometer long, but the combined speed of the two trains passing one another was three hundred kph.

Dad, are you making this up?

She told me her grandmother was aboard a train once called the Cannonball Express, where an escaped convict moved between cars like a bobcat. None of the passengers knew he had crept aboard, and he blended into the crowd. In those days rich people slept in private roomettes, but your great-great-great-grandmother and her husband were poor. My Grandma B told me that your triple-great-grandfather was a blacksmith who became a taxicab driver way back when automobiles replaced horses. You've seen automobiles on *The Ancient History Channel*, haven't you?

Yeah, they had four wheels and smoked up the place.

Well, your triple-great-grandpa eventually learned to drive what they called an Ess You Vee; I'm not sure what that means, but long before this he'd been looking for a chauffeur's job far from home. They ate in the dining car and slept in their seats in the coach section of the Cannonball Express for two nights, and the second night they heard the woman behind their seat cry out; then her voice turned all bubbly, and when they looked behind them they saw that her throat had been slit.

Dad, that dust cloud, it seems to be getting closer.

Aw, c'mon, Sonny. You must be—

But Sonny wasn't kidding. Boyd focused his tele-photo lens on something—was it a mirage? Gray dust floated above a spot about ten kilometers away. The drizzle was turning into a light rain as the sky dark-ened.

Without a word, they mounted their mopeds and took off east over the open desert. At first dodging bushes and shrubs, gunning their bikes to full throttle seemed like fun. Their mopeds' wheels grabbed hold of the damp sand as they reached a speed of twenty kph, kicking up a modest spray of dust despite the wetness. They disturbed a herd of Wild Valley Nags grazing, munching wildflowers, before they took off at a gallop; the spotted lead nag looked ornery, Boyd thought, when it tossed its head back over its mane in his direction and nickered, showing its teeth.

He looked back at the dust cloud, which seemed to be gaining headway. He wanted to nicker, to neigh like a stallion.

Before long they met up with an east-west hard-pan road Boyd had never encountered in his Valley rambles. Now there were no obstacles in their path. They gunned their engines and lengthened their lead on whatever was behind them. As they hurtled past the ground cover, Mount Marvelous slowly seemed to approach. The tall towers and steel blades of Windmill City loomed. At this distance the mills looked like nightmare pinwheels that could slice your head off. There were too many to count, and already he could see their blades spinning, glinting in the hit-or-miss sun.

Look, he said.

Yeah, Sonny said. I've never seen them up close.

In the central Quonset hut Hayes greeted them at the front desk:

Ho, Boyd, ho, Sonny!

Ho, Hayes!

How's Dolly?

How's Willy?

Never fear—

—Guv'na Brush is here!

After they exchanged high-fives, Hayes walked them into a windowless room with a worktable. On it sat an unfinished clay model of a windmill.

Where's Dolly? Boyd said. Sonny began to shiver—was he coming down with the flu?

No, Hayes said, I asked you first: *How's Dolly?* I thought you might know.

Boyd could hear a thunderclap outside. You mean she's not here?

No, not here, Hayes said. Sonny began to shudder.

Where's Mom?

I wouldn't know, said Hayes. She didn't show up for work today. Neither did Suzy. I don't usually sit in the front office, pretending to be a receptionist! Boss asked me to sit out there as a special favor. A *special favor*, he said, like I don't do special favors for him every day.

Hayes made a sucking sound as if he wanted to spit out a plug of tobacco. I clean up after him, I keep track of wind speeds and mega-wattage, I climb up inside those big birds and turn their wings on and off. I mean, what more does he want from me? Let him raise me to twenty-five Bees an hour, and I'll wash his durn persnickety underwear! But you didn't bring Sonny along to hear me gab. You wanna go take pictures. It's not the best weather—hoo, listen to that thunder—but Boss has a pair of slickers you could borrow if you've a mind to shoot Old Forty-nine. Nice bird she is, especially in this wind.

No, it's bad weather for shooting, Hayes. If it's OK with you, could Sonny and I just sit back here and wait out the storm? Look at him, he's feverish.

Boyd knew this was not true, but Hayes quickly departed, after customary goodbyes with high-fives.

Boyd found a workbench and sat Sonny down beside him. He put his arm around the boy, but he couldn't find anything to say. They huddled like that until the storm passed.

Outside, they found their mopeds soaked but still leaning on their kickstands. Whoever had followed them was nowhere to be seen. Maybe the whole incident was an illusion. Maybe it was a nightmare, and they were still asleep under their blankets in Rattlers Parish. Maybe the word *maybe* accounted for everything under the sun. Although clouds still hung over The Valley, here and there chinks of sunlight said *maybe*.

On their ride back home, they stopped at a Broil Station to fill up their bikes. They lunched in Cactus Vale; Boyd had chicken livers, and Sonny had *Cuisse de Poulet*, an adventurous choice, considering that he usually preferred deep-fried nuggets. As they neared Rattlers Parish when Sonny said it would be good to get home and see his mother, Boyd thought of The Big Maybe, and when he opened the front door to his condo and shouted, *Dolly?* the silence was no surprise.

At least Sonny had stopped shuddering. As though he knew the truth would eventually set him free— but at what cost Boyd couldn't imagine—the boy rode off in the afternoon sun to play nine holes of miniature golf with his friend Jilly. They had met like this on Saturday afternoons for the past few weeks, and there was no reason they shouldn't meet today, even if Dolly's absence may have been causing a lump in Sonny's throat that felt like a golf ball. Engrossed with the notion of uncertainty, Boyd thought that Sonny would cope with whatever happened. If The Big Maybe ruled, The Great Whatever was an inevitable corollary.

In any case, Sonny had mopeded south to meet Jilly, and Boyd was on his way north. He knew where he was going. He kicked at dogs that lunged for his ankles. He smelled the same sour odor he'd noticed earlier—and had been aware of every time he passed through Rattlesnake Alley. Today, though, a girl wearing black rags, who must have been about the same age as Sonny, was hanging what looked like grimy overalls on a clothesline. As Boyd putt-putted by, warding off a mutt, she held both hands over her head and waved to him.

He found her in the schoolyard, chucking stones at the bedraggled smoke tree just inside the barbed wire fence. She must have heard his moped in the driveway, but she continued hurling small rocks, the way women throw things, distinctively, with a stiff elbow—so that she looked like an awkward warrior, hardly capable of stoning a Looter. She had abandoned her olive-drab uniform for a tight-fitting denim jacket and blue jeans, with desert boots. Hardly military, Boyd thought.

He let down his kickstand, parked his moped beside her bicycle, and pulled at his cowlick. While continuing to pitch stones, they exchanged greetings:

Ho, Mr. Boyd.

Ho, Mrs. Kissman.

How's Sonny?

How's Mr. Kissman?

Never fear. Guv'na Brush—

—is here!

After they exchanged high-fives, he picked up a fair-sized rock and flung it, knocking off a branch.

Oh my gosh, he said. I didn't mean to do that.

She dropped the stone she was set to throw and led him to the school door. She used her key and let the door groan open. The sound sent a shudder through his mountain lion skin leg wear.

I've been waiting for you, she said, as they made their way into the teachers' lounge.

I'm sorry. Sonny and I got caught in a thunderstorm. I'm late.

Yes, I could see thunderheads over Windmill City from here; we got only a sprinkle.

She put a kettle on the propane stove, moistened her lips with her tongue, and fingered one of the gold buttons on her denim jacket. While we're waiting for the water to boil, why don't I show you something.

Yes, why not? he said.

She used her key to open a closet door he hadn't seen. It was a small door, perhaps a mini–broom closet, no more than a meter high, tucked between a trashcan and someone's rusted-out bicycle leaning against the wall.

From the closet she removed a rolled-up document that looked like a scroll. Unwinding it flat-out on the stained carpet, she started humming a tune.

What's that you're humming? he said.

Oh, it's a very old song, *Don't Fence Me In.*

It's catchy.

Yes, she said, unrolling the colorful whatsamajiggy. By setting four heavy pots of ficus trees on its curling edges, she was able to stand back without it rolling up like a window shade.

There, she said, have a look.

He studied it, a rectangle that measured approximately one-by-two meters. Sky-blue segments edged the left, right, and bottom, with five blue blotches toward the middle, but the center was more interesting. Divided into segments of all shapes and sizes, each of which had a separate color—tan, violet, yellow-green, and so forth—the whole thing gave the impression of being the blueprint for a shield, some sort of armor you would use to ward off an antagonist. The bottom right had a small tail that stuck out into another blue blotch—maybe this tail was a sexual organ; if so, it would be hardly adequate for Down-in-the-Mouthing. The top right-hand portion of the chart also ended with a protuberance, as did the lower middle, which dipped low, though not so embarrassingly as the bottom right.

The only words on the multicolored thingamabob

were printed over the five blue blotches toward the center: *The Great Lakes*. The whole thing was probably a jigsaw puzzle someone had made into a design for a buckler to be used by a person looking for water.

He stood back but couldn't stop gazing at it. It's pretty, he said.

Yes, I agree.

What is it?

I'm not sure. But look at this one.

Still humming *Don't Fence Me In,* she removed another rolled-up scroll from the closet. This one was much smaller, so she used little cactus pots to hold down its edges. Words studded this scroll, and he recognized it.

Here we are, she said, pointing to more or less the middle of the bottom half. And here's Mount Marvelous to the east. West of the mountain, he could make out the words *Teepee Village* and *Cactus Vale,* below two crosshatched black lines that stretched across *The Valley* to *The Great Ravine* split by what looked like an arrow, a *gravel road* that pointed west to *Desert Center* and *Camp Wonderful* to the southwest, where a smaller *gravel road* skirted the *Camp*.

Again, he couldn't stop gazing—at the *golf course*, *Windmill City*, even a straight line below the words *10 kilometers*. The whole printed version of *The Valley* wasn't as colorful as the big scroll with *The Great Lakes*, but he could make sense of the small scroll.

Hmmph, he said, why haven't I seen this Valley thingamajig before now?

Against Guv'na Brush's orders.

But what about the other one?

Against Guv'na Brush's orders. This closet has stayed locked for as long as I've been here, until a few days ago after you visited, when I decided to take a peek. Winters ago when Mr. Heetclit gave me a skeleton key to the school, he made me promise never to open this door.

I wonder why. There's nothing bad about this stuff.

I agree. And I think Mr. Heetclit also agrees. But he made me promise—*Swear,* he said, *you must swear upon the Bible and the* Guv'na's Good Book *never never to open the closet!*

Hmmph, you're an amazing woman, Mrs. Kissman.

Call me Cathy, she said. What's your first name?

He told her. Bill Boyd, she said. That has a nice sound. It reminds me of someone.

Cathy Kissman sure makes my ears ring.

Ha ha! It's funny you should think so. So does Mr. Heetclit. But my maiden name's not Kissman. I've never thought of myself as a Kissman. My husband works for Mick's Comestibles in Desert Center. He used to be a jeweler until Guv'na Brush cracked down on

> *Bad ornaments that would make us fools:*
> *Bracelets, necklaces, all jewels.*

Yet I see you're wearing a wedding ring—as I am.

Well, that's an exception. But, I don't know, ever since Johnny started working up at Desert Center, he's been worse than ever. I don't think of myself as a Kissman.

What's your maiden name?

If you really want to know, it's Vallée.

V*a*l*l*e*y? he said, spelling the word.

No, V*a*l*l*é*e, but it sounds the same as v*a*l*l*e*y.

That's strange.

Minutes ago the kettle had whistled; now the tea had steeped long enough. She filled both of their cups and motioned him over to a tattered couch. She sipped tea and crossed her legs before speaking:

My parents used to get together with the Kissmans on Saturday afternoons to play golf. Old Man Kissman was a jeweler, and my father worked night shift for *The Evening Star Wrap-up*. For some reason the Kissmans and the Vallées got along, especially on the links. One fine Saturday afternoon—my mother told me the weather was *delicious*—they came up with an idea. At that time Johnny and I were still in school. He knew he wanted to take over his dad's business; with his manual dexterity and a flair for jewelry design, he knew he could set up shop in Ye Olde Towne Square. I thought I wanted to be a dancer, but my father sat me down one day and said, *Cathy, you can be anything you want to be, but let's face it, being a dancer is tough.* I agreed, but I told him I was tough; my body was sturdy. I biked to school, I cleaned house, and took care of a large garden where we grew beans, squash, and melons—during the days when private kitchen gardens were permitted.

Obviously, my father prevailed. I still plié and pirouette in private, and I love to sing. I can't tell you how much I love to sing. But you see what's become of me. Not that I loathe teaching. Despite old Mr. Heetclit on bad-mood days, I love watching Sonny come out of his shell and quit using spoonerisms. I love listening to Jilly's questions about the evening star.

My parents died in the Pneumonia Plague sixteen winters after the Fourth War of Excision, but not before Johnny and I were married in The Little Church on the Square. We honeymooned in a cabin off a dirt road on the north slope of the Great Ravine. Even then, my husband was a bit of a fusspot. He was always, *Cathy-this, Cathy-that.* I was either fetching his tea or ironing his pillowcase. He asked me to smuggle paper from the school supply room; he asked me to get Mr. Heetclit to put in a good word for him at Desert Center.

Cathy Vallée removed a hairbrush from her purse. First on one side, then the other, she brought the brush down her bowl-shaped flame-red coif. Her tresses reached the nape of her neck and the line of her jaw. Once again, Boyd wanted to whip out his Leica and shoot her over and over, but, alas, he'd forgotten to bring his camera. The sound of her grooming, straightening the part in her hair directly above her left eye, reminded him of Mindy standing before a mirror in the bathroom. But Cathy Vallée didn't need a mirror. He hadn't seen her use cosmetics, though her cheeks glowed and her lips seemed to sparkle when she moistened them. She plumped her hair with her hands and removed a small book from her purse.

This belonged to my great-grandmother, she said. Come closer, look at her handwriting.

Boyd scooted over until he could feel her tight thigh muscles against his own; at the precise instant they met, a shock of static electricity startled them both. Despite the lack of heat in the lounge, he fingered the mole on his left cheek and felt feverish.

The book reeked of mildew. Its cover had been separated from its binding, and its first page squiggled and squirmed. Can you read this or should I try it aloud? she said.

He shrugged his shoulders.

Well, then, she said and started to read aloud:

August 9, 1974: Today I woke up thinking of myself as an old lady. Yesterday at my thirteenth birthday party Grandma C said I was getting to be "a real beauty"— her exact words. She gave me two Barbie dolls, a Liza

Minelli T-shirt, and this book. Dear diary, I don't know how to tell you how happy I've been with Mom and Dad back together and Aunt Jocelyn raising a toast to them, "May they live happily ever after!" On TV we watched the 37th President of the United States and his wife step into a helicopter, make his Vee-for-Victory sign with the fore- and middle-fingers of both hands, and leave the White House forever. Well, that was cause for celebration. There's so much to be thankful for: the end of that horrid war in southeast Asia, the hilarious "streaking" craze that's driving college students to dash around in the buff, the wildness of that sculptor Joseph Beuys who came to the United States and fenced himself in for a week with a live coyote at his art gallery. These are exciting times, but I was most excited to learn about my own past. For all these years I've had a hankering to sing. I've liked the Osmonds, the Captain and Tenille; I've especially loved Joan Baez and Joni Mitchell—but where does all this come from? My being a New Yorker? No, Laura and Sondra tell me it's more than that. They're from the Big Apple, too, but they don't obsess about music like me. Well, last night I think I found out. Grandma C drew me away from the living room for a minute to tell me that Dad's French-Canadian side of the family, the Vallées, is related to a famous singer of the 1920s—I never even heard of him, but he has our last name. Dear diary, his first name was Rudy.

She looked up from the book. Well, what do you think?

I don't know what to think, Boyd said. I don't understand it.

I don't understand it completely either—my mother never said a word to me about her grandmother—but it sounds vivid, doesn't it?

Boyd shrugged his shoulders.

What I really like is my great-grandmother's use of *August 9, 1974*. I've heard the word *august* refer to Guv'na Brush, but what could this mean?

It's probably some sort of mood.

It's not a place, because my great-grandma mentions *New York*; I think that's a place.

Maybe it's a time frame, Boyd said. Like, you know, when *The Evening Star Wrap-up* mentioned the sandstorm occurred on Thursday.

Yes, but who needs to know anything more about the storm's time frame than that? It happened the day before yesterday on Thursday, just as The Valley Quickshake happened yesterday on Friday.

And my sister Mindy has been gone since she was kidnapped by Looters seventeen winters ago.

And my parents came down with their first bouts of pneumonia, so my mother told me, because of the Fourth War of Excision's lingering effects.

So it is with war, he said.

So it is with war!

Now that they'd expressed customary condolences, Boyd sipped his tea. As usual, it sparked a certain feeling in him.

Apparently, Cathy Vallée felt it, too. She closed her great-grandmother's book, put down her teacup and turned toward Boyd. She was staring straight at him with half-shut, slitted eyes as if it she were in a trance.

Bill, she said.

He leaned over and touched his lips to hers. They embraced, and she put her tongue in his mouth. No one had ever done this, and Boyd wasn't prepared for it. As their bodies pressed together, he let her explore his tongue, his mouth's ridged roof, the palate and uvula way back in his throat—until he thought he might gag. Instead, he relaxed and reciprocated with his tongue, rooting and roaming. He felt her flame-redness infuse him from his desert boots, up through his lion skin leg wear and his sweater, to the top of his head. He was afire with her smell, the taste of tea in her mouth as he tongued the inside of her cheeks, delving underneath her tongue and touching the soft spot on her *front floor,* rubbing it to produce saliva that mixed with his own in a dozen slippery undulations like nothing he'd ever felt—as his hands fumbled with the gold buttons on her denim jacket, and hers grabbed at his brass belt buckle before giving up, stroking him below the belt where he wanted to be licked, bitten by a diamondback rattlesnake, ripped asunder. He would never forget the surge of his muscles and nerves, the crazy, laughable struggle to rip off his clothes, the thought—with their lips locked together—that he would end up making love to this wasp-waisted nymph with his desert boots still on. He would always remember the sound of her moans, the groan of floorboards, and the squeak of the lounge door opening like teeth grinding when the old man hollered:

Ho, Cathy!

I said, *Ho, Cathy!!*

Later that afternoon at the swap meet he shuddered when the wind played with his cowlick. Clouds were blowing in from the west, over the Great Ravine into The Valley. He fingered the mole on his cheek and removed his camera from its case. His light meter pointed to an f-stop of eight, but things were finicky. Before long, it would register four. Nevertheless, he focused his telephoto lens on the wooded north slope of the Great Ravine, scoping for a honeymoon cabin. Oblivious to the crowds that swirled around his booth, he shot an evergreen grove he thought might be the place.

He was startled by a familiar voice:

Ho, Boyd.

Ho, Dolly.

How's Sonny?

How're you?

Never fear, Guv'na Brush—

—is here.

As they exchanged high-fives, he noticed how tired she looked, older than when he'd last seen her. Was it her unbrushed blond hair, which she'd recently cut short? Was it her cheeks, sallow without rouge, her eyes that darted from his to the crowd surrounding the booth? She'd put on weight, yet she appeared gaunt.

You're looking good as ever, she said.

You, too, he lied.

Is Sonny OK?

He's with Jilly. They went over to her house.

That's good, she said. That's really very good.

He misses you.

No, Boyd, don't tell me that.

I miss you, Boyd said.

No, please don't tell me that.

When're you coming back?

I don't know. Maybe—

But he couldn't hear the rest. The taste of hot tea and Cathy Vallée's open-mouthed kiss gave him pins and needles, and he was deaf to the swap meet. The sensation of being struck, poisoned by a wasp-waisted, forked-tongued nymph bore him on a desert wind toward The Great Ravine. Just as abruptly the squeak of the school lounge door opening like teeth grinding brought him back to the principal hunched in the doorway, his walking stick upraised, his voice rough as a gravel pit. His scarred face had been contorted, and when he barked out an order that they stop what they were doing, smoke seemed to issue from his ears, and he looked as though he might fall to the floor weeping in a rage.

How could you do this to me? he'd stormed.

When he saw the open closet door and the charts unrolled on the carpet, he used his walking stick to hobble over to a folding chair in the corner.

How can you do this, Cathy? he murmured. If Boyd had ever needed a photo titled *Crestfallen,* here it was in this old man collapsed in a chair.

What am I to do now? he said. What good would it do me to report you? What good would it do me to let you get away with this?

Never once had he taken his eyes off Cathy Vallée. Rumpled, blushing red as her flame-red hair, she appeared to shrink down on the couch.

Finally, he seemed to recognize Boyd, who'd buttoned his sweater wrong, so that it was lopsided. The old man pointed at Boyd, while still staring at Cathy Vallée, and said, And who's this dude, Cathy? A lumberjack straight from the olden days?

Much later, Boyd would connect these events—saying goodbye to Dolly and being caught by Mr. Heetclit— as a photographer connects the end of one exhibition with the beginning of another. Truth to tell, a continuum wedded one experience to the next, just as every event in his life, from the day of his birth thirty winters ago, had been linked to where he was standing now. Winters later he would see through the notion of immortality, the lie that the white dots in the night sky were the eyes of Guv'na Brush's loyal followers after their death. He would gaze at the not-really-invisible celestial white object changing shape, larger than the evening star, and he would say its name. For now, he felt like a man with a ring on every finger, connected to The Big Maybe and The Great Whatever. For all he knew, the mole on his left cheek was a dark evening star to make a wish on. The cowlick he could never brush down stood for something, just as the part of him that stiffened below his belt stood for something else.

That night over TV dinners Sonny and Boyd watched *The Evening Star Wrap-up*. The reporter made no announcement that a *lumberjack* was on the loose in Rattlers Parish.

Where's Mom? Sonny said, though his tone of voice seemed to know.

Boyd compacted the metal plates to be recycled. How was it with Jilly?

She beat me at giniature molf. Then we went to her house to watch TV.

Anything interesting?

Actually, we weren't matching wuch.

Oh?

Jilly's mom was at her cook blub, discussing *The Book of Esther*.

That's nice. Did you have a snack?

Dad, I don't know how to say this. Mom's not here, and she's probably not coming back. Not that I could tell her, but—

What's on your mind, Son?

Sonny had begun to tremble, as he had earlier.

What's up, Sonny?

Oh, I don't know, Dad. Everything so— It's just so— Did you ever, like—? When you were my age, did you ever kiss—?

I was twelve, your age, when I first kissed a girl.

Really?

Well, I'd kissed your Aunt Mindy and my grandma. I'd given a birthday kiss to someone. But I was twelve when a girl named Ginny and I mopeded out to a date palm grove and necked one afternoon. I don't know how we did it without being seen. All I remember is kissing Ginny, lying on my back, and looking up at the palm trees. Those clusters of dates sure looked sweet way up high. They looked like little brown babies, and I sure wanted to photograph them. This was before Guv'na Brush leveled the grove to make a chicken farm—The Cockerel, you know, south of Rattlers Parish. He'd always preferred poultry, and one night on *The Evening Star Wrap-up* a spokesman said,

Don't waste yourselves on figs and dates!
Be chicken-eaters and be greats!

What happened to Ginny?

I don't know. She moved away. Maybe she was killed in the Wars.

So it is with war, Sonny said.

So it is with war!

Sonny began to sob. Where's Mom? he said.

After Boyd tucked him in bed, he got out his camera and went into the bathroom. Other than when he washed and shaved, Boyd never paid attention to himself. Tonight, he looked at himself in the mirror. Through his Leica's viewfinder he traced his hairline, his dusky complexion, the cleft in his chin. Did he have what Dolly called *a lantern jaw*? Was the bristle of hair over his lip what Grandpa A called a *toothbrush mustache*? Were the shoulders under his T-shirt *broad*?

He had used his last flashbulb winters ago, and it was too dark in the bathroom to take a good snapshot. Still, he continued to study himself in the mirror under the florescent light, focusing and unfocusing his lens, until it was bedtime.

The imprint of Dolly's head still creased her pillow, he noted, as he slid under the covers. Tomorrow he would dispose of the rest of the nude photos he'd taken of her, but he would never be able to throw away his memories of her massaging his back with her sculptor's hands, calling him Boyd, as though he were someone she barely knew, a buckaroo. Her smell lingered in the sheets, along with the strange aroma of lemons.

Toward midnight he thought he heard Looters rummaging outside. But it was only his neighbor's wind chimes.

Sunday

Whenever he tried to brush them off, they came back and wriggled up his desert boots. It was no use kicking at these wrigglies; they continued to crawl up his ankles and legs, under his blue jeans and the ridiculous leather chaps he was wearing. The fact was, New York bore no resemblance to The Valley at all. There were no mountains surrounding a desert, no towns like Rattlers Parish. For some reason the Guv'na there—surely not the sensible Guv'na Brush—had designed the city as a monumental piece of fruit, a gigantic hollowed-out apple, in which condos and wickiups stood side by side, and Desert Center, if you could call it that, existed as an enclave near the apple's core. Instead of going to school, young people gathered around gramophones with tuba-like resonating sound horns to hear singers perform renditions of the tune, Don't Fence Me In, that sounded like a hundred staticky song sparrows peeping and trilling.

From his window inside the apple he tried to peer out at a vast prairie, which, on second thought, looked more like a salt flat. But the wrigglies inside the apple kept crawling up his legs, worming up his thighs. As fast as

114

he tried to brush them off—brush brush—*they crawled back. He couldn't spend any time studying the apple's interior, much less the surrounding countryside. All at once a horse with three heads—one that looked like Myrna, one that looked like Dolly, and one that looked like Cathy Vallée—loped outside his window in a place called The United States. Just as he was about to lean his own head far out of the casement and give each horse's face a diamondback rattlesnake's forked tongue-kiss, a wriggly made it up to his groin and bit off his penis.*

At breakfast with Sonny, his neighbor's wind chimes irritated him as never before.

You're shivering, Dad, Sonny said. He was chewing a chicken bone, actually eating it.

Boyd sipped his tea. He couldn't stop shaking. The thought of that last wriggly in the nightmare haunted him. Apples were never as common in The Valley as citrus fruit, and he believed then and there that he would always go in fear of apples.

He let out a fake sneeze. Oh, I don't know, Sonny. Maybe I caught a case of the sniffles yesterday in the rain.

Hey, that wasn't a real sneeze. You never get colds.

Well, one way or another, we're going to church today.

Maybe we'll get to see Mom sing in the choir.

That would be nice. But don't get your hopes up.

They sipped tea in silence while a breeze continued to jangle their neighbor's wind chimes; the noise seemed to be coming from everywhere.

By the time they reached church, amid the clanging of gigantic cowbells, most of the congregation had gathered on individual stone stools, which formed pews. Boyd took one of the last remaining seats in the back alongside Sonny and scoped out the congregation. He could barely see the pulpit, much less the great mass of worshippers in front of him. For a moment he mistook a redhead for—but no, that was somebody else. Mr. Heetclit was there, though; Boyd could make out his head, from which an all but imperceptible veil of steam seemed to rise as if from a simmering teakettle.

In the incense-heady air an orchestra of Jew's harps twanged, accompanied by a soloist who blew on a piece of tissue paper pressed to a comb while a women's chorus droned *A Mighty Master Is Our Brush*. Boyd had always loved the melody to this hymn, and he hummed along with it while Sonny craned to see if his mother was among the singers behind the altar. Distances tricked your eyes in The Little Church on the Square; certainly its name was deceptive. The building, constructed entirely of sandstone, was a gargantuan orange-yellow cathedral that took up two whole city blocks. Towering high enough to contain four Windmill City Old Forty-nines atop one another, long and wide enough to enclose more than two thousand individual stone stools—no one had ever counted them; to do so was forbidden—The Little Church on the Square was a marvel of gargoyles and photomurals of Guv'na Brush. Its crannied apse was said to house, among other relics, the remains of The Original Prairie Chicken tragically hunted down long ago north of The Valley. If you stood under The Great Glass Window at the back of the apse in late afternoon on Mid-winter Sunday, you could see the Prairie Chicken's meticulously preserved, mottled brownish plumage glow as if on fire. You could pray *for the lost flock in the brush.* And you could go on your errands *for the rest of your life without fear of cosmic brush-off.*

The Right Reverend Chew Lee Annie at last rose to deliver his sermon. Given the cavernous extent of the church, it rumbled with echoes—which some Rattlers Parishioners referred to as The Halo Effect. At any rate, Boyd and Sonny bowed their heads while the Right Reverend pontificated:

Our text for today, Exodus 14:21, recounts the flight of Moses from Egypt. Having arrived at the shores of the Red Sea, he reached out his hand, and the LORD caused the sea to go back by a strong east wind all that night, and made the sea dry land, and the waters were divided. Good people, this is nothing more than a foreshadowing of our leader's struggle with the forces of evil from whence he came. To be sure, he went west, not east like Moses. And he came neither with followers nor companions. Nay, he walked and rode alone to encounter rivers and hills, woodland and whatnot. Some say he came out of the bowels of insurrection and iniquity. Others say he left a place of myrrh and spices, his Egypt in the East not a place of evil—for then howsoever could he be good who came from Sin City? I say it is not for us to quibble with such intricacies, which would bend us out of shape and turn us into hunch-backed question marks. I say we should be as decisive as the dot at the bottom of the question mark. We should believe in him and aspire to be like him, a forder of rivers, a turner-back of Red Sea tides. For, the waves of annoyance that lap at us are nowise as buoyant as the salt savor of this sun-dried land. Here in The Valley we have escaped Pharaoh's enslavement. East of Mount Marvelous, west of Camp Wonderful, men and women remain chained to customs looted from the past. Only we here in The Valley look forward; we alone are free. In the name of the Guv'na, the Brush administration, and Desert Center, I say to you, Never crush—

—Guv'na Brush!

The choir intoned these last words with tremendous fervor, as if they'd never said them before, as if they were a discovery waiting in the aisles.

With tears in his eyes Sonny turned toward his father and whispered, Mom's not up there.

Outside, they joined the throng of worshippers lined up under the mid-morning sun. The smell of defrosted barbecued chicken did nothing to dispel every parishioner's pious smirk. Decked in their Sunday-best denim and cowboy boots, they schmoozed and wrenched their necks to eye Mr. Such-and-Such and Mrs. So-and-So.

She's not here, Dad, Sonny whined.

No, but look over there. That's someone we know!

The buckskin-clad oldster who approached them fingered his string tie and undid his bandana to wipe his forehead.

Glad to see you two here this morning, he said, dispensing with customary greetings. He put his arm around Sonny's shoulder and drew him close.

Bonjour, my boy! How are you today?

I'm OK, I really am. It's just that—

Don't you think I know? She's not here. This is the first time she's ever missed Sunday services.

Boyd clucked his tongue. Sir, I'm guessing you know the truth—

—*shall make you free*, he said. He lowered his voice: Or perhaps it would be better to say, *the truth that shall make us free. Bien sur*, I know what's going on. I've known what's been going on since she confided in me. She said she was powerless to resist, said she felt bad about it. I told her I felt it was the worst news I'd heard since I learned about her mother's death. I told her I hated what she was about to do with her life, with *my little family*. She wept, she begged me not to say anything, not to report her. And what kind of a person would I be if I reported my daughter? Believe me, this has tested my allegiance. As a physician, I must cure myself of this sadness.

A mousy woman, with streaks of gray in her hair, broke away from the food line and approached. She smelled faintly of lemons. Tied back in a bun, her hair, as well as her dress's prim, lacy collar, gave her the severe appearance of a woman who had been on her own for eons.

Good morning, Dr. Stone, she said. Hello, Mr. Boyd. How are you, Sonny. You don't know me, but—but I need to dispense with formalities and speak from the heart.

She was trembling, Boyd noticed. Like Sonny, like The Valley floor during the Quickshake, she was twitching. The other members of the congregation seemed to vanish.

The woman continued: Dorothy couldn't make it today, the woman continued. She wanted me to tell you that she loves you, but she couldn't face you. She may never be able to. I can't tell you what it's done to both of us. We've both been fired. I don't know how we'll manage. Any minute Guv'na Brush's troops could haul us to Desert Center. All these winters I've tried to do things right. I've even flirted with Hayes and the Boss—little good that did me! But when Dorothy stepped into the Quonset hut that first day, as a receptionist, I can truly say that I *received her.* I exchanged customary greetings, but my heart went out—

It went out, did it? the old man said. *Sacre bleu,* the heart is an organ in our chests which pumps blood to the body. It is nothing more. Young lady, what you are doing is going against Nature, not to mention Guv'na Brush. For, Guv'na Brush is merely trying to enforce Nature's laws. Besides, do you see what you have done to this boy?

She burst into sloppy tears. I see, oh, I see what I've done to Sonny.

Do you see what you've done to my son-in-law?

Oh, yes, Doctor, I see.

And what about me, an old man with a few more winters at most?

By now she had taken out a purple bandana to wipe her eyes and blow her nose. It was such a display of tears that people in the congregation munching on barbecued chicken came into focus again. They glared and gossiped loudly:

Who's she?

What's she doing with Dr. Stone?

Why's she neighing like a Wild Valley Nag?

When's she going to stop?

Where's she from, for Brush's sake?

Before anyone could answer, the Right Reverend Chew Lee Annie intervened. And how are we this morning? he boomed. I'm thankful the wind died down and the day brightened up, aren't you? I've been meaning to make an appointment to see you, Doctor—but, wait a minute, aren't you retired? My wife has this awful problem sleeping, and I thought something you could prescribe might— The thing of it is, she wakes up every night in the wee hours, lies beside me with her eyes wide open, and sobs—I'm ashamed to say it—*Rudy! Help me, Rudy!*

In the parking lot Boyd put his arm around Sonny and said, Well, now that's done, and I'm sure glad it's over.

Ho, Boyd, ho, Sonny.

Ho, Hayes.

How's Dolly?

How's Willy?

Never fear. Guv'na Brush—

—is here.

Now that they'd exchanged customary greetings with high-fives, Boyd saw Hayes in a new light. He'd shaved his beard and looked younger, neater than ever. Clad in a white shirt with a bolo tie, in chaps and cowboy boots, he was barely recognizable.

Where's Willy? Sonny said.

Home playing with his toy soldiers.

Listen, Hayes, I've been meaning to ask you some-thing, Boyd said.

I don't need to be a chicken scientist to know what's on your mind, pal, said Hayes. I asked you *How's Dolly?* and you want to know.

Well, I think I already know, Boyd said.

Yeah, Mr. Hayes, Mom's not coming back home—ever.

Then you must know the situation at Windmill City. Sheesh!

Listen, Hayes, I've been meaning to ask you if the Boss's invitation for me to shoot Old Forty-nine still stands.

Yeah, heck, it sure does still stand—just like Old Forty-nine herself! Pretty bird she is, too. It don't make no difference that Dolly's gone. Boss doesn't believe in guilt by association, if you know what I mean.

Hayes spat a wad of tobacco over both Boyd and Sonny's mopeds; it landed like a beetle on the gravel. You've got a standing invitation to come up and shoot all you want. You don't even need an appointment. Boss says to me, he says, *Just you tell that Boyd he can bring that Luca, that whatsis, his camera, up here when-ever the bojams he wants.*

That's great, Hayes, Boyd said.

Dad, look! Look over there! said Sonny, pointing to where the parking lot of The Little Church on the Square gave way to an olive grove.

At first Boyd couldn't see anything but sand and trees, with indistinguishable gray forms; they were shadowy, barely visible. Then, in a flash he made out at least six—he couldn't count them—unkempt characters picking olives, stuffing them into their pockets and scurrying in the shade of the branches. A few were popping olives into their mouths, only to spit them out. Every Valleyite knew those black olives were inedible if you picked them off a tree. Without brine and a lot of work they were *ptooey!*

You wait here, Boyd said.

Abruptly all six or seven of them broke into a sprint. Boyd *tsked*; he realized he should've taken his moped—even though he'd had enough trouble biking through the desert yesterday. Now he gave himself to the task of running with the zest of an antlered elk pursuing a skulk of foxes—no, he was flying as swiftly as a red-tailed hawk swooping down on a mouse.

The olive grove sloped up a bit, giving the lie to his image of a hawk descending. He was running on his toes, thereby gaining headway on his quarry. This was one secret he'd learned long ago, sprinting on a gravel road south of town. It was this knowledge that put him in the lead during Brush-country races with his schoolmates. Knowing how to spring forward on the balls of his feet, using his toes, gave him an advantage over his flat-footed competitors. The second secret was knowing how to breathe right, to inhale and exhale evenly, rather than struggle like the rest of the gulpers and wheezers. Back then, outside a schoolhouse that had recently been leveled to make way for a Broil Station, Boyd had been known as the fastest kid in Rattlers Parish, a title which, he flattered himself, he still held twenty winters later.

In the midst of toeing the olive grove and breathing in long, slow arcs, he let himself think, *You can run like hell all you want, Looters or whoever you are, but I'm gonna catch you, slit your throats with a sharp rock, and drag your damned bodies back to the authorities to string you up and leave your bodies to rot.* Rather than slowing him, the virulence of these thoughts, the forbidden curse words, urged him on. Unleashed, with a new freedom, he bounded over the crest of the olive grove and plunged full-speed into a modest gully washed out by an arroyo. He couldn't hear Sonny and Hayes behind him, but he caught sight of two gray figures disappearing over the top of a dune on the other side of the gully. While his desert boots gained purchase on the dune, he trampled over a couple of gray rags, garments that appeared to have dropped from the escapees. Good, he thought, they're leaving me a trail of tatters. By the time I reach them they may be naked. He recalled the stash of nude photos he'd taken of Dolly, the portraits he'd wanted to shoot of Myrna, and the ones he believed he was going to shoot of Cathy Vallée.

Again, rather than deterring him, the thought of Cathy Vallée spurred him up, up, over the dune's side, only to go full tilt down into a stretch of open desert. The ground was packed hard, allowing him maximum speed, but the Valley floor sported a well-worn vest of mesquite. Worse, he could no longer see the gray figures—where had they disappeared?

Barely slowing, he scanned his surroundings. He remembered the trail and followed a sprinkling of gray fabric to a slightly misshapen sand dune on top of which a rosemary plant secured its roots. The sand had shifted around its base, but the plant had long ago declared squatter's rights and stood its ground, jutting up like a featureless head topped by a thatch of blue-green hair.

But look, on the far side of the plant someone had thrown down a raft of boards with a metal handle. Why would anyone do that?—unless—

Boyd grabbed the handle and swung open a trap door. Inside, he could see a flight of wooden planks, below which lay darkness. What the hell, he thought, and began to descend, keeping the hatch open for whatever sunlight lasted. He was no more than a few steps down when he noticed a light bulb screwed into a socket attached to the wall. He blinked as his eyes adjusted. Far down what appeared to be an under-ground hallway, a row of bulbs glimmered, revealing a ceiling reinforced with corrugated steel strips and walls that felt as though they were made of dried clay or adobe.

He took off at a sprint on the balls of his feet, passing a light bulb every ten meters. Evenly spaced, they flickered every now and then but continued to emit candlepower. Boyd had been in caves on cliffs and under rocky escarpments, but he'd never been in a tunnel. Still, the electric light bulbs accounted for a cozy glow, an atmosphere that probably surrounded fireplaces where people used to congregate in the olden days—on *The Ancient History Channel* he'd seen pictures of hearths and wood-burning stoves, which the Guv'na had declared were anathema to the interests of Brush Electric.

As if to blank out these thoughts, the tunnel seemed to stop dead fifty-or-so meters away, where the bulbs gave out. He slowed, listened for footsteps, and resumed at a brisk jog, only to see that the tunnel didn't end here; rather, it turned a sharp corner. Ahead of him lay another dimly lit stretch, with no one in sight. The floor began to descend.

Despite its lamp-lit cozies, the tunnel was dank, cool enough for him to run without effort. He heard the crunch of his desert boots on the packed sand floor. He smelled nothing except the odor of electricity he'd noticed one day in a generator room at Windmill City. Then, too, a faint aroma colored the air. It was nothing like the stench emanating from

Rattlesnake Alley, but it made him think of a couple of wild pigs that had been caught in a brush fire he'd once photographed. The smell was enticing, almost pleasant.

All of a sudden he burst into a well-lit room with a high, dome-like ceiling, a circle of chairs covered with deerskin, and a fireplace that looked just like the one he'd seen on *The Ancient History Channel*. Shelves built into the walls brimmed with books. What's more, a full-sized refrigerator stood alongside a propane stove, on which a teakettle sat next to a large metal implement that was bubbling, with steam escaping from under its lid. He'd never seen anything like this large thingamajig; ubiquitous tin plates for microwavable Mick's Comestibles were waiting to be recycled on top of the mountain Old Man Boyd had dubbed *Thunderhead*, but the whatsamajiggy on this stove was different. When Boyd removed its lid, the implement—some sort of cauldron—contained something like what he'd sniffed in the tunnel. If this wasn't chicken, what was it? Its dark, simmering sauce brimmed with bits of meat, potatoes, carrots, onions, and—yes, he could recognize them from an old catalog—mushrooms. The dinner table and chairs, the sofa covered with sheepskin and bits of old clothing—rags!—reminded him, oddly, of home. Except for Sonny, Dolly, and the whoosh of wind through drafty windows, this underground habitation could have been an upgraded version of his own condo. The only thing missing here was a TV. There was no screen sitting on a table, no drone of news wrap-ups spoiling the silence.

He spooned a dollop of whatever was bubbling on the stove, blew on it as if it were any old chunk of chicken tetrazzini, and sampled a bite, remembering his grandmother's words, *O taste and see!*

Later, after he'd retraced his steps, climbed the ladder back out the trap door, and found Sonny and Hayes, he regretted blabbing. To notify the authorities in Rattlers Parish had been wrong.

While a fleet of mopeds carrying bumble-bee-striped uniformed guards in sunglasses from Guv'na Brush's Bureau of Protection whisked Hayes, Sonny, and Boyd to Desert Center, he had second thoughts: What if he had just shut up? Would Hayes have believed the lie that he'd lost sight of the scruffy figures? Would Sonny have believed his father's story that he'd tripped on a cactus and knocked himself unconscious?

Ye shall know the truth, he said to himself. But whether the truth would make him free was another thing.

Sitting in a sidecar in a procession of mopeds, he knew he'd made a mistake. Sonny would be absent from school tomorrow, not to speak of the trauma this whole event would be for the kid. A day or so ago he lost his mother—and now what? Thanks to Boyd's big mouth, Hayes would miss a day of work and might even be fired. Since Sonny and Hayes had been labeled *witnesses*, they were players in an event that would no doubt be featured on tonight's *Evening Star Wrap-up*.

When the uniformed guards undid his handcuffs outside Sandstone Manse, Boyd put his arms around Sonny and Hayes's shoulders. I'm so sorry for saying anything, he said. Look what I got us into!

Sonny and Hayes massaged their uncuffed wrists. Consarn it, Hayes said, we'll be OK. Boss might even like it when he sees me without a beard on TV tonight; it's good PR.

But where were the reporters? The uniformed guards returned and stood at attention by their mopeds, while the three supposed heroes huddled under the arched portico of SM, beneath a plaque that read, *Blessed Is The Man Who Walketh Not Among Looters*.

Before long a pudgy mustached man who looked like an undertaker opened the Manse's large redwood entryway. Boyd recognized him, but the others didn't.

Gentlemen, please. Ahem, why are you standing outside like this? You should have knocked. Come in, come in!

Once inside, when the door shut with a slam that would have split the beaverboard walls in Boyd's condo, he let his eyes roam, from the oil portraits and statues of Guv'na Brush in the foyer, to the chandelier that hung from a cathedral ceiling and lit the gallery. A marble flight of stairs, wide at the bottom, narrowed as it ascended in the shape of an hourglass, to widen again as it reached the second floor, barely visible from where Boyd stood. On the main floor to one side of the staircase, three hallways branched off, each with its own chandelier, as well as propane gas lamps in wall sconces. On the left, one hallway had a royal-blue carpet, on the right a second hallway contained a wall-to-wall rug as yellow as an egg yolk, and in the middle the third hallway sported a burgundy runner split by a flame-red linoleum strip that reminded Boyd of Cathy Vallée.

From hidden loudspeakers, piped throughout the manse from a phonograph, the scratchy rendition of a song met Boyd's ears. He'd never heard it, but he recognized its lyrics: *I'm Just a Vagabond Lover.*

Gentlemen, the mustached man said, won't you please, 'hem, follow me.

He pointed to the middle hallway and led Boyd, Hayes, and Sonny down the linoleum strip fastened to the hardwood floor with some polished brass fixtures. Boyd tried to walk a tightrope on the linoleum strip while glancing back at Sonny, who was having a harder time, stumbling over the burgundy runner, only to have Hayes give him a hand. All three proceeded in silence, except for the melody warbled by some old-time crooner on the intercom.

Gradually, the hallway narrowed and got darker due to the distance from its main chandelier and reduced lighting from gas lamps. Soon the dusky reaches of the corridor began to resemble the tunnel he'd run through earlier. As he followed the mustached man, Boyd didn't know whether to hum along with the intercom or turn around and lead Sonny and Hayes back out the door they'd entered—was it minutes or eons ago?

Just as Boyd was about to ask his host a question, the corridor opened out into a vast hexagonal chamber. Lit by a single candelabra set on a huge dais, the chamber was far duskier than the dome-like room in the underground passageway he'd discovered. Either the tapers contained incense or someone had sprayed the room with aerosol, but the place smelled of mesquite after a rain. Thank Brush, the crooner's ancient ditty no longer could be heard. Boyd faked a sneeze to judge the size of the room, and his achoo echoed from all six sides of the chamber. Without rugs or tapestries, without decorations of any sort, the sanctum sounded as though it was thirty meters wide, excluding its six dim alcoves.

Gentlemen, won't you please be seated.

Boyd sat at a small table in front of the dais. He looked over at Sonny, who was stifling a sob, rubbing his eyes with his fists. Hayes slouched, beardless, inscrutable.

The mustached man climbed up a stepladder to the dais and sat down at a desk. From somewhere Boyd thought he heard a woman cry out. He was sure he heard someone coughing—a familiar *ah-hag ah-hag*.

Hear ye, hear ye! We are, 'hem, called today before God and Guv'na Brush to deal with Messrs. Boyd and Hayes, as well as Master Sonny Boyd. Because Guv'na Brush has been detained elsewhere in Desert Center, he has chosen me, his spokesman, to ask you some questions. First of all, you have apparently, 'hem, stumbled upon a tunnel east of Rattlers Parish this afternoon. Is that correct, Mr. Boyd.

Yes, sir, it is.

Second, we have been given to understand that this tunnel is inhibited, 'hem, I mean inhabited, by Looters.

It would seem so, yes, sir.

Don't say, *It would seem so.* Please just answer the questions, yes or no.

Third, is it true that you are the husband of Dorothy Boyd, née Stone?

Yes, sir.

Fourth, are you aware that your wife has been consorting with the receptionist who works for Brush Electric at Windmill City?

Yes, sir. Boyd knew Hayes was tapping his fist on the table more from the vibration than from the barely audible *whap whap whap.*

The mustached spokesman said, OK, boys, bring them in.

Before Hayes could raise his fist, three uniformed guards in sunglasses from Guv'na Brush's Bureau of Protection led two women and an elderly gentleman into the hexagonal chamber. The mustached man bade them sit at a table next to Boyd's. Sonny glanced at them and began to sob in earnest.

Ladies and gentleman, welcome, thank you for coming.

Considering that the women were wearing handcuffs, Boyd thought the mustached man's welcome sounded odd.

First of all, sir, Guv'na Brush thanks you especially for your help.

De rien, Monsieur.

You are aware, Dr. Stone, of the phrase *contra naturam?*

Oui, Monsieur.

I thought so. You speak an old language. I thought you'd be aware of an even older one.

Boyd would have interrupted, but the three uniformed guards in sunglasses from Guv'na Brush's Bureau of Protection seemed to be focusing their mirrored shades on him.

Do you have anything to say about this, 'hem, lamentable situation?

Oui, Monsieur, I can only say what grief these proceedings give me. When I think of *ma petite famille,* I have no words to express my *douleur.* I don't know why my daughter let herself go like this. Her husband may not be the best provider, but he is brave—remember what he did the other day with two Looters at the golf course; witness what he did earlier today underground. As for my grandson, I'm at a loss. Why would she cast off this boy on the verge of his manhood? Why would she say no to being a mother? My own wife left me many winters ago. She departed without customary goodbyes, but never in this way, never in an unnatural way. I am proud to serve Guv'na Brush in ridding The Valley of unnaturals, but—*pardonnez-moi, Monsieur*—I cannot continue.

Grandpa A wiped his eyes with his bandana and fixed his gaze on Sonny, who had nested his head in his arms and was trembling.

Very well. And what do you have to say for yourself, Mrs. Boyd?

Boyd noticed how in a couple of days she had blossomed into a blubbery something-or-other—he was afraid to make a comparison. Even at this distance, he sniffed the familiar trace of her perspiration.

Mrs. Boyd, I will repeat my question. What do you have to say for yourself?

Nothing, sir.

You are aware, 'hem, that nothing will come of nothing?

Boyd thought this a weird turn of phrase.

Well, then. OK, sir, I'll say this: Ever since I was a little girl—no, that's not it. I was too young to remember my mother. When she died, she—no, that's not it. Ever since my father sat me on his lap and told me about men and women—no, sir, that's not it!

What is it, then?

I don't know, sir. I've been harboring feelings. I've always looked the other way. I found myself alone one day in front of a mirror. I married because I was afraid of what I saw. At first I loved him. I did things. I thought I could mold myself, thought I was clay. Sand, silt, stone, salt. I thought I—

That will be enough. Please sit down, Mrs. Boyd.

Boyd saw Sonny peek through the nest he'd made of his arms and glance at his mother. Grandpa A was coughing hard into his bandana, *ah-hag ah-hag*. Hayes stared at the ceiling.

And as for you, 'hem, you are a receptionist, right?

Yes, sir.

For the second time that day Boyd noticed how stick-like she was, with a no-nonsense hairdo; how she smelled vaguely of lemons.

Why, for Brush's sake, would you jeopardize your position at Windmill City?

It wasn't anything I could say no to, sir. It wasn't like curse words or forbidden food. It was pure pullet. When I saw Dorothy walk through the door of that Quonset hut, I became what I always was without knowing it. Without letting myself go, I stepped—well, sir, I'm sorry for the expression, but suddenly there was a valley. And I'm so, so sorry. Look what I've done to Sonny and his father. Look what I've done to Dorothy's father. Someone once told me about an old song that went, *If you knew Suzy like I know Suzy*—but nobody knows Suzy, except maybe me. In Article Five Guv'na Brush stresses how dangerous it is to have self-knowledge; we should get to know others, get to know the Guv'na and The Valley. I should've known better than to peer within.

OK, that's enough, Miss—what did you say your last name is?

Anthony.

Well, Miss Anthony, would you and Mrs. Boyd please follow these uniformed gentlemen out of the room? They have something they need to tell you.

No! Sonny stood up from his chair and shouted, Don't mo, Gom!

Dolly! Boyd said, and he said it again: Dolly!

But the uniformed guards in sunglasses from Guv'na Brush's Bureau of Protection led the women through the left of the three large marble doors, the blue one behind the dais. Boyd tried to compare the door closing to something, but all he came up with was an image of the giant portal of The Little Church on the Square slamming shut. Sonny was making a commotion that sounded familiar, perhaps like Boyd's own cries when he found out about his parents' death in Teepee Village, cries he thought he'd long forgotten.

He leaned over and hugged his son. It'll be OK, kid. They just need to tell her something. Then they'll let her go.

Ahem, gentlemen, you may leave now. That is to say, Mr. Hayes and Master Boyd are free to depart. Please use that door over there, the mustached man said, pointing to the right of the two marble doors, the yellow one behind the dais.

While the mustached man was negotiating the stepladder down from the dais, Hayes handed something fuzzy to Boyd. It felt hairy and sticky. Put it in your pocket, Hayes whispered before he and Sonny disappeared through the yellow door.

Mr. Crabbe, where are they going?

Home, of course.

But Sonny can't take care of himself; he's just a kid.

Don't worry, Mr. Hayes will be instructed to take care of him. I, 'hem, understand that he has a son, Willy. I'll bet you twenty Bees that your son and Willy will have a good time tonight. When the cat's away, the mouse will you-know-what. In Sonny's case, both mama and papa cats will be away.

Away? I don't understand, sir. I have no idea what those guards intend to *tell* Dolly. I helped you by telling you about a tunnel. Why are you keeping me here?

Clarence Crabbe tweaked his mustache and giggled; his portly bulk shook. We have no intention of keeping you *here*, he said. Won't you please follow me.

Boyd followed him out the red center door into a corridor lit by gas lamps. As they descended into what appeared to be a poorly lit cellar, Boyd was aware of the presence of life-sized clay figures lining the hallway, as if Dolly had been commissioned to do work down here. But no, they were uniformed guards standing at rigid attention, wearing sunglasses as always. Boyd thought he heard them snickering as he passed, though he wasn't sure. One thing was certain: they weren't budging from their posts.

Now, Mr. Boyd, would you kindly step, 'hem, inside. We all realize what a hero you were earlier today. But the Guv'na has asked that you be detained here for further questions he himself will ask. You might want to consider these quarters, 'hem, a temporary vacation hideaway. No need to worry about sunburn down here, ha ha! But then you're sure no albino, are you? Anyway, have a look. You'll have all the comforts. Later you'll sup on chicken cordon bleu. You'll slumber, 'hem, like a bunny, and tomorrow will bring what it will bring. As your father-in-law might say, *Très bien!*

It was only after Crabbe minced off into darkness that Boyd heard muffled voices from nearby:

Ho, Mr. Boyd, p-poke your arms through the b-bars.

Let's see your muscles, pal. You're supposed to be a hulk.

Here's one for the hangman: *Fuck Guv'na Brush!*

Boyd pretended he didn't hear that last remark. He glared up at the TV bolted to the wall, locked in the On position. It wasn't yet time for *The Evening Star Wrap-up*, but Clarence Crabbe had already commandeered the podium outside SM and was answering reporters' questions about the latest sightings:

No, it's already been leaked: he didn't actually see them, but, 'hem, he invaded their habitat, so to speak.

Yes, 'hem, the Guv'na is pleased to hear the news, though he is disturbed at how many of our belongings have been looted to maintain their way of life.

No, neither the Guv'na nor I—nor, I presume, any Valleyite—is pleased to hear that they've tunneled underground and, as it were, have undermined The Valley. In the Guv'na's words:

Use sticks and stones, slingshots and peashooters
Against our enemies, the Looters.

Before Boyd could reach up and put his fist through the TV screen, someone whispered, *Hsst!*

Boyd whipped around. An imposing man in a clerical collar stood at the bars, accompanied by a uniformed guard who let him inside Boyd's cell with a key.

Ho, Boyd.

Ho, Reverend Chew Lee Annie.

How're Dolly and Sonny?

How're Mrs. Chew Lee Annie and Lev It Ickus the Kitty?

Never fear. Guv'na Brush—

—is here.

Now that they'd greeted one another with customary high-fives, the Right Reverend led Boyd to his cot, where they both sat down.

The Reverend proclaimed: I am here to counsel you on This Great Day of Discoveries.

Yes, sir.

Far more softly, so the guard couldn't hear, he said, You must understand what every Valleyite is thinking.

Yes, sir. I'm trying to understand.

Well, then, Boyd, the hero is scorned on his own turf. He is jailed because he threatens the powers that be, the valley of shadows, the crumbling brush. Forget about his wife, who has changed, be she ever so supple. The hero himself shall be recognized.

I'm ready to do what has to be done.

And your delight will be in the law of the LORD, and in his law you shall meditate.

But sir, meditation is not enough. I must act.

Indeed, yes, Acts 27:24. As it was spoken, Fear not, Boyd; thou shalt not stay to be brought before Guv'na Brush, and lo! thou shalt be given them that ride with thee.

But how shall I know when?

Even before the evening star has risen. Even before that unnamable white object rises over The Valley tonight. Thou shalt know the when and wherefore, the slowness and rush.

Thank you, sir. Never crush—

—Guv'na Brush.

During a Mick's commercial before *The Evening Star Wrap-up,* Boyd asked for tea. Although he'd been in his cell only a little while, already he felt like a caged beast. He'd imagined how it was to be confined behind bars one day when Grandma B took him and Mindy to a small zoo on the north side of Rattler Parish. Wild Valley Nags trotted around a corral surrounded by an electric fence. The noise of their neighing had been more than he could bear. One spotted colt kept trying to nudge what must have been its mother, who shied away from it.

What do you think of those nags, Mindy? he asked

She said something he remembered more than twenty winters later: Sure, they look sad, Little Bro, but at least they have all the horsefeed they need.

When the guard returned with a full cup of tea, Boyd grabbed him with one hand and unlocked his cell door with the key ring he wrenched from the guard's belt. Before he could cry out, Boyd smashed the man's head against the bars. He ran down the row of cells and freed three ragged detainees. With Hayes's fake beard and hairpiece glued on, he and the freed captives tiptoed up a corridor. They easily overwhelmed the lone sentry stationed by a rear door that opened onto an alley in Desert Center. Boyd realized he was putting distance between himself, Sonny, and Dolly, who might never be able to follow him. This realization was at least as painful as the dull ache someone might feel thinking about going to a dentist to have a tooth extracted.

Huddled in the shadows of Sandstone Manse, the oldest of the detainees, a man with a real beard, said, Let's split. It'll be harder to find us.

A swarthy young man dressed entirely in rags, who had trouble speaking, stammered, N-no, l-let's—

I agree, Boyd said. We're stronger if we stick together. No man is an island—Grandma B had taught him that one. We won't be able to find mopeds, but if we take off at a run, we should clear the Ravine and be in The Valley by midnight.

They set out at a medium-fast jog down back streets, avoiding the Gaslight District and the Opera House, where Boyd could hear a contralto belting out the closing strains of *Sunrise Gold* over and over, as if she were a stuck gramophone.

Once they reached the city limits, whenever a moped passed, they took to the dark wooded stretches beside the road. The wonder of it, Boyd thought, was that no uniformed guards had been dispatched—perhaps because they would have had to remove their sunglasses at night! A likelier explanation was that Boyd and his comrades had neatly dispatched the innermost guards, who weren't capable of setting off an alarm. Hardly any traffic plied the gravel. As they cleared the eastern edge of the Great Ravine, Boyd peered up a dirt road, hoping to see the cabin where Cathy Vallée spent her honeymoon as Mrs. Kissman. At dusk the railroad tracks that ran alongside them looked like two pairs of blacksnakes sunning in the darkness side by side; their heads lay behind them in Desert Center, and their bodies stretched downhill across The Valley floor to the east halfway as far as Mount Marvelous.

From here on, the downward slope was a trifle— *rien,* thought Boyd, letting his legs take over. His mates, too, seemed to be exhilarated by the descent.

Hoo, one of them said, I feel like a Wild Valley Nag!

Ha! Bet you smell like one, Pete.

Save your breath, boys, because—

A moped whizzed by, taking advantage of the downward slope, not coasting but putt-putting at full throttle.

Jeez, that guy's doing fifty kph, Pete said.

I doubt that, the bearded one said—Boyd didn't know his name.

Say, Mr. Boyd, the young man said, I-I can't believe this. I'm losing my c-clothes.

When Boyd glanced behind him, in the semi-darkness the young man's shirt seemed to be falling apart.

These r-rags'll leave a trail, he stuttered. Maybe I should quit now before r-ruining your c-chances.

Boyd had no energy for a speech. He grunted, No.

And that was that. The oldest man huffed, but the rest fell into a stride, breathing evenly, jogging on the balls of their feet or running on their toes. The young man, whose name turned out to be Karim, continued shedding his rags. Long before they reached The Valley floor, Boyd looked behind him and lo! Karim was naked. Except for some worn-down desert boots, he was trotting in the buff, grinning with buckteeth like a Wild Valley Nag.

In due time, they headed south over the desert, careful to cover their tracks by stopping now and then to spread sand over their footprints. Whatever rag trail Karim left in The Ravine was no longer a problem. Accordingly, Boyd slowed his pace to a fast walk. In the darkness the evening star was his beacon. He headed toward Rattlers Parish, though he knew his companions might have preferred to go in other directions. Rattlers Parish was closest to the Great Ravine, and even if the others hailed from farther east, Cactus Vale and Teepee Village were smaller and would provide less cover.

The oldest man muttered, I'm from Teepee Village, but you won't get me back there again. I killed two of the Guv'na's guards on patrol the day after they slit my wife's throat. She was sick of them hanging around when I was away on Moped Vac duty. They'd been stealing our grapefruits, and one day she was foolish enough to call them something, probably cursed them out. Course, the guards denied they killed her, said a couple of Looters did it. They've got wanted posters with my bearded mug all over Teepee Village, calling me Guv'na's Public Enemy Number One, even though I've been in jail a week, waiting to be hanged. My daughter's been living with her aunt, but I can't go back.

The middle-aged one, Pete, who Boyd had thought resembled the single photograph of his own father, which Grandma B had kept on her chest of drawers, mumbled something in the darkness.

What's that? Boyd said.

Pete removed a bandana from his mouth. He

coughed distinctively, like a goat, Boyd thought. Couldn't take that dust while we were running, Pete said. Sure am glad we've slowed down. Don't know what I'd do if I was to go home again. No family, no one. Just a battalion of recruits at Camp Wonderful. You know, the great thing about that place is, if they give you five minutes' leave you can stroll up to a little hill and look out at the sagebrush to the west. Never did learn the name of that neck of the desert. Never did anything but peel off my uniform one day in the sage. Wanted to go for a walk, go bird watching.

Boyd glanced back at Karim, hoping for his story, but the boy was silent.

Before long Boyd led them to a palm grove surrounding a pool of spring water—one of his photographic jaunts had taken him here last winter. As they approached, an animal hissed and bolted away into the darkness. The men flung themselves to the ground and sucked up whatever water they could, sputtering. Pete coughed in long spirals like one of those squat hunting dogs—beagles—barking.

Boyd found some dates that had fallen to the ground. He washed them in spring water, and all four of them fell to, yumming as if the sugary fruit were Mick's buffalo wings lathered with hot sauce and blue cheese dressing.

Best damned meal I've ever had, said Pete.

Call me chicken shit if that ain't right, the oldest man said. From that moment Boyd determined to call the old man Chicken Shit. Later, he learned the old man's given name was Andy, but Boyd continued to call him Chicken Shit.

Karim sat back surrounded by date pits the men had spat on the sand. I-I wonder, he said, do you suppose we—do you think we m-made *The Evening Star Wrap-up?*

No TVs out here, said Chicken Shit.

No, Boyd said. But if you look up there, you can see the real evening star all wrapped up.

Karim stretched out on the sand. Y-yeah, but what's it w-wrapped up in?

Hey kid, Pete said, don'tcha know your school stuff?

No, Boyd said, go easy on the kid. Thing is, the books say those bright thingamajigs up there are the dead eyes of Guv'na Brush's followers looking down on us.

Yeah, Pete said, so in a sense we never die.

B-but we're not G-Guv'na Brush's followers. Does that mean w-we don't go up there w-when we die?

Good question, said Chicken Shit. And I in my aged wisdom haven't the shit's whiff of an answer.

Boyd cleared his throat like Clarence Crabbe: Ahem, in the olden days some guys named Gally Leo and Ein Stine explained what's up there, those white dots. If what they said is true, the *Guv'na's Good Book* would be false.

Aw, c'mon, Boyd, said Pete, what cactus juice've you been drinking?

I know it sounds stupid, Boyd said. If the *Guv'na's Good Book* were wrong, those dots wouldn't mean anything. They'd be up there, that's all. And it wouldn't only be dudes like us, but everyone, even the Guv'na's faithful supporters, would die and be gone forever. That doesn't make sense. I mean, if you believed that, there wouldn't be any point in life. Think of it, everyone might take off their clothes and head for the sagebrush west of Camp Wonderful—where would that get us? Everyone might take a razor and slit the Guv'na's guards' throats. The Valley would be a bunch of crazies, Wild Valley Nags like us, and there'd be nothing to prevent them, no—well, I don't know what to call it, there'd be no thou-shalt-nots, no Articles—

You mean like, Thou shalt not kill the Guv'na nor any of his minions?

Yeah, Pete, that's what I mean.

Or the Article, Thou shalt not commit fornication out of wedlock unless sanctioned by the Guv'na for procreation's sake.

Right, Boyd said.

I see your point. Things would crumble—

—like they did in The Valley Quickshake on Friday. Only, it would be much worse. There'd be plagues of locusts, floods, and a fire like we've never seen, a sandstorm twenty times as scary as the one we had the other day—

—and it would bury The Valley in dust and ashes, Pete said.

—and there'd be no one to call criminals bad, Boyd said.

Chicken Shit broke in, And a voice would be heard throughout the land, saying, *Fuck Guv'na Brush!*

Karim hadn't said anything. When the others looked over at him, he was asleep, snoring softly. Boyd stripped off his Sunday shirt and covered the kid with it as best he could. The night air had turned cold, and the wind began to kick up little funnels of sand, rattling the spikey fronds of the date palms.

MONDAY

Boyd removed his beard and hairpiece with a single rip.

As groggy as he'd felt, he couldn't fall asleep. Or else he was asleep, dreaming of himself lying there on the sand, wide-awake. During the night a large animal returned to the pool and, afraid of the men, hissed and growled. Boyd was sure that a rodent hopped onto his chest, and he sprang up, slapping the air. An owl hooted in the darkness on and on, then flew away, because the next thing Boyd knew an oppressive silence settled over everything, muffling the men's snorts and gurgles. Later, when he opened his eyes, the wind had resumed soughing. He could no longer see the white dots overhead or connect them to the evening star. But he could hear a voice booming,

Ho, Little Bro.

He wanted to reply, but his lips were paralyzed. He could see her in focus, seated at a desk in a king-sized bedroom. Yet every time he tried to speak, her yellow school uniform grew blurry and her bloody nose seemed to grow large as an orange. Every time he tried to approach her desk, she arose from her chair and retreated on invisible feet into the recesses of the room. He wanted to ask her where she was, for Brush's sake. He wanted to hold her, be held by her, as they had held onto one another in Grandma B's condo.

Ho, Little Bro, she said again. Don't try to speak. Don't try to move. I'm here for you to say I love—

—Don't you dare say you love him! Dolly blurted; her cropped blond hair haloed her face, and she was wearing a see-through nightgown. You always told him you loved him. You and Grandma B. There was hardly room for me. He hardly paid attention. After Sonny was born he—

—Mom, where are you? Mleeeze Pom, don't leave me—

—You must return *tout de suite,* Dorothy, *voici le moment!*—

—I can truly say that I received you, Dorothy, but now I say with all my heart, *Return to your family, you must return.*

Boyd wanted to add his voice to this chorus. He wanted to embrace the crowd that circled overhead, whining like magpies, and say, Hush, listen to me! But the voice that didn't whine, the face framed by her bowl-shaped flame-red hair that made Boyd stiffen in his sleep—she wasn't there, squabbling among the others. If only he could dream of her wasp waist and tongue-moistened lips. If only he could taste that tongue and feel the top of his head fly off as she showed him a diary and told him about a little girl in the olden days long before the Wars of Excision, when Guv'na Brush was Rudy Newhouse from a place called Can Ah See and there were lakes in Jersey, gramophones playing, *East side, west side all around the town,* and Cathy Vallée was the tiniest speck in the mind of her great-great grandfather.

Instead, Grandma B shushed the others. It was as if she covered him with a patchwork quilt and said, *Good night, sleep tight, wake up bright in the morning light, and do what's right.*

The sky was the color of a tin shack. Boyd rubbed his eyes. The others were already awake, washing dates, gathering pods from the flowering mesquite that surrounded the oasis.

Although he was chilly without his Sunday shirt, Boyd decided to let Karim have it. The kid was spitting out pits, and the shirt was so large that it fit him like a tunic, reaching his knees.

H-ho, Mr. Boyd, he said.

No need to go through formalities here, Boyd said.

Yeah, said Pete, pocketing mesquite pods. If I was to be formal, I'd say my back's killing me, how's yours?

Not too bad thanks, Boyd said.

Ha! You sure are something, said Pete.

Chicken Shit, who'd been rinsing his beard in the spring water, said, Naw, you just have to find a spot in the sand and curl up. All night I dreamed of dogs circling a spot before they lay down. Wouldn'tcha know it, I couldn't stop circling. Anyone got one of those pain poppers, whaddya call 'em, the Guv'na's Feelgreat Pills?

Ha! Pete said, handing the old man a mesquite pod. Why not pop one of these.

After Boyd finger-brushed his teeth at the spring, he made sure his beard and hairpiece were reattached—what kind of stick-on material was this that Hayes had given him? It was endlessly regluable. He motioned the others over to where he planted himself in a squat.

He looked back over his left shoulder at the Great Ravine. Here we are, he said, making a dent in the sand with his index finger. And here's Rattlers Parish. If we get going, it shouldn't take us more than an hour to get there. We'll need to avoid Ye Olde Towne Square and Rattlesnake Alley. There's a back way, some arroyos, he said. We'll circle around a bit. We'll steer clear of the main roads. If all goes well, we may have a place to stay for a few days.

Pete began to sing, Oh, give me a home, where the chicken snakes roam—

Hey, stop that! Chicken Shit yapped. It gives me the shakes. What the hell is it?

I don't know, Pete said. Learned it when I was a tyke.

A tyke? What the hell is that? said Chicken Shit.

I don't know, Pete said.

Soon they set out, with Boyd in the lead and Karim in the rear—he hadn't said more than three words all day. If Boyd couldn't understand what *tyke* referred to, Karim must have been even more at a loss. The kid appeared to be a couple of winters older than Sonny, so he was just that much further removed from the olden days when, presumably, Pete had kept his ears open. As young as he was, Karim might know *Sunrise Gold* but probably not *Don't Fence Me In*. Without gramophones, with the advent of Article Nineteen prohibiting all songs except The Valley anthem, the younger generation had grown up on *Sunrise Gold* and little else, except for their parents' recollections of golden oldies. Two winters ago Guv'na Brush had sponsored a contest for anyone to write a song titled *God Bless Guv'na Brush*. The winner would receive a prize of one thousand Bees, plus a three-day vacation in a wigwam villa high on the south slope of the Great Ravine. The fact that nobody had won the contest might have had less to do with Valleyites' lack of musical aptitude, Boyd thought, than with their fear that, if their contest submission were deemed faulty in any way, they would risk jail sentences or even having their throats slit. How well Boyd recalled the images, on *The Evening Star Wrap-up*, of corpses sprawled outside Sandstone Manse, rotting on the ground. Whether they belonged to Looters or various enemies of Desert Center was impossible to determine, given their decomposition. To be sure, these TV spots were infrequent, say, once every week or so, and they were broadcast without the usual voice-over that explained things in dulcet tones. But viewers could tell, from the way a raven plucked out a corpse's eye, that these images underscored thou-shalt-nots as potent as any in the *Guv'na's Good Book*.

Wafted on wind currents that slapped at Boyd's bare shoulders, a quartet of buzzards circled high above the four escapees. He needn't point out these raptors to his companions, or mention that he and his comrades could comprise a banquet for the birds. Again, he recalled Dolly mimicking the cry of a song sparrow. How had he failed to keep her attention? He had gone his way with a camera, while she had gone hers with a handful of clay. That was the way it was supposed to be; the Guv'na wanted women to be productive, especially when they were not pregnant, which the *Guv'na's Good Book* seemed to imply was unproductive in his maxim, the first footnote to Article Thirty-Four:

> *Women, don't be stagnant;*
> *Get to work, get pregnant!*

As it happened, after Sonny's birth Dolly was unable to conceive, so she turned to something she'd pursued since she was a schoolgirl building sandcastles: sculpture. Rather than seeing this as a fault, rather than calling her *barren*, as a second footnote instructed a husband in such circumstances, Boyd had encouraged Dolly to do what she most loved to do. As an artist, he was by definition financially challenged, so why shouldn't Dolly and he band together like a couple of thieves? She seemed to take pride in her work. Even if she hadn't been chosen to contribute even a cowboy boot as part of the Guv'na's statue in Rattlers Parish, the folks in Windmill City had backed her. Boyd had tried to support her every day, telling her, *Gosh, that seated figure is a beaut'!* and, *I can't believe you sculpted the mole on my left cheek so accurately and with—whew!—such feeling.* Even when he knew she'd been sleeping with Suzy, he was prepared to bid Dolly a gentle farewell. He couldn't understand why she'd spurned him. He would never learn the truth, which could free him from ignorance about this. As he strode past some juniper and creosote bushes, he believed he would never see Dolly again.

Stalled in the shifty rumor mill of the sky, the sun wasn't giving out any secrets. Boyd guessed it was still early when he saw the steeple of The Little Church on the Square loom in the distance. A few kilometers from Rattlers Parish the desert seemed to change. For one, there were footprints here and there; hiking clubs sponsored day trips for retired government workers who played at being ornithologists and plant lovers. As far as Boyd was concerned, they might have been veterans of the Latter-day Wars That Have No Name with a penchant for fresh air, lectured at by guides who said, Here is a barrel cactus, here is a roadrunner. See the roadrunner dart behind the barrel cactus?

Boyd chewed on a mesquite pod and realized that in fact he was a runner of roads, disappearing behind barrel cacti. No, that would be far too small for him to hide behind. He was as stealthy as a smoke tree whose stick-thin limbs were so pale you could see through them; however dense and numerous, they were all but invisible. His friends would slither over the sand like lizards, too quick to catch. Pete might look like a pet iguana, but he could dish out venom like a Gila monster—while Chicken Shit and Karim zoomed over anthills and gopher holes like mopeds at full throttle.

At first they mistook the putt-putting of mopeds for animal noises, but Boyd led them into a gully west of town. Again, thanks to his photo outings all over The Valley, he knew this gulley gradually wound its way south, skirting the main road and Rattlesnake Alley. The mesquite pods seemed to quench their thirst, though Pete expressed a wish for a tall glass of iced tea with six lumps of sugar! It won't be long now, Boyd said, though he knew there might be problems getting into his condo and raiding his fridge for ice cubes.

As they emerged from the gully, what surprised him most was the absence of the Guv'na's guards outside his house. Meters of yellow tape ribboned off his driveway, and there was a large yellow sign posted on his front yard; its black letters howled, KEEP OUT! GUV'NA'S ORDERS! Yet not one official moped sullied his street. His neighbor's wind chimes kept time with the stiff breeze, but nobody appeared to be home. Bantam Court looked like one of those model *Brushup Village* streets he'd seen, all vacuumed and glittering, on *The Evening Star Wrap-up*, with false façades; those faux lanes and cul-de-sacs were supposed to lure hundreds of migrant workers from north of the railroad tracks. Perhaps the bumblebee-striped uniformed Sandstorm Troopers were busy patrolling one of the Guv'na's *Brushup Village* streets this morning! Although he didn't yank off his beard and hairpiece, Boyd had no need of a disguise today.

In any case, he and his comrades ducked under the barrier of yellow tape. Boyd used his door key, and the group trudged over the threshold.

Shit! Boyd said when he saw it: the carpet ripped from off the floor, the furniture overturned, smashed, and the walls smeared with what looked like blood. But there was something else, as well as blood: in the living room someone had stripped off the wallpaper and streaked the words, *Never Crush Guv'na Brush!* In the kitchen the toppled fridge lay alongside the white sheetrock wall that stank with the slogan, *Never Fear, Guv'na Brush Is Here!* Someone had painted words with the straw end of a broom loaded with excrement.

The others fled outside, where Boyd could hear them hacking and wheezing. He pinched his nose shut and stepped over the microwave that had been hurled from its counter. He touched a small button on a wooden panel that looked like molding; a spring clicked, and a small drawer snapped open. He sucked in one fetid breath through his mouth and lifted the case out of its hiding place with both hands. He unzipped it and removed its lens cap, focusing out the cracked kitchen window. Through his viewfinder he glimpsed Dolly's outdoor family statues that had been crudely beheaded, robbed of arms and legs, and knocked to the ground. They lay, three hunks in the sand that had already begun to cover them, thanks to the wind.

I've gone and found a tunnel hideout for the Guv'na, he thought, and this is my reward! The Guv'na must think I'm some sort of monster. Or he's getting back at me because of Dolly's infractions with

Suzy. Why else would he turn on me like this? For roughing up a couple of his troopers?

He fished his last rolls of film from the drawer, rammed them into his camera case, and joined his comrades outside. By now they had reconnoitered on the driveway. When there was no mistaking the putt-putting of mopeds as belonging to the Guv'na's guards returning, they took off at a sprint toward an arroyo Boyd said wound around toward the golf course.

Again, as they had last night, they ran with the wind at their backs. Again, Boyd had the sensation that he was flying. He sensed that from the vantage point of a hawk he and his comrades might have looked like four gophers skedaddling into a dry riverbed that looped from one nest of condos to another.

Not even Chicken Shit was breathing hard when they sprinted the last few meters up a macadam driveway to a large condo's redwood door. Boyd rang the bell, and when he heard nothing he knocked three times. After a decent interval, he knocked again, harder this time. Somewhere, a horse nickered.

From behind the door a voice boomed, Coming! Boyd *tsked*.

What's going on? Pete said. Where the hell—?

Boyd knocked once more; solid as it was, the redwood portal shook on its hinges.

Once again a voice boomed, Be right there!

C'mon, Mister! said Chicken Shit.

When the door flew open, Boyd was not so much irritated as shocked at what he saw. It was as if the old man's face had collapsed, as if he'd aged ten winters. No matter how jovial his *Bonjour* sounded, he looked as though he'd been crying.

He did not exchange formal greetings with Boyd but merely motioned him inside. His comrades looked sheepish, so the old man snapped, *Entrez!*

They'd never seen a condo like this. Against the living room wall a huge TV sat next to a baby-grand piano playing an obscure old ditty by itself—no one occupied the black piano stool, but there was printed sheet music on the wooden stand. Oil paintings decorated the walls: landscapes of cactus-studded washes and hills with ocotillos in bloom. A large portrait of Grandpa A as a young man, posed alongside a blonde who radiated an aura that was all but tactile, hung over an ornamental gas fireplace. Over the Brushwinters Boyd had sat on the leather sofa; he'd reclined on the chaise longue, walked over the antique Persian rug, but he'd never heard the piano tickling the ivories by itself. The others must have thought it magic; their eyes lit up, and even Karim, who was hardly dressed for the occasion, looked dignified, under a spell. For that matter, stripped to the waist, Boyd felt his curiosity lend him a modicum of equanimity, if not formal wear.

Alors, you boys look as though you've been through Hades, the old man said. And what is that fake beard and hairpiece all about, Son? Let me get you a new shirt. Can I pour you some tea, young man?

Yes, sir, with three lumps of sugar please, said Pete.

When Grandpa A retreated to the kitchen to put on the kettle, Chicken Shit said, Wow!

You sound like my son, Boyd said.

Who is this old guy? said Pete.

When Boyd explained, they fell silent, picking at their clothes. From outside Boyd heard it again, a nickering. He was about to peer out the back window when the teakettle whistled and the old man returned, bearing a tray, four cups, and a bowl of sugar cubes.

Voilà, he said as he handed his son-in-law a new mountain lion skin shirt, which Boyd put on.

They're here, you know, he said to Boyd, while pouring tea.

Who's here?

The Guv'na's troops looked the other way.

What're you talking about, sir?

It's funny how five thousand Bees can unlock men's hearts. The old man smirked. It's odd when we normally consider money to be the root of all evil, *n'est pas?*

I'm sorry, sir, I don't understand.

Boyd's comrades were busy slurping. He barely heard the old man snap his fingers and whistle as if to a dog.

When they entered holding hands, the others slopped tea on their saucers. But Boyd stood fast. He was prepared for their handholding, for their shorn hair. If he needed to wear a fake beard and hairpiece, they were entitled to their shaved heads. Much as he did not hate seeing her without her tresses, Boyd knew he'd done something very wrong to deserve this. He was reconciled to their standoffishness, and he accepted his share in having brought it about.

The others blurred in the background as she strode to him by herself. How are you, Boyd? she said.

He felt like Karim with a terminal stutter. He looked down at the carpet.

Dad took us in. He hates us, I know. But they won't kill us now.

OK, he said. As soon as he said it, he realized how dumb it sounded. Here the old man had saved their lives, and all he could say was OK.

She again grabbed the hand of her skinny partner—come to think of it, Dolly appeared to have lost some weight overnight, though she was not nearly as thin as Suzy.

OK, he repeated. I'm OK. How are you?

We're alive, she said. How's Sonny?

OK, he said. I guess. That's partly why I'm here. I thought he might be here with you.

Mais non, il n'est pas ici, she blurted.

Not here? Boyd asked. Then where? *Où? Où?* How had he learned these words?

I'm guessing, Dolly said, he's with Hayes—

—up at Windmill City! Boyd said.

That's right, Boyd. And I don't know if we'll ever see him again, unless your beard, somehow—

—makes me incognito.

There he was again, finishing up her sentences, as he'd done lo! those many winters they'd lived together!

Grandpa A interrupted. Look, the Guv'na's guards have stolen our mopeds. We're under house arrest here, and we only go out to shop, to walk to minimarts. But what I have in mind is this. He motioned Boyd and his tea-sipping comrades to his back window. Outside, the source of the nickering Boyd heard earlier stretched its spotted head toward the window and neighed as if it wanted to be petted.

Hein, it's still a bit wild. One of my patients captured it and gave it to me last week; I had a corral built, never thinking there would be this *cauchemar*. But I have some rope outside.

Karim had come to the window. He put down his teacup on the sill and gazed at Boyd. I-I, he said, I think I—

You think you what? Boyd said.

He thinks he can show you something, said Pete.

Yeah, can't you see that? He knows something, Chicken Shit said.

M-Mr. Boyd, let's g-go, he said. It's a m-mare.

Outside, while the others watched from behind the fence, Karim knotted the rope into a lasso. He didn't have to use it, though, or struggle with the nickering mare; she came to his hand outstretched with a lump of sugar as if she recognized him. Wild Valley Nag that she was, she nuzzled his hair and whinnied when he mounted and rode her bareback around the corral, whispering into her ear. Before long he called Boyd over, and she let Boyd touch her bristly forelock and stroke her mane. Soon she let him mount and ride her, grasping her withers with his legs, sitting up straight and tall as if he were an accomplished equestrian. She trotted around the circle without reins or a rope, listening to him whisper, *Giddyap* or *Turn around* or *Easy there, Mrs. Kissman*—for some reason he chose to call her Mrs. Kissman. And when she completed circling, prancing like a filly, he dismounted and gave her velvety muzzle a kiss.

Later, after he'd swigged tea, gobbled a chicken potpie along with the others, and slung his camera case over his back, he marveled at his luck. If he hadn't freed Pete and Chicken Shit, whom he'd introduced to the others as Andy; if he hadn't come across Karim, none of this would have happened. Was it fate that found Pete and Chicken Shit a home as guardians of Grandpa A and the women? Was it predestination that bound Boyd to Karim as they rode Mrs. Kissman together that morning?

She bucked at first and broke into a trot up a remote gulch. When she reached the open desert beyond Rattlers Parish, she loped at a steady forty kph, Boyd guessed. Dodging snake holes and rocks, her hooves seemed to know The Valley as if she'd learned its lessons thousands of winters ago, perhaps before it was a Valley at all. Perhaps she'd picked up her knowledge when Mount Marvelous was an active volcano and the desert was the floor of an inland sea, according to certain ancient books. If so, she swam over sand dunes like an amphibian, though not like any Boyd had seen in the Desert Center Natural Brushtory Museum.

To be sure, she galloped into a cold north wind that augured rain, but nobody followed her. No dust cloud or moped, or whatever had followed Sonny and Boyd the other day, tailed him and Karim this morning as they rode toward the railroad tracks and Windmill City. Karim sat huddled behind Boyd, hugging him and his camera case, chanting in a language Boyd couldn't understand.

It was getting on toward noon when they reached the tracks and turned east. For the umpteenth time Boyd mouthed the word *east*; saying it made his lips widen into a smile. What was it that Grandma B had told him about the East, about women who wore burqas and men who wore colorful headgear and robes, sheiks who swilled tea in a desert vaster than The Valley? Myrna and he making love in her tent, the notion of himself as Rudolph What's His Name the sheik? With Hayes's ridiculous beard and hairpiece, he couldn't easily finger the mole on his cheek. He couldn't compare himself to anyone but a man with a camera, with a boy named Karim hanging onto him, hightailing it toward Brush Electric at Windmill City.

Something surged through him when he saw the mills in the distance. He pointed them out to Karim, who seemed impassive, too busy watching the desert floor fly by beneath him to pay attention. As they approached, he tapped Boyd on the back and pointed them out himself, as if to ask, What are those pinwheels up ahead?

The steel blades of most of the forty-nine mills were revolving in the wind. Boyd could see that several towers had toppled, while men in yellow uniforms busied themselves hoisting one fallen tower with a steel crane mounted on the back of three Miramar mega-peds chained together.

He dismounted and left Karim to hitch Mrs. Kissman to a post. Once Boyd entered the central Quonset hut, he expected to see Sonny. Instead, a new receptionist so gussied up in a dress festooned with chicken feathers that she looked like a walking billboard for Mick's Comestibles said, Ho, who goes there?

Ho, my name is Boyd.

Ho, Boyd, my name is Ruthie.

Ho, Ruthie. Never fear. Guv'na Brush—

—is here.

After they gave one another high-fives, Boyd asked about Hayes and Sonny.

Well, you could stay here and chat with me awhile. But since you really want to know, Hayes and the white-haired kid are out by Old Forty-nine. Weren't you supposed to take pictures of her? Boss left instructions—

Boyd wondered what had become of Dolly's sculpture, but he didn't dare enter the adjacent workroom to find out.

After exchanging formal goodbyes, he stepped back outside, only to find Mrs. Kissman tied to the post without Karim. At first Boyd didn't fret about the kid's disappearance. The horse had obviously not broken away to follow Karim, who might be studying windmills behind the Quonset hut. Later, Boyd regretted not calling Karim's name, mounting Mrs. Kissman, and galloping off to search for him.

Now he simply rode the horse over to Old Forty-nine.

The immense steel blades of the big old bird revolved in time with the other mills in working order. As soon as Sonny saw his father approach on horseback, he yelled, Dad! and dashed toward Boyd.

Ho, Sonny!

Oh, Dad, it's you!

Ho, Boyd.

Ho, Hayes. Let's cut the crap with formalities.

Where have you been, Dad? I'm so glad to see you I need to pee. Where's Mom? What's that Wild Valley Nag you're riding? Is it fun? Can I ride up there with you?

Boyd hoisted Sonny off the ground and seated him in front of himself on Mrs. Kissman's withers. She whinnied with what sounded like pleasure, and Boyd let her approach Hayes, whose armpit she nuzzled.

You sure look weird in my beard and hairpiece, Hayes said.

You sure look weird without a beard or hair, Boyd said.

Oh, Dad! It's so hood to gav you back! Sonny said.

Hayes tied Mrs. Kissman to a pole while Boyd circled Old Forty-nine, shooting it from twelve angles. He had the feeling that the windmill was winking at him with its whirling silver blades. The hum of an electric turbine inside the shack at its base reminded Boyd of one particular creek's dull *vroom* at the base of Mount Marvelous. He was expecting Karim to show up any minute, to materialize like a dervish. The longer he lingered below Old Forty-nine—the more he began to think of the venerable mill as a kind of whirling dancer—the surer he was that Karim had vanished and would not be coming back.

A crew of men in yellow uniforms hailed Hayes. He yakked with them awhile until Boyd broke in and asked if they'd seen a disheveled boy.

Nope, one of them said.

Nope, said another. Hey, that's some spotted horse over there. Looks like a Wild Valley Nag.

Once was, said Boyd. Now we're using her as a plaything for the kid.

On his return to Rattlers Parish, with Sonny seated in front of him, Boyd took the long way, closer to Mount Marvelous, just west of Teepee Village. Still clad in his false beard and hairpiece, he slowed Mrs. Kissman to a fast walk and touched Sonny's head.

Those huts over there, Boyd said.

Yeah, Dad?

See that one teepee house way off on its own, with blue and red paint patches?

Yeah, Dad?

I knew two people who lived in that one.

You did?

Uh-huh. Do you see that house, the third one to the left of that building with the sandstone arch, Bee Rush Academy?

Yeah, Dad? It's half-collapsed.

I also knew someone who worked in the house near that Academy.

All at once two mopeds putt-putted up. Mrs. Kissman reared.

A couple of Guv'na Brush's bumblebee-striped uniformed guards with sunglasses leaped off their bikes and shouted, Halt, who goes there?

George and Willy Hayes.

Ho, George. Ho, Willy. We're Lucky and Buck.

Ho, Lucky. Ho, Buck.

What's your horse's name? Looks like a Wild Valley Nag.

Uh-huh, her name's Windy.

Ho, Windy. We're looking for a big guy named Boyd.

Never heard of him. Work up at Windmill City. On our way to Rattlers Parish for Monday evening prayers at The Little Church on the Square.

Uh, OK. Never fear. Guv'na Brush—

—is here.

They putt-putted away, and Boyd brought Mrs. Kissman to a slow trot. When he fingered his beard— and found it had slipped part way off—he murmured to himself, Fuck Lucky and Buck!

Did you just say something, Dad?

Mrs. Kissman whinnied and broke into a lope.

Boyd would have liked to have whipped out his camera and shot Mount Marvelous beheaded by clouds. He would have liked to have snapped the distant spires of The Little Church on the Square from

Rattlers Parish, or to have focused on the overcast early afternoon light that painted the golf course gray. His Brushachrome black-and-white film would catch subtleties the eye missed. No matter what Grandpa A said, Boyd's photos would be larger than life, not a fraction or reduced distortion of it. Instead, he patted the Leica slung over his shoulder and began to hum. Before long, he was singing:

> *I dream of a tent in The Valley*
> *Where I could be happy and dally*
> *With Sonny and Windy and Dolly.*
> *But if I can't do that, by golly,*
> *I'll look for a kiss, my finale,*
> *From somebody else, Cathy Vallée.*

Dey, Had, what's that supposed to mean? Why're you singing?

Haven't you ever wanted to sing just for the heck of it?

Well, yeah, but I never just, you know, busted out into song like that. And who's Cathy Vallée?

Just a name, Sonny. Someone I made up to fit the song, to rhyme with *finale*.

What's *finale* mean, Dad?

Boyd quelled his impulse to yodel. He slapped Mrs. Kissman's thigh, and she broke into a gallop.

In a matter of minutes they'd hoofed it through an unusually deserted Ye Olde Towne Square and were trotting through Rattlesnake Alley. A couple of stray dogs took one look at Mrs. Kissman and ran off in the other direction, yelping. Again a girl wearing black rags was hanging some sheets and towels on a clothesline outside of her wickiup. When she saw Boyd and Sonny, she waved and sent out a high-pitched *Hallooooo*.

Boyd peered at the desert east of town. There it was, as always, the inscrutable domain of sagebrush and mesquite. Gullies and arroyos blended into a pattern of shifting sand. He thought he saw a sooty figure planted atop a dune, but it turned out to be a Joshua tree.

Hey, Dad, isn't that where you found the tunnel?

I was looking for it, too, Sonny.

You know, sometimes I think I see things that aren't there. Or else I don't see things that are there. Sometimes I think I'm doing stuff that isn't real.

Me, too, kid.

Will Mom be at Grandpa A's place?

As a matter of fact, Mom was not at Grandpa A's place.

When Boyd dismounted and walked the horse to her corral behind the house, he told Sonny to stay outside and take care of Windy. No one came to the door, and the condo seemed deathly quiet. Boyd sniffed the air, which carried none of the odor that had wafted from his own house earlier today.

The front door was unlocked. As it swung open, Boyd could hear something playing on Grandpa A's phonograph. There were still several vinyl disks on the spindle, but the scratchy ancient lyrics that filled the condo were

> *Wait till the sun shines, Nellie,*
> *When the clouds go drifting by.*

Sir? Boyd said, removing the needle from the record—*zzzt!*—shutting off the phonograph.

Sir? he said, louder. Hey, Dolly, Pete! Hey, wake up, house!

In the bedroom Boyd found him with his throat slit, bloodying his sheets. Judging by the record player and red stuff still oozing from the old man's neck, Boyd figured he'd met his murderers only a few minutes ago. The liver-spotted backs of his hands were still warm, and his body hadn't yet begun to stiffen into an effigy, a photo perhaps titled, *Old Man Permanently Reclining.* Although a faint smell tainted the air, no one had scrawled slogans on the walls with feces; no blood was smeared anywhere, and the furniture was intact.

Boyd searched the condo. In the bathroom he found a scribbled note taped to the underside of the toilet seat. It read:

I no somethin bad is goin to happen. They been parked outside, passin a bottle back and fourth. We beged the old man to joyn us, but he said he payed five thousand Bees. He been frens wit the Guv'na for eons and was not about to be ambooshed. We could escape thru the back door, he said. He was to old to be a roderunner. He would reeson wit the Guv'na's troops. The fore of us ought to reach Mount Marvlus by nightfal. Regards to Sunny, and remember, I'll be wit you when the crow caws!

Pete's signature was all but illegible.

Outside, Sonny seemed to sense what was happening. He didn't cry for his mom; he didn't ask about Grandpa A. He let Boyd hoist him onto Mrs. Kissman. In a flash they were galloping again, but Boyd wasn't saying anything, even though he felt a frisson of rage when he thought of his father-in-law supine on the sheets.

At their pace, they would arrive all too soon. Yet Boyd couldn't stop time from slowing down, opening up like a wide-angle lens. As real as the cholla bushes that whizzed past him, Boyd recalled his father jigging him on his knee. There was gramophone music in the background as his father held up a big blue book. He pointed to words in the book, ink squiggles, and, once, he read lines that Boyd could still hear as loudly as Mrs. Kissman's hooves:

That time of year thou mayst in me behold
When yellow leaves, or none, or few, do hang
Upon those boughs which shake against the cold,
Bare ruined choirs where late the sweet birds sang.

For the life of him, Boyd had never made sense of these lines. Not that he spent his life trying to decipher them. He'd mainly forgotten his father—what he looked like, how he smelled. Grandma B hadn't kept photos of his parents, and other than Grandma and Mindy's stories, Boyd's impressions of them were vague. Still, the four lines of that thingamajig—unlike any song he liked to make up—had stayed with him, along with what his mother said when she found Old Man Boyd reciting from the book: Honey, what're you doing with little Bill? He can't understand a word of what you're saying.

His father had put down the big blue book, jigged Bill on his knee, and said, Sandy, I'm an old man; I know not what I do.

Why was it these words echoed in his mind? How was it they lingered when nearly everything else about his parents was a blur? If Old Man Boyd was a writer, did he see pictures in his head, too? Did Boyd inherit his father's love of images, those yellow leaves that Boyd could visualize like sandstone ledges on the lower slopes of Mount Marvelous, those bare ruined choirs he could see like The Little Church on the Square without its roof and spires? One thing was clear: Boyd was no writer. If he burst into song and yodeled every once in a while, he never wrote down the lyrics. He could read fairly well, and write sentences better than Pete in his note about Grandpa A.

But he would never think up anything memorable to write. With the libraries and bookstores gone, who cared about writing?

He must have been dreaming. Sonny nudged him and said, Dad, we're here. The boy slid off the horse and ran toward the group of kids balancing stones on their forefingers in the schoolyard. Mrs. Bissman, I'm kack! he yelled.

Jilly had been jumping rope. Now she threw down the rope and started to jump up and down on her own. She ran over to a group of girls, and they all began to giggle like chickens.

Cathy Vallée stood off to one side of the schoolyard. Her flame-red pageboy lit up the gray afternoon. She wasn't wearing her olive-drab uniform today. Rather, her tight black sweater and blue jeans played tricks with Boyd's eyes. First they were there; then they weren't, giving him the impression that she was, at least at intervals, naked.

He used Karim's rope to tie Mrs. Kissman to an ocotillo by the schoolhouse entryway.

Cathy Vallée approached timidly. Will he bite? she said.

I see you've dispensed with formal greetings, he said. And by the way, he's a she.

Will she bite?

Pet her and see for yourself!

But she's a Wild Valley Nag. They're fierce.

She loves to be petted by fierce people.

Cathy Vallée stroked the horse, who bobbed her head up and down as if to say, Yes, do it again.

What's her name? she said.

Windy.

Ha! I wonder why you call her that?

Now, don't be a fusspot.

School's out in a minute, she said. I hope you can stay for tea.

Just then a rusted-out bell emitted a series of bongs so ludicrous they sounded like two tin cans smacked together. The kids rushed inside to get their empty lunchboxes and satchels, while Sonny waited outside.

I take it Sonny was absent for good reason, she said.

I'll write you a note tomorrow—handwritten, with plenty of squiggles, said Boyd.

Her laughter was another bell, perfectly cast from lip to crown.

Jilly grabbed Sonny's hand. You're coming with me, she said, leading him to her bike. She set him on the seat in front of her, and they pedaled away, along with the rest of the noisy school kids.

Cathy Vallée led Boyd to a couch in the teachers' lounge and put a kettle on the stove. Mr. Heetclit went to church yesterday, but I stayed home, she said. I biked over here to clean out that closet. He'd be furious with me if he knew I got into it again. But then

I guess he'd already cleared it out. He made off with those charts and my great-grandmother's diary; I was so flustered I left it in the lounge. Maybe he burned the stuff, or he turned it in to the authorities. I have no right to be angry about this, but I am. I have no idea why he left one piece of paper in the closet.

The kettle whistled. She set out tea for both of them and opened her purse. Before she began reading from a single sheet of paper, she arched her neck in a way that reminded him of Mrs. Kissman. He was waiting for her to nicker, but she glanced at him and moistened her lips. Did she sense that he was growing rock-hard? The sound of her voice, her peculiar *chirp*, had a bodily effect on him. He needed to keep himself in check, like Mrs. Kissman tied up outside. He needed to hold onto himself tight. He unslung his camera case from his shoulder and set it on the table.

They sipped tea in unison. She read aloud:

December 25, 2041. Last night we gathered by the tree to open presents. Tommy was sweet enough to buy me two pairs of support hose; I crocheted him a pillow embroidered with the words, "For My Loving Son." I gave Sally and Timmy matching sweaters. Thanks to their hand-bound letterpress copy of King Lear, *I shall re-read the play and see how foolish and vain a golden ager like myself can be. Best of all the good news, my darling grandchild, my dearest Catherine, gave birth last night up the street at Mount Sinai. Her gift to us all:*

a seven-pound daughter she hasn't named yet. But I've bet Tommy that his new niece will be named after her mother; that's what she told me last week when she was as pregnant as a blimp. Thank God these glad tidings blot out the news we've all been trying to forget. For a change yesterday we didn't turn on the TV. New York City has pretty much seceded from the Union, but this doesn't dispel my feeling that our nation, not just our family, faces a new birth. If the White House continues the way it has, no doubt violence will break out. It still seems years away, though, and from the standpoint of an eighty-year-old, five years are an eternity. Despite Harry's death last summer, despite Catherine's widowhood, I will not cease believing in hope. This country will be reborn from its ashes, not die like a film cut to pieces on the director's floor. Who knows but that I may be around to see many another snowy day in Central Park, to rock my great-granddaughter in my arms, and to listen again to her mother's favorite old twentieth-century Christmas carol—no one plays it much anymore—the one about the reindeer with the shiny nose—what's its name? I must be having a "senior moment"!

Well, what do you think? she said.

I don't know what to think, he said. What does *December 25, 2041* mean?

It could be a code, she said.

It could refer to a system before Brushwinters.

She let her eyes rove over him, which must have

showed her how he was feeling. Yes, she said, I'm thirty-two.

I'm thirty, born in the Winter of the Big Rains, so my grandmother told me.

Right. I was born during the Winter of Waning Peace.

Can you remember the Fourth War of Excision?

Barely. I recall the Guv'na's troops standing at attention on TV.

Well, you're an old lady! My first memories go back to the Battle of Teepee Village during the final days of Fourth War. I saw it on *The Evening Star Wrap-up*. That must've been during my third winter.

Tiny tot, then you have no memory of the Retaking of Desert Center in the early stages of the Fourth War.

That was a bit before my time, I'm afraid, he said. Matter of fact, I don't remember much of any of the wars; I hung out with my grandmother and took photos. Again, he felt her eyes roving, making his cock leap to attention.

Poor boy, she said.

Ten hut! he barked, saluting like one of the Guv'na's uniformed troops. Give me my sunglasses, my moped, and a swig of pulque!

It doesn't look as though you need pulque, Bill!

Ah, Cathy, you—

They had scooted together on the couch, when a

loud *Ahem* erupted from the lounge doorway. Was this Clarence Crabbe?

See here, Cathy, this is the second time I've found you and Mr. What's His Name on the sofa! The last I heard you were a married woman, but that's beside the point in this day and age. My point is, the lounge is not for horseplay. You may be the last teacher in Rattlers Parish, but that doesn't allow you to be first to get special privileges.

As he spoke, once again Boyd thought he noticed smoke coming out of the old man's ears. Was it an optical illusion due to the flickering florescent lights?

What I can't understand, the old man continued, is how Mr. Kissman lets you get away with this. That he lets you out of his sight is something I can't comprehend.

By now Boyd had a chance to study how very decrepit the man was. He was much older and more shriveled than Grandpa A. Hunched, rheumy-eyed, with wispy white hair and a glaring red scar on his left cheek, he was the oldest man Boyd had ever seen, perhaps more than a hundred winters old. Yet today he carried no walking stick and bristled with an indignation Boyd associated with men half his age.

He growled, What I can't understand is how I've let you go on like this, teaching here for all these winters while the rest of my staff was whittled out from under me. The Wars of Excision ended nine winters ago; some say the Wars broke the bank. Guv'na Brush had good reason for his cutbacks since then. But I kept you on.

Suddenly, he broke into a toothless grin. Do you know why I left you that page from the diary, the one I knew you'd steal from the closet? He pointed his twig finger at the sheet of paper she had placed on the table beside her teacup.

I got rid of the charts and the rest of the diary—who needs them? They're castoffs from another era you don't want to know about—you and your tall, dark gentleman friend, that is. I'll give you this, Cathy, your friend is a lustier catch than Mr. Kissman—what's his name? Johnny? I could never understand what you saw in him. Sure, he has connections in Desert Center, but as a human being the man is a rhinestone.

But I'm getting away from the subject: that page in the diary. I need to tell you something, if you haven't already guessed. Have you guessed what I'm getting at, Cathy?

No, sir, I haven't.

Well, then. Maybe I shouldn't bore you and this young man. After all, an old stone doesn't need to be turned over. The ants underneath it don't want to be disturbed, and they may cause you to faint.

What do you mean, sir?

I mean, my dear, that there is more than you can imagine under your lovely nose. Do you smell a rat?

Cathy Vallée seemed to shrink. Mr. Heetclit, if you're trying to scare me—

Boyd leaned forward on the couch, as if to stand up.

Now it was the old man who shrank back. All right, he said, I'll leave it at that. Let me just say that I knew the woman who wrote the diary, as well as her favorite granddaughter. I knew them well. Which is why I haven't reported you to Desert Center, my dear. I'm a doddering Methuselah, but my heart's still beating, and I could never—

Outside the wind kicked up, and the rusted school bell gave out a series of tin-can bongs.

Is it just me, or is it getting colder? the old man said.

No, I feel it, too, she said, and I'm wearing a sweater.

I've noticed, he said. I remember long ago standing in front of a store window; I think the store's name was Racy's—no, it was Lacy's. Well, one week in winter I planted myself in front of that store window every day after school, looking at the sweaters on the fashion models. Lacy's had these mannequins, you know, mostly women but a few men, too, and they wore jerseys, turtlenecks, cashmere V-necks, gray cardigans with gold buttons. I stood out there day after day, and I had my eye on a hand-knit yellow wool whatsamajiggy, the warmest, most comfortable sweater imaginable, that is to say, I imagined myself wearing it, sitting by a fireplace in an apartment, with my parents chatting about books—there were plenty of books back then, you know. We would be listening to Elton Johnson and the Gee Bees on the radio, or maybe it would be Lady Gaggis—no, no, I don't have her name right! The fireplace would crackle, and I would nestle into my sweater, feeling as cozy as apple pie—and since you don't know what apple pie is, you'll believe me when I tell you it's cozy!

Every afternoon that week during the winter we'd begun fighting what we called the Afghanistan War long before the Wars of Excision, I zipped up my hand-me-down pea coat and left Lacy's to trudge back to our walkup on Eighth Avenue in a neighborhood called Hell's Bitchin'—but our house was not hot as hell! That winter the holding company that owned our redbrick tenement had refused to replace the building's boiler when it gave out. My father and I used to go down to the basement and try to restart the dead old hulk. It was no fun flicking the restart switch and hearing nothing, no fun trying to call somebody downtown to report the owners to the authorities, no fun putting on every stitch of clothing in our drawers and closets so we could layer ourselves against the cold. Even bundled into seven layers of skivvies, long johns, T-shirts, button-downs, pullovers, windbreakers, greatcoats; even with two woolen caps folded into one another and jammed onto our heads, when we lay under blankets or waddled around our railroad apartment looking like roly-poly boulders, we felt it creep through our clothes, through our three layers of socks, and settle into our foot bones, where it radiated up and out to our gloved hands and capped heads. That's right, the cold oozed; it was like a mudflow reaching everywhere. And I knew I would leave that city as soon as I could. I would hitch a ride with the sun; it was westward-bound, and I knew I would be going west; young man, I went west!

Boyd shook himself, as if from a trance. Are you talking to me? he said.

Was it smoke that issued from the old man's ears? Yes, I'm talking to you, he said. That Wild Valley Nag tied up outside. It's yours, isn't it? She's a mare; I know one when I see one. What in Brush's name do you mean to do with her?

Boyd shuddered. Stay warm, he said.

Ha! Stay warm?

That's right, Mrs. Kissman and I—

Ha! Mrs. Kissman! You must be aware that her name is Cathy.

That's right, but I—

I call her Cathy, the old man said. In my heart of hearts I have always called her Cathy.

Cathy Vallée blushed. Outside, Mrs. Kissman tossed her head as the wind rose in a low howl. She snorted and whinnied in protest.

And now if you'll excuse me, I'll go back to my office for my afternoon lie-down, the old man said.

Dispensing with formalities, he hobbled out of the lounge.

Boyd *tsked*, I was hoping to— But now—

I know, now I don't feel like it either.

She went to close the window; a chunk of its pane was missing. His eyes trailed her.

Oh, dear! she said. She's gone.

He leaped to her side. It was true, amid the clatter of sticks and sand being blown about, Mrs. Kissman no longer stood tied to the ocotillo by the entryway.

Boyd flew out the front door and thought he saw her loping east of the schoolhouse. Was someone riding her? He couldn't quite make out.

Look, Cathy, I've got to run. Literally! Why don't you bike home. With luck I might catch Mrs. Kiss—I mean, Windy, and meet you at your place later. You live on Chicory-Chick Way, right?

Right.

And Jilly lives down the street, so you can check on Sonny, right?

Right.

Au revoir, ma chérie! Where had he learned to say that?

He set out at a sprint, but once he got his footing on the loose sand, he slowed his pace to a brisk jog, breathing easily, evenly, in long, slow arcs. The north wind tried to blow him sideways without success. Without his Leica, which, he realized, he'd left in the teachers' lounge, he felt naked. He wouldn't be able to catch Mrs. Kissman. But he could follow her tracks, at least until the blowing sand covered them up. With Mount Marvelous looming ahead, Boyd caught his second wind and felt a kilometer melt underfoot.

The faster his desert boots churned, the slower time seemed to tick. How many winters had he been running after glimpses? With his light meter and viewfinder, he'd slowed life to a halt—just as Mr. Heetclit had been frozen in front of Lacy's store window. How many winters ago had that been? He hadn't said. He said he'd known the woman in the diary, but what did that mean? What did it mean to freeze under layers of clothing, when one sweater was enough to keep you warm in The Valley? How had the old man kept going all these winters, living in his office, working for the Brush administration, supervising his only teacher, when he might have fired her for any number of reasons and hired somebody else, perhaps even Dolly? Not that Dolly was much of a teacher; she didn't read or write nearly as well as Cathy Vallée, but at least Dolly had a child and knew about kids.

For a time, as he followed Mrs. Kissman's hoof prints through the desert, Boyd let himself drop into overdrive and think of Dolly, who had taught him to lick and lip. She'd taught him that he could lose himself in her and then lose her to someone else; that he could go on somehow, feeling wretched but rinsed inside, because she'd instructed him, she'd shown him the truth that freed them both. Long ago he must've been aware of this truth, but he'd buried it under a cactus plant thorny with false smiles. He'd hidden it under countless empty gestures, *Ho, Dollys,* and bear hugs in the evening. Free as she was of him, how long could she and Suzy escape the authorities? What would she think when she learned about Grandpa A—if she didn't know about him already?

At the rate he was running, he would be in the foothills of Mount Marvelous before the sun went over the Great Ravine. Kilometers of scree and sandstone, rocky outcrops and crags would give way to slopes, dips, and the bare, brown cliff side that looked, from a distance, like the tawny back of a cougar but was really a mishmash of boulders and batholiths, loose dirt and deer tracks. He cleared a gopher hole with a leap and thought of the lamp-lit room with a high, dome-like ceiling in the tunnel he'd found yesterday. Whoever lived there had skedaddled without turning off the stove. The smell of meat and vegetables simmering had been tantalizing, especially now that he was racing just south of Mick's Comestibles.

The facility north of him was the largest in The Valley. Its barbed wire fence, its one-and-a-half square kilometers of whitewashed wooden coops,

surrounded a sprawling redbrick building—The Chicanery—whose towering stack belched black smoke.
The smell was anything but tantalizing to Boyd, who
gulped air through his mouth and, even so, caught
the scent of flesh and feces. Although he was more
than a kilometer away, he thought he could hear the
puck-puck of hens that would never lay another egg or
hear a rooster cry at dawn. Of the six facilities in The
Valley, this one had been built most recently. After
the First War of Excision, the Guv'na had constructed
The Chicanery to keep up with East Valleyites' insa-
tiable hunger for poultry. The Guv'na's words etched
into a stone pedestal by the main gatehouse were
unforgettable; all school children took field trips to
Mick's facilities, and Boyd had been lucky enough to
visit The Chicanery as a kid. Like every student, he
had climbed Watchtower One and, of course, he had
memorized the words:

> *Yo ho! Mick's gives you scrumptious chicks*
> *From farms, not four, not five, but six!*

Now, it was all he could do to avoid gagging. As
appetizing as they were on recyclable tin plates, they
were disgusting in the raw. Because of The Chicanery, Rattlers Parishioners could have a chicken in
every microwave, and they were spared the task of
devising diverse menus. If the underground inhabitants of the tunnel he'd broken into yesterday did

more than heat water for tea on their stoves, wasn't this a sign of their barbarity? Maybe their bubbling cauldron smelled OK, but—well, he wasn't sure of anything anymore.

Thankfully, he was beyond the north wind's chicken stench now. He upped his pace when his desert boots found a stretch of sun-baked clay pocked with hoof prints. All at once the tracks vanished in a pebble field, but a few large brown turds steaming in the cold told him Mrs. Kissman was not far away. Before long, he was jogging around boulders, running underneath granite overhangs. He thought he heard her whinnying up ahead, but it might have been a bird or the wind whistling through a creosote bush. As he ascended, the vegetation thickened. The closer he got to the watershed near the snow-capped volcanic peak of Mount Marvelous, the shrubs and trees grew larger. Although he doubted he'd be able to reach the line of evergreens hundreds of meters above him, they loomed like a giant green beard glued to the mountain's face. If he were to shoot a photograph of Mount Marvelous as a portrait, rather than a landscape, it would be of a huge, shaggy countenance with a snow-white cap of hair: Old Green Beard, who might have looked a bit like Mr. Heetclit in disguise.

There it was again, that whinnying. Only, this time it was no bird, no wind. It sounded as though it came from right beyond a bend in the trail. Behind the boulder wedged under a cliff, Mrs. Kissman was neighing all right, and the sound was bouncing off the rocks, echoing like faraway thunderclaps.

As soon as he cleared the boulder, he saw an entrance so hidden, so unexpected, that it could have been invisible: an aperture, like a camera shutter's open eye, in the mountain wall. Whoa! he blinked twice and rubbed his eyes: the circular opening was wide and tall enough for three Mrs. Kissmans to enter. He fought off a twinge of panic and looked back; he could no longer see Rattlers Parish or The Chicanery. He had dead-ended here, and there was no going back.

He felt a drop of icy water hit his forehead and looked around to see uncountable white flakes swirling and whipping almost horizontally in the wind. Come what may, he shook himself like a horse and let loose a whinny he thought she might hear.

Stumbling over loose rocks as he made his way to the black maw of whatever it was, he thought he heard a crow cawing. As snowy and dark as it was outside, inside it was darker. Water dripped from the rock walls, and he could hear himself breathing, though he couldn't see his breath in the cold. When his eyes got used to the dark, he saw he'd entered a large cave. Its central passageway stretched back as far as he could see, but there were corridors that branched off. Each of these branches glowed, lit from within.

He could smell her now, along with other aromas. The odors of perfume and sweat, firewood and the stuff on the stove he'd whiffed in the tunnel yesterday—all this accosted him. As he made his way down the main passageway, which descended ever so slightly into the mountain, he had an impulse to cry out, but held back. You must keep yourself in check, he thought. Don't loosen the reins!

At the opening of the first turnoff, he glanced into a lamp-lit room with a high ceiling. Couches surrounded a hearth in which a fire crackled, emitting the smell of mesquite. Shelves lined the walls, shelves filled with books. Although he couldn't read their titles, he could see their yellow spines, black spines, smallish books with dust jackets alongside oversized books shoved lengthwise onto the shelves. A low table between four wicker chairs was heaped with paperbacks, slim volumes and hefty leather-bound editions. In a chaotic pile, dozens of books had spilled over a desk onto the floor carpeted with fleece and deerskins.

Neigh! He heard her again, but not here, not in this room apparently reserved for horses of a different color.

He made his way back into the dark central passageway, following his ears, as well as his nose. When he stuck his head into the opening of the second room, he recognized her right away. Hitched alongside at least ten other piebalds and palominos, roans and dappled-grays, she was not just another Wild Valley Nag. Her mouth nuzzled a pail of something or other, but when he *tsked* at her, she lifted her head and eyed him, munching all the while. The others didn't budge; they were feeding or sleeping on their feet amid a clutter of hay and oats. But she continued to eye him, blissfully, he thought, if horses felt bliss.

Ah, he addressed her, at last I've found you!

Ho, Boyd, you've found me, too, Pete said, appearing behind him. I knew you'd get here. Didn't think you'd get here so fast.

Ho, Pete, but let's cool it with the formalities. Boyd embraced his friend.

Well, c'mon back, then. I've got something to show you.

Will Mrs. Kissman be OK?

Who's Mrs. Kissman?

Never mind.

Boyd followed Pete back through the central passageway into another room.

They were sitting at a table with their backs to him, so he wasn't sure at first. But when Pete cawed like a crow, they turned toward him. He counted their faces like the fingers on one hand, and he recognized five of the six people seated there.

As if they'd known he was coming, they lined up to say hello, dispensing with formalities.

How're ya doing, cowboy? Chicken Shit said, with an abrazo.

I knew you'd make it, Boyd, said Dolly, ruddy, redolent as a cactus flower. She kissed him on the cheek. He began, but stopped himself from saying anything about her father. No use bringing up Sonny either.

Why not join the feast, Suzy said, less emaciated than when he'd last seen her.

I-I'm so glad to see you again, M-Mr. Boyd, Karim said. I was too scared to w-wait for you at the w-windmills. I borrowed a h-horse from Tunnel One and followed you to the s-schoolhouse with my friend here. We were afraid to w-wait for you when the wind started to b-blow, so I took your h-horse. I'm sorry about that. Let me introduce you to m-my friend, Adze.

It's a pleasure to meet you, said Adze, who looked as though he could be Karim's big brother. Both were sinewy, with lank hair that reached below their shoulders. But whereas Karim had found new rags to drape over his wiry frame, Adze was decked in sheepskin. For that matter, Dolly and Suzy had found some ragged bits of fabric or animal skin to protect them from the damp, and even Chicken Shit and Pete had done something to their attire—Boyd wasn't sure exactly what, but their junky jeans and desert boots, their sweatshirts, looked as if they'd been mended more durably than ever.

Boyd fingered his lion skin shirt. Ho, Adze.

Won't you please join us for supper, said Adze, who led Boyd to a ceramic basin in an alcove, where he washed his hands and rinsed his face with hot water.

The others made room for him at the table, where Adze set out a clean china plate and spooned something from the cauldron on a propane stove. He passed Boyd a basket of nut-smelling thinly sliced brown bread.

What? No Mick's? Boyd quipped.

The others were too busy saying *yum* and *delicious* to answer.

When Boyd forked a piece of whatever it was into his mouth, he began to *ooh* and *ah*. He'd never tasted anything like this. Chunks of something-or-other swam in a rich brown gravy into which he dipped his bread and tasted its grainy essence steeped in a flavor ever so much more pungent and wonderful than chicken. What was this meat so tender and tasty that he had a moment in which he remembered tasting it in another lifetime, an instant which Grandpa A would call *déjà vu?* What were these red and green cooked goodies that tasted like the earth—along with this freshly baked brown dough so crusty and delectable that he felt as though he would be relishing it for eons? And this long-stemmed goblet? Adze was pouring red liquid into it that was no pulque, no sir! Not that Boyd shunned fermented agave juice, but this was something else. Dolly and Suzy were sipping it, murmuring under their breath. Pete and Chicken Shit were clinking their goblets with Karim's and Adze's—so Boyd joined them and blurted, Here's mud in your eye, though he had no idea what that ridiculous phrase meant or why anyone would want mud in their eye. But between bites of bread, when he quaffed some of the red stuff, he knew he'd drunk it too fast. This was liquid you wanted to imbibe slowly, reveling in its fragrance as well as its taste. It slid over your tongue and excited something way back there, as Cathy Vallée had. It wasn't sweet like Mick's Juicywoosie Brushycrushy, but it wasn't sour or bitter either. It reached down deep and warmed you, made you feel that your life was beginning again, like a roll of film after you removed it from your camera and readied it for your darkroom, only to load a new roll onto your Leica's film spool—and feel a kind of rebirth. What was this beautiful liquid which, when you lifted it in a goblet, glowed redder than a sunrise? Here you sat, in a dank mountain cave, overwhelmed with light!

Cheers! said Adze. There's something I think you should know. But first please pour some more for yourselves.

Later, Boyd would understand the meaning of an entrée with wine. He would even become a bit of a snob when it came to venison and a red wine referred to as Burgundy. He would never again scorn grapefruits and oranges as *junk fruit* or recite Guv'na Brush's proverb,

> *Of all junk fruits the worst is an orange,*
> *Because it doesn't rhyme with anything.*

He would learn about the savory delicacies from the sea and especially covet one known as sockeye salmon. One evening he would sample a type of foreign combination, which his host referred to as *sushi*, and he wouldn't be sure he liked it, though of course he ate it graciously. Of shellfish he would prefer the variety known as *mussels*, served with garlic butter, steaming in their shells; he would remove their tender pink innards shaped like tiny pudenda, and spoon up their broth, which, gritty as it was, tasted like the ocean. Eventually, he would become a *connoisseur*—a word Grandpa A would have liked—but Boyd never took for granted a simple green salad drizzled with vinaigrette. He never became blasé when it came to cherry pie and his old standby, tea.

Adze remained in his chair and picked at his sheepskin garment. The others, also seated, stared at their wineglasses, as if bored, but they were listening.

I think you should know, Adze said, that things were not always like this. You didn't live in condos, teepee houses, or wickiups, and we didn't live in caves. Ever since the Hundred-and-One Revolutions rocked the planet, things have more or less become the way they are in The Valley. Give or take a few cities vaster by far than Desert Center, the inhabited world comprises Valleys and Highlands, Waterside Outposts and Prairie Encampments. How do I know this? Do you think our roomful of old books taught me this? Important as those books are, they stopped being published long ago. Do you think *The Evening Star Wrap-up* taught me what I know? Look around, and you won't see a TV here or in any of our habitations. We have read books by daylight and by lamplight with electricity poached from Windmill City. We have heard of *The Evening Star Wrap-up*, but what we know we have witnessed with our eyes and the ears of our forebears.

You have seen horses tied up in the next room. Listen, you can hear them nickering, Wild Valley Nags we have tamed and used to take us to hayfields and apple orchards, rolling meadows of alfalfa and barley: we grow grain and sugar beets in out-of-the-way places. Think of every Broil station from Teepee Village to Desert Center, all relying on petrol. Think of every petrol rig from the eastern seaboard to the western beaches: behind every station and hole in the ground, tucked away between hedges and rock walls, are gardens, pastures, and vineyards hidden to those who think they are useless. Think how much smarter our horses are than their Miramar mopeds, how much more agile the meanest of our drays is, compared with their bikes. Don't tell me you haven't noticed our tunnels underlying The Valley. Don't tell me you haven't noticed us, but it's true, no one notices what is truly unimaginable, distasteful, or unknown. In a way, we are invisible; for all their palaver, they cannot see us. How often it has been like this throughout history: Did the people of central Asia recognize what Genghis Khan's warriors were all about when they first appeared on the horizon? Did Montezuma really see, from the start, what Cortez aimed to do? Because our people thrive on Valleyites' castoff books, furniture, old china dishes, teacups, and sources of power for light and heat, they call us Looters. I say it is they who long ago looted the world, and we remain right under their noses, ready to recycle their rubbish.

Many years ago after the Hundred-and-One Revolutions, our forebears emerged from ghettos and reservations. From slave camps and military bases, we hopped boxcars and buses—when such modes of transportation still existed—and made our way willy-nilly to rundown farms and abandoned racing stables. You might say we were equestrians unequalled in our sense of equity; we galloped against greed. Our only weapons were rocks, cudgels, and horse sense. We have nothing to do with the razors and switchblades of our antagonists. The only knives we know butcher fish, meat, fowl—or else dice various goodies, some of which you just tasted.

Thanks to your discovery of Tunnel Seven yesterday, Boyd, and thanks to your father-in-law who warned some guards about Karim before they slit the old man's throat, Guv'na Brush and his troops are in a constant state of yellow alert. It is easy for them to denounce an enemy from afar as an abstraction, a necessary scapegoat. It is easier still for them to pursue the real thing—two dark-skinned scarecrows sighted at a golf course—then break into a tunnel inhabited by our people. They have ransacked Tunnel Seven and have begun to fill it in. The lone and level sands will stretch as they were before our burrowing, but I'm glad to say that tunnel doesn't link up with any others. Unlike Tunnel One, which runs alongside the railroad tracks and bisects much of The Valley from east to west, or Tunnel Two, which connects north with south, our seventh underground lifeline was a modest two kilometers in length, dug after the Third War of Excision by dozens of our number who had a fondness for the environs outside of Rattlers Parish. Well, they are long gone, victims not so much of the Fourth War as of their curiosity. Some of them wandered outside without canteens early one summer day and died of heatstroke that afternoon.

I won't bother you with details, how I, for example, acquired my name. Our mothers—who have moved from tunnels to a cave not far from this one— our women named us after saints. We were John or

Teresa, Mark or Mary. That is the way with our wom-
en; they are dreamers and poets. Karim forswore his
given name and chose a new one as did I, out of what
used to be known as street smarts, an intuition that
lurks in us as it does in our animals.

But, lest you think me a Bighorn Bag of Wind in
sheep's clothes, I need to tell you that my mother
bore me in a southern wild that used to be known
as Mexico. She and my father mounted their horses
during a dry season and, so she told me, rode into the
north wind for days till they found themselves in a
canyon oasis with fan palms, dates, and mule deer.
They rested there among other horsepeople who had
hitched their hopes to a new land. They hunted and
fished in fresh-water creeks that poured down from
the mountains. My mother bore two more children,
stillborn brothers. But she was restless; I can still remember her pressing her lips to my cheek, saying, *I
want a girl.* In due time she got her wish, a living baby
daughter who killed her mother in childbirth. Well,
we broke camp and rode north out of that canyon
soon thereafter, and I hardly recall my sister saying
anything. By the time we homed in on these horsepeople and settled outside Tunnel Four here in The
Valley, she was *gooing* and *gahhing.* But, alas, one day
the next year when my father left me to ride with her
up to these caves, they were caught by the Guv'na's
uniformed guards and dispatched, along with the

piebald mare they were riding. A group of us found them by a wash east of Teepee Village. I can't tell you how horrid they smelled, how wretched they looked with their eyes pecked out by vultures.

Boyd stood up from his chair. Please stop, he said. I can't understand most of what you're saying, and what I understand I can't bear.

Aw, c'mon, pal! said Chicken Shit. Toughen up!

But Boyd saw that Dolly was leaning heavily on Suzy, who was in tears. Pete's head wobbled on his neck; his eyes had turned into slits, and he looked as though he might fall off his chair, dozing.

Karim coughed—just like a horse, Boyd thought— and said, M-Mr. Boyd, don't be afraid, G-God is good, it is a beautiful night.

Now Adze stood up from his chair. I agree, he said. Why not let Karim and me show you one more thing; it's full tonight. Then we can hit the bunkhouse. You will need all your energy tomorrow. After the destruction of Tunnel Seven, we've had enough. Once and for all, we're going to—how did your mother say it, Karim?—kick the enemy's butt. Our scouts have left them notes of fair warning as to where and when. They will find out about our caves up here, but we'll kick them so hard they'll leave us alone at last. From his sheepskin boots to his fleecy cap, Adze scurried with Karim to lead Boyd and his companions out of the dining room into the central passageway. They strode up the dirt floor to the mouth of the cave. Boyd felt his jaw go *clickety-clack* in the cold. He glanced back at Dolly, whose jaw was also clacking.

Look, said Adze, you can barely see it through the snow and cloud clumps.

The wind blew infinite numbers of tiny white flakes almost horizontally; they had already coated shrubs and rocks with something like fleece. Boyd tried to peer through the snow and ignore the wind's blast, the deafening whoosh that filled his ears and made his jaw clack faster.

C-can you see it? Up there between the r-rocks?

It was Pete who saw it first. He crowed, though Boyd could barely hear him.

Then it was Suzy. Oh, my gosh! Dorothy, look! she said.

Finally, Dolly and Chicken Shit joined Boyd in glimpsing it between the V of two ledges.

No wonder they call this Mount Marvelous! Dolly shouted.

What the fuck, it looks like a big egg! Chicken Shit cried.

I've never in my life—What's the real name for that thingamabob up there? Boyd hollered.

TUESDAY

Late into the night he heard them tying up their horses in what must have been nearby stables, clanking pots and utensils in the dining room, filing into the cave where he lay tossing. There must have been hundreds of them; he could smell their sweat and hair. And the cave must have had numerous bunkrooms to house them. Adze had mentioned that women and men normally shared caves and tunnels throughout The Valley. But there was a yellow alert, and some of the women had retreated to care for the children in safer quarters. Ever since Desert Center had reliable sightings, Adze and other leaders, both women and men—known as The Dearly Beloveds—had advocated separation for safety's sake. Adze and Karim's seeming to feel comfortable with Dolly and Suzy suggested that separation of the sexes was not an everyday policy. Before saying goodnight to Boyd, Adze had mentioned that he'd known many women who preferred their own company, just as he'd been friends with men who'd chosen one another to live with. Bunkhouses might not be the most private love nests, but communal living never prevented loved ones from coming together.

Think of it as *joy*, Adze had said. The smooching you hear tonight will involve males. Their joyous noises will be accompanied by the voices of men and women inning and outing, as will be their wont, in our caves and tunnels when life gets right again. Now, life is on yellow alert, and we are all up here in caves and will need to rest for tomorrow.

It must have been well after midnight when Boyd, lulled by grunts and heavy breathing, warm under his deerskin blanket, forgot about the shrill wind and let himself drift on a snowflake higher than Mount Marvelous toward the—but he had already forgotten the name of the enormous round egg in the night sky.

Wake up, Pete said. Couldn't you hear the crow cawing?

Aw, c'mon, that grape juice we drank— I don't know, Boyd said. He hadn't had a headache as bad as this since Mindy accidentally crowned him with a stone she'd lobbed at a jackrabbit.

No kidding, Boyd, you need to get ready. You know the story.

Boyd nursed his head in his hands. Where are Dolly and Suzy?

Bundled off to another cave.

For Brush's sake, where are Sonny and Cathy Vallée?

Hey, cut that *for Brush's sake* shit; we're on our

own here! Last night you said something about Sonny staying with his girlfriend. And who the hell is Cathy Vallée, if I may be so rude to ask? I mean, what a strange name!

Boyd stumbled to a large basin of water and doused his face. *Brrr,* that's better, he said.

Now c'mon, let's get breakfast. The others have already left, as you can see.

Boyd saw: the bunkhouse was as empty as it had been when he'd lain down last night across from Chicken Shit, Pete, and Karim.

As he sat over tea and butter-and-honey-covered thingamajigs called hot cakes, Karim joined him.

G-good morning, Mr. Boyd. Would you like some t-tea?

Sure, why not? I don't usually eat breakfast, but this stuff—yum!

I've s-saved your horse for you.

Why, thanks, kid. I guess we've got stuff to do today.

Yes, w-we don't need TVs to tell us what's going on in The V-Valley. Adze left; he told me to wish you G-God speed.

Boyd pushed back his plate and swigged his tea.

P-Pete and Andrew will be staying behind. Pete's got a c-cold, and Andrew, well, he told me he's c-chicken shit.

Ha! That's a good one, Karim!

As they entered the stable, she nickered. Just don't give me a love bite, he thought. Your choppers would cut through my lion skin shirt.

Karim's roan stallion and Mrs. Kissman's spots would have made a nice snapshot, Boyd thought. But he'd left his Leica at the schoolhouse, and today would surely be too chaotic to capture on film. Still, he had the feeling he'd had yesterday, that he'd often seen Mrs. Kissman standing next to a roan stallion in a stable like this, that she'd been waiting for him since the olden days and might well nicker at the stallion until the end of time.

Now their hooves clopped up the central passageway to the brightening exit in the rocks.

At first Boyd couldn't see anything. It had stopped snowing. But he was used to the dim, lamp-lit cave, and everything outside was so white he rubbed his eyes, which started to tear like a schoolboy's. Stop it, he thought, but he couldn't stop crying. When he finally began to cope with his snow-blindness, he saw that Karim, too, was weeping, wiping his eyes.

It gets b-better, Mr. Boyd, believe me.

Sure stings, though.

Yes, but look at those b-branches covered with snow. That juniper's s-shagged with ice.

Right you are.

Mrs. Kissman made headway down the slope, sticking to a narrow trail Boyd had hardly noticed on his way up the mountain yesterday. But she followed the hoof prints of horses that had preceded her, and Karim's roan stallion Abdul tailed Mrs. Kissman with more than competence. Despite his being larger than she as she descended, he was downwind of her. Boyd chuckled when he thought of her other name, Windy, which fit her quite well this morning after what must have been a breakfast of corn and beans. Karim didn't say a word, but Boyd guessed he was aware of what Abdul might have relished.

The snow thinned out as they approached The Valley floor. It was blustery, but the sun had come out from behind the clouds as they'd descended.

Ah, Mr. B-Boyd, the hillside's dew-pearled.

Hey kid, what's gotten into you? You never talked this way. I took you for a silent guy.

Sure, it's f-fun to be silent. I like to think about things, let them steep, you k-know, like tea. But Abdul and I also like to s-sing.

Aw, c'mon, horses can't sing.

Listen to Abdul, Mr. B-Boyd.

Karim put his mouth to the horse's ear and whispered something. All at once, Abdul whinnied musically. Mrs. Kissman perked up her ears, and Boyd couldn't identify the melody, but—whew!—after a while he recognized it as the opening section of *Don't Fence Me In*.

Boyd couldn't believe what was happening. It

wasn't just a horse singing; it was that he was becoming someone he'd never been, someone who talked as strangely as Karim. He'd begun remembering lines and phrases his father and Grandma B taught him from old books—sometimes he couldn't avoid reciting these lines in his head. He had never thought of himself as anyone other than an ordinary Valleyite, a freelance photographer, Sonny's dad, and Dolly's hubby—he hated the term *hubby*, but he clung to it; he thought it fit him as a spouse. But if now was the time to cast off expressions like *for Brush's sake,* it was time to talk and think in ways that seemed righter than ever, in tune with his new friends and whatever was happening to him. He wasn't really Dolly's spouse anymore; neither was he strictly speaking a photographer. The leather sack full of sticks and stones cinched to Mrs. Kissman's haunches bespoke a rougher profession.

Don't look back, Mr. Boyd. We're coming to the base of the mountain, and we'll be turning north soon. But I thought you should know a few things about me in case, well, in case things don't work out for me.

How strange! Karim was no longer stuttering.

Adze told you about his trip from Mexico. I had a long journey, too, from back east, thousands of kilometers on the other side of this mountain. Guv'na Brush named it Mount Marvelous—not true, I say.

It was anything but marvelous to find after our trek through the salt flats back east. But I can tell you this: my mother was from a long line of explorers. After her husband's death in the Old Country ten thousand kilometers across the eastern ocean, long before I was born, my mother said she was fed up. Fed up with eating? I once asked her. She laughed and said, No, back then she'd been fed up with burqas, bridegrooms, and the idea of babies. She had—how do you say this?—her tubes tied as soon as she arrived in this country, or she thought she had them tied! She had always loved athletics, especially one sport in which you throw a ball through a hoop. One day she met a man after one of these games, and they—how do you say this?—shot hoops. *Toom, toom, toom,* the ball sounded as it hit the court. She was so good that she scored three-pointers. She liked to tell me that she *kicked his butt*! But they loved one another, I think, and they set out for the great prairie grassland sometime after the so-called Fourth War of Excision. They must have been kicking each other's butt very hard, because one morning she woke up and vomited. Every morning after that she vomited. She couldn't believe it when her belly started to swell. Much as she fancied her ballplayer, she stole his horse and took off one morning he slept late in a shack where they had been living while he gave sports lessons to *local yokels*—that's what my mother told me he called them.

212

The next months she made her way west, stopping in villages to cook and clean house for yokels. Sometimes she would stay a week, sometimes a month. And before you knew it, in the basin territory east of The Valley, I was born. I can barely believe the stories she told me about how hard it was for her to get over the mountain—you call it marvelous, she called it malevolent. She lost four of her toes from frostbite and nearly slipped off a snowfield into a canyon, with me tied to her back. She felt the mountain rumble and thought she saw smoke pouring from its top. An avalanche came close to burying us both. In a sense, she never made it beyond the mountain. She settled on its western slope with the horsepeople in Cave W, for women. She cooked and cleaned, she taught me how to ride and whisper to horses—isn't that right, Abdul? And she died in one of Guv'na Brush's raids west of Teepee Village a few years ago—I know you do not understand the term *years*, but it is the same as *winters*. I will not bother you with awful details about her rape and what the Guv'na's guards did to her throat.

Boyd was about to let loose with a curse when Mrs. Kissman shied. A few kilometers north, on the other side of the railroad tracks, he could see a cluster of horsemen. Although he couldn't hear them, Mrs. Kissman could. She stomped her right front hoof in the sand by a palo verde tree; Abdul did likewise.

Then they were off in a blaze of gravel over the tracks and up the rutted trail towards the horsemen. It's happening again, Boyd thought, though he had little time for thought. The Valley floor rose slightly into an area of badlands beyond which it was impossible to see. Much as he knew what lay to the north, he was afraid to speculate. He could no longer rely on fixed foci. Things had become too unpredictable to measure the light with a meter and say Windmill City was dead ahead.

Yet there it was, with dozens of horsemen spread out before it. As Abdul and Mrs. Kissman galloped side by side over a barren stretch of rain-warped hillocks, the ragged band of horsemen came slowly into focus, facing the gated enclosure of windmills whose steel blades gleamed. The horsemen couldn't have heard Boyd and Karim at their backs, but if they had, they might have welcomed the two latecomers into their ranks. Whomever they were facing Boyd couldn't see, though he knew this was a major stand-off.

The badlands ended with an eroded creek bed, which Abdul and Mrs. Kissman leaped over, and the enemy burst into view. It was hard to count Guv'na Brush's elite Sandstorm Troopers in their bumble-bee-striped uniforms with special epaulets, but Boyd estimated at least a hundred. Stretched out behind the guardrail topped with barbed wire, they outnum-

bered the horsemen three to one. In their yellow hel-
mets, with sunglasses, they gunned their mopeds—
Boyd could hear them now—and the combined
revving of their engines sounded thunderous. Obviously, they weren't going anywhere; they couldn't
leap the guardrail or moped en masse through the
narrow gateway arch. They were guarding the mills
against intruders, and they might have looked like
peacemakers, were it not for their implacable scowls.

Boyd and Karim managed to squeeze between the
motley ranks of the horsemen, who were not, he saw,
exclusively men. Although every rider's horse toted
a leather bagful of sticks and stones, every second
or third horse carried a woman. With shorn hair or
locks tied in a bun under a ragged scarf, their gender
was unmistakable. Boyd scanned the ranks for Dolly
and Suzy in vain, but he could make out the buzz of
furious female voices:

That one raped my mom.

That one killed my boy and burned our fruit trees.

That one put my man in jail and made the Guv'na
hang him.

Clad in sheepskin, with a headpiece that sprouted massive, curved horns, Adze sat atop his black
stallion in the front line directly opposite the arched
gateway. He seemed about to raise his hand, which,
Boyd could see, grasped some sort of rock.

Whoa! Boyd snapped. Hang on, Adze!

Well, it's about time! Adze said. He seemed not to notice Karim, who looked more childlike than just a minute ago, as if he might start stuttering again.

Listen, maybe I can talk to them, Boyd said.

Ha! Talk to these stinkbugs?

Well, it never hurts to try. I'm no pacifist. But look at those switchblades and slingshots with razors. We've only got— He patted his leather sack.

All along the line the horses were whinnying, restless. Who knew but that their brood mares or colts had been slashed by these guards? Who knew, Boyd thought, but that these Wild Valley Nags were eager to give the Guv'na's uniformed guards the kicks and bites they deserved ever since Rudy Newhouse's horse-hating followers slaughtered their forebears?

Look, Boyd said, give me a minute. I think I see someone I know behind their lines. Boyd pointed to a man twitching on the banana seat of a Miramar mega-ped alongside the motionless hulk of Old Forty-nine behind the troops.

OK, go, said Adze, lowering his hand.

Take care, kid, Boyd said to Karim and nudged Mrs. Kissman.

At a slow *clop clop* they approached the archway. When the guards revved their mopeds in unison, he smiled so broadly his cheeks hurt, took his fake beard and hairpiece out of his pocket, and waved them as a peace signal. This produced gales of laughter from the Guv'na's guards; perhaps they'd seen white flags, but never a scraggly disguise. Well—why not?— Boyd joined them in laughter. It was as if he'd brought back the remnants of a Looter, not the full head, but its follicles.

Ha ha! Yes, this is funny, he thought. Now all I need to do is have a powwow. I'd love to beat you fellows over the head, but my grandmother once told me that true heroes beat their swords into plowshares. Before I let out a war whoop, I'd like to give peace the tiniest chance. He pointed to the man behind the lines seated on the mega-ped, obviously the boss.

The word *boss* made Boyd think of Hayes. Here he was playing with Hayes's whiskers and wig, but where was Hayes? Where was the Boss?

Although Boyd *tsked*, nobody could have heard him. His smile evaporated as he prodded Mrs. Kissman through the arched gateway; the Guv'na's troops parted to let him through. They'd stopped laughing, too; their mirrored sunglasses glinted this way and that—sometimes they caught Boyd square in his eyes. Still, he proceeded, high above the men on mopeds, whiffing Broils petrol fumes, trying not to cough.

Lord, let me not sneeze, he thought. He noticed he'd invoked the LORD, rather than Guv'na Brush.

As Mrs. Kissman ambled up a little hill below Old Forty-nine, which overshadowed Boyd and the man on his mega-ped, the wind abated. Yet the other forty-eight mills, give or take one or two that were still under repair, were twirling like pinwheels.

Ho, Boyd.

Ho, Mr. Crabbe.

How's, 'hem, Mrs. Boyd?

How's your mustache?

Never fear. Guv'na Brush—

—is a dead tarantula if he thinks he can get away with butchering these people.

Oh, c'mon, Boyd, you don't mean to say you've been fooled by these Looters!

Sir, I'm no man's enemy. Not your Troopers', not Guv'na Brush's. But you know as well as I that *there's a purple stile that little yellow boys and girls are climbing all the while.*

What are you talking about, young man?

I'm saying that *two roads diverged in a yellow wood.*

In the name of the father, the son, and The Burning Brush, what is this gibberish?

I'm telling you that *my days are in the yellow leaf; the flowers and fruits of Love are gone,*

Boyd, 'hem, you need help!

Clarence, it's you who need help. I'm just speaking from the heart, stuff I thought I'd forgotten that my grandmother taught me. But you and your yellow-bellied troops; you and your lemon-colored pet canary, Rudy Newhouse or whatever he's called—he's not even a real person, is he?—he's a figment—you and your yellow journalism, your *Evening Star Wrap-up*, your father's mustache, your mother's hemming and hawing: I say cease and desist with these my people; I say *Fuck Guv'na Brush!*

The troops must have heard this last remark. They whipped around on their banana seats, incredulous, as the wind gusted. Boyd glimpsed Hayes half-hidden behind a tiny curtained window midway up Old Forty-nine. He must have been at the controls, which had been turned off. All at once the giant steel blades of the mill caught the blast of west wind and started to twirl with tremendous momentum. It all happened so fast that no one moved a muscle. Boyd got caught in one of those time-lapse photos he'd found himself in lately, but it didn't last long. A single mill blade came down precisely where Clarence Crabbe sat poised on his Miramar mega-ped. At the last instant Boyd yanked Mrs. Kissman back and turned his head away. Clarence Crabbe was in the middle of a *'hem* when his voice broke and his skull was cloven. It sounded like a grapefruit split up the middle, only there was no cutting board for the knife's blade to knock, only a squish, then the squeak of Clarence Crabbe followed by his mega-ped hitting the ground, *ker-thump!* Boyd glanced up at the curtained window, but Hayes was nowhere to be seen.

A roar of dismay went up through the bumble-bee-striped troops just as Boyd's outnumbered comrades, led by Adze, charged the guardrails. Boyd watched half a dozen horses bolt through the arched gateway, while a gaggle of them leaped over the barbed wire. The troops gunned their mopeds but couldn't very well leap over the rail. Neither did they have time to turn around and vamoose. Many of them sprang open their switchblades and tried to load their slingshots with razors, only to be rammed off their mopeds and trampled by the horses, agile enough to regain their balance.

Boyd watched this melee for a few seconds. He would never photograph a scene like this or see one like it on TV.

Then he slapped Mrs. Kissman's rump, and he was busy trampling as many troops as he could, whacking helmeted heads with a pinyon cudgel. One Trooper, who'd lost his sunglasses and slashed Boyd's leg, glared at him and, before mopeding off to the west, growled, *You'll be dead by nightfall, shithead!*

As it turned out, most of the troops mopeded away, wounded and cursing. Finally, Adze shouted, Whoa!

Boyd counted the casualties: at least ten dark, ragged men and women, not to mention four times as many Sandstorm Troopers. The surviving horsepeople dismounted to sling corpses over their nags, rope together the riderless horses, and travel back to the hills. He observed all this, as if through a telephoto lens, while he continued to bleed through his lion skin leg wear until Karim, who had a gash on his forehead, approached with a rag.

Wait, Boyd said, don't use that! I'll get infected.

Don't w-worry, Mr. Boyd. This rag is clean. All our rags are clean.

And how in God's name is that?

You see that c-canvass bag over there? It is full of r-rags we have boiled in water and soaked in alcohol. Also, there is this a-aloe plant. I used it on my h-head.

Boyd let him roll up his leggings, clean his wound, and wrap it in a gauzy material. How Karim managed to wrap everything up was information unfit for *The Evening Star Wrap-up*!

On the trail south, Adze thanked him. Now you're one of us, he said. Thanks to you, I believe Karim and I suffered few wounds. You must return, feast with us, spend the night. We are your new friends, along with your—how do you call them?—your *buddies*?

Give them my regards, Boyd said. I'm sorry I need to turn down your gracious invitation for now; I know I'll see you soon. His leg wound chafed beneath his lion skin breeches.

It was still early when Adze and Karim turned east up the trail toward their caves. The sun hadn't cleared the snowy summit of Mount Marvelous when Boyd slapped Mrs. Kissman's rump, and they proceeded to canter south toward Rattlers Parish. The Valley's sunny kilometers to the west seemed to be filled with water, a lake he knew to be a mirage. Still, he let himself go and suddenly recited another line Grandma B had taught him: *The day is like wide water, without sound.*

Funny how Grandma B had remembered all that stuff. It was as if he was an old rain barrel that had once been full of her recollections. Now, in dry weather, the barrel was empty, but it retained an unfathomable aqueous sheen. Until the moment he'd stood alongside Clarence Crabbe and burst forth, he'd never known he was a repository of such words by dead men. Dead women, too, for that matter. He couldn't remember her name or the man she was writing about, but a woman had described her friend's face as a *yellow bronze mask all draped upon an iron framework.* Now, if that wasn't as vivid as a snapshot! Words like that were worth a thousand pictures!

Right now he'd trade his memory bank for a glimpse of Cathy Vallée. She'd look good in lion skin, he was sure, as long as it didn't cover her pageboy. He loosened his sweater's buttons and let the winter wind have its way with him.

By the time he loped through downtown Rattlers Parish—careful to avoid Ye Olde Towne Square—the sun had cleared Mount Marvelous. The desert brightened for all of a minute before a cloudbank lowered, casting everything in a gray glare. The sky looked threatening again as Mrs. Kissman slowed to a trot through Rattlesnake Alley. The dogs were nowhere to be seen this morning, but the swarthy ragamuffin was, as usual, outside her wickiup, taking stuff down from a clothesline. She waved, but this time she dropped her clothespins and dashed over to Boyd.

Ho, sir.

Ho, little girl, what's your name?

I don't have one. I'm just called Little Girl.

Don't you have a mother and dad?

No, I live alone here. She pointed to her wickiup.

But that's impossible. Who takes care of you?

I do. I wash and dry their clothes. She pointed to neighboring huts.

Whew, I wish I could—

Sir, don't worry about me. I stopped you today because there's something funny going on around here. You look like a nice man, not like those guards with sunglasses or those guys who come skulking around my door at night.

Why don't I—

No, believe me, sir. I can take care of myself. I even hope to go to school one day in Rattlers Parish. But it's funny, you know all the dogs around here? They're gone. Do you think coyotes ate them?

I doubt it.

My neighbors doubt it, too. Mr. Pebbleshook

doesn't know what to think; he's in a wheelchair and lost his terrier. She pointed up the street to a hut even more decrepit than her wickiup. Terriers are small, but Mrs. Sandstrom can't find her dog either, and he's a cross between a Rottweiler and a St. Bernard.

Tell you what, Little Girl, I'll look into this. I've got things to do first, but we're, like, neighbors, and, well, hang on a bit!

He nudged Mrs. Kissman on to Jilly's condo. Curiously, the streets were deserted, as if the Guv'na had declared a curfew. Yet there were no bumble-bee-striped uniformed guards patrolling on mopeds.

Brittlebush Boulevard was more upscale than his neighborhood—Boyd shuddered to think of his trashed condo—but more modest than Grandpa A's. Little good the doctor's corral and whirlpool bath did him, Boyd thought, hitching Mrs. Kissman to a gate-post.

He should have known, from Jilly's door chimes, that trouble lay beyond the entryway. *Sunrise Gold* boinged like a reminder to stand at attention. By habit Boyd turned into a ramrod and saluted properly by placing the palm of his right hand over his mouth as the door opened. The tall blonde who greeted him wore a black satin dress festooned with silver buttons. She would have been attractive if her face didn't appear to be squashed to one side. At first Boyd thought she might have had a stroke, but he rapidly realized that she was smirking at him, as though she were smoking an invisible cigarette—though cigarettes had long been banned.

Ho, Mr. Boyd.

Ho, Mrs. Mack.

How's Mrs. Boyd?

How's Mr. Mack?

Never fear. Guv'na Brush—

—is here.

Now that they'd exchanged customary greetings with high-fives, Mrs. Mack said, I don't know why I'm bothering to be civil with you, Mr. Boyd.

I've just come to pick up Sonny. Aren't he and Jilly—

Haven't you seen the TV?

No, I've been out on some errands.

I should say so! *The Morning Star Wrap-up* has been broadcasting yellow alerts about you all day.

Is Sonny here? I'd like to—

They said you'd be riding some Wild Valley Nag. Not a bad specimen tied up out there, I'd say. What's his name?

Mrs. Mack, would you please—

I will do what I please, sir. You don't look like the sort of Looter who would rape me and burn down this house. But I might as well tell you that you've wrecked things here. My husband and I were supposed to have luncheon with Mr. Crabbe's assistant in Ye Olde Towne Square, but thanks to you, he had to cancel and has been called back to headquarters. Look at this dress: do you think I'd be traipsing around in it if not for luncheon?

Luncheon, what's that?

Why, you silly man, where's your education? Luncheon refers to chicken salad sandwiches we eat between breakfast and supper.

Oh, you mean lunch? he laughed.

What's the use of talking to a violent man who can't speak the Guv'na's mother tongue?

Mrs. Mack, I'm not here to debate the *un* in luncheon. I'm here to pick up my son. Boyd winced at how his words rhymed.

Well, I'm sorry to tell you that Sonny's not here? My husband made sure of that. The Guv'na's guards have taken your boy in for questioning.

Boyd slapped his forehead. How dare they do that? Sonny had nothing to do with what happened at Windmill City.

Please don't get hysterical, Mr. Boyd. I'm truly sorry your son is under arrest. He's such a nice albino boy, really he is. And I think Jilly agrees. I read books, you know; I'm no dummy.

She unscrunched her smirk and called out, Jilly, oh, Jilly, would you please come out here?

Jilly stepped from behind the living room curtains. I've been right here all along, Mom.

Would you please tell Sonny's father what happened?

Boyd noticed how Jilly didn't resemble her mother. Not only was the girl shorter, which would be normal for her age, but she was plump, with a face Boyd would call cute but not striking like her mother's. She had dirty blond hair that would probably turn auburn as she got older, and the bone structure of her face reminded him of Mindy's long ago. Either Jilly took after her father or she was an adopted child.

What happened? You want to know what happened, Mom?

Jilly swiveled to face Boyd. I wish I knew. Sonny and I were watching TV, talking about his mom, if you want to know. In the middle of playing Spin the Toothbrush, all of a sudden a face comes on the screen wearing a fake beard and hairpiece, Mr. Boyd. At first we're too busy playing to notice, but then Sonny pulls away from me and says, Dad! That's Dad! Right away there's another photo of a clean-shaven man; he's bald. And there's this notice under both of your pictures that says, Wanted! Five thousand Bees for any information leading to the arrest of these two men. Then before I can button my blouse, some guards are at the door.

They led Sonny away without a struggle, Mrs. Mack said.

No, Mom, that's not true. He kicked one of them you know where, and they led him away in handcuffs.

***

Outside, the street was still deserted. They must be looking for me on Mount Marvelous, Boyd thought. How much easier to follow the hoof prints of dozens of nags up the mountain than to see that one set of prints veered off toward Rattlers Parish. Hayes had apparently escaped. As for Hayes's Boss, Boyd had never seen him. For all Boyd knew, the Boss might be one and the same as Guv'na Brush, if not the late Clarence Crabbe. Hayes may never have bothered to mention this to Boyd, but now that he pondered, it seemed to make sense. Clarence Crabbe might have hemmed and hawed his way into every sandstone cranny in The Valley. This might explain the TV yellow alert issued by an underling, as well as the absence of troops in the streets. Rudderless without their leader, the Guv'na's troops in sunglasses may well have decided to doff their bumblebee-striped uniforms and become civilians.

If this was wishful thinking, it was better to wish upon a cloud, however threatening, than to think of Sonny behind bars, guarded by an army of the Guv'na's followers. Nevertheless, Boyd tapped Mrs. Kissman's rump and glanced over his shoulder as they trotted over to Chicory-Chick Court.

Damn! he said when he saw a moped by a bicycle outside a nondescript condo. The moped port's caliche driveway divided a grassless front yard without olive trees or cacti. Surrounded by white sand so flawless it might have been mopeded in from the renowned dunes west of the golf course, a rock garden glittered in the gray afternoon light. After Boyd dismounted and tied Mrs. Kissman to one of the moped port's posts, he couldn't help noticing how the rose quartz and mica glinting in the variegated rocks had been carefully piled to simulate something—he wasn't sure what. He blinked at the optical illusion. Was this a mirage, or was he too fatigued to make sense of what he saw?

He knocked at the front door and looked back at the pile. No, it was no mirage. The rock garden had been arranged to resemble jewelry arranged on a necklace.

The short towheaded man who opened his door took one look at Boyd and tried to slam it shut. Fortunately, Boyd's desert boot served as a doorstopper. With no formal greetings, he stepped inside and grabbed the man's arm; he was brandishing a small switchblade.

Now, why would you want to do that? Boyd said.

Ow, you're hurting me! the man said, dropping the knife to the floor with a clang.

That's because you were planning to hurt me.

Yeah, but you didn't have to break my arm.

Where is she? Boyd said, noting the man's pinkie rings. He was also wearing a silver ID bracelet, which

Boyd was sure had gone out of fashion after the Latter-day Wars That Have No Name. Boyd didn't need to glance down to know who this man was.

He fingered the mole on his left cheek and said it again: Where is she?

I have no idea who you're referring to.

Boyd pulled at his cowlick. Mrs. Kissman, who else? He sniffed and caught her aroma: the ever-so-subtle smell of a pine grove.

The TV says you call your horse Mrs. Kissman.

Boyd *tsked* so loudly the man winced.

OK, Mr. Boyd, I'm sorry. I guess I cared too much about that old war song, *When Johnny Comes Marching Home*. I thought I could march back here after my work at Desert Center, and everything would be OK. She would say, *hurrah hurrah*—or is it *hooray hooray*?

What're you trying to tell me, Mister?

That my wife's not here. She left me.

Boyd pocketed the switchblade and strode from room to room, opening closets, looking under the bed.

Are you satisfied? the man said when Boyd finished checking. It's not enough that she had her fling with old scar face, Heetclit. Now she's got you. How do I know this? Do you think she tells me? No, sir, but I've got antennae. I've got a flair; my mother taught me how to read peoples' minds. I can tell what you're thinking right now.

Sure, pal, and I can tell you're Guv'na Brush! Your wife didn't leave you. She was forced out—

You're crazy!

She was stung by a couple of bumblebees with sunglasses!

You're nuts, you know that?

Johnny, I hardly know you, Boyd said, and shoved the man against the wall so hard that the framed display of an enormous rhinestone wedding ring broke loose from its hook and slammed down on his noggin, causing a burst of white sky-dots—the dead eyes of Guv'na Brush's patriots—to cascade over his head, accompanied by the squawk of a caged parrot.

Boyd tied Mrs. Kissman to an ornamental hitching post by a defunct diner just south of downtown Rattlers Parish. The Chicken Coop had finally closed when a glitzy Chick-O-Pea bistro opened on Ye Olde Towne Square, making it tough for competition.

Finding a bucket and a hose connected to a spigot that still worked, Boyd set out water for the horse. Now you be a good Mrs. Kissman, he whispered in her ear. I'll be back and we'll ride again soon.

He could still hear her snorting in his mind's ear as he ducked and dodged between alleys. When he finally made it to the door of the courthouse and city jail, he was surprised to find it unlocked. The Valley may have officially been in a state of yellow alert, but a Tuesday-afternoon lull hung over Rattlers Parish.

Inside, a floor-to-ceiling tapestry woven into an image of Guv'na Brush dominated the lobby. With his smile-slash-smirk meticulously depicted in cloth, from his boots to his ten-gallon hat, he presided over the receptionist gussied up in a chic outfit whose fabric appeared to resemble crispy fried-chicken skin. At first she didn't recognize him in his fake beard. The lobby was deserted.

Ho. Who goes there?

Ho, Johnny Kissman. How's the Mister?

Ha! I'm not married. And you don't look like Johnny— Say, haven't I seen you before?

Mebbe. Where, Boyd thought, did I come up with the laughable word *mebbe*?

Well, whoever you are, Mrs. Kissman's not here.

I know, I left her at a hitching post.

Huh?

Never mind. I guess I was thinking of an old friend I wanted to get hitched to. She jilted me.

Who'd ever jilt a man like *you*, for Brush's sake?

But you say my wife's not here.

Nope, two guys made off with her.

What about the kid she came with?

Oh, the albino? He's back there, she said, pointing to two swinging doors.

Boyd pivoted before the receptionist could exchange formal goodbyes.

He swung through the doors and was hit by a whiff of pulque. Inside an anteroom, with his legs propped on a table, a paunchy Sandstorm Trooper sprawled watching a TV bolted high on the wall. He glanced at Boyd and said, Ho, c'mon in, why don'tcha.

Boyd clenched his fists but the bumblebee-striped Trooper removed his sunglasses and said, Howdy pardner!

Where's my son? Boyd said.

Now don'tcha worry, fren. Your kid's in the back, safe as all get-out. The Trooper began to hiccup.

I'll get him fer ya in just a sec, hic. But canya believe this boolshit? Ever since that buncha Looters lambasted our Troopers this mornin', there's been a hullabaloo like I've never, hic—

With his legs still on the table, he motioned Boyd over to the TV monitor. Boyd gazed up at a huge crowd that surrounded Sandstone Manse. There was no voice-over, only video images of people chanting, carrying signs, *Down with SM!* and *Let Brush Eat Mush!*

Where's Sonny? Boyd roared.

Here, hic, take these keys, said the Sandstorm Trooper. Canya believe this bool—hic!

Dad, I'm in here! Sonny yelled.

Boyd used the key and flung open the cell.

Oh, Dad, I heard your voice. They took Krs. Missman away.

But she's hitched— Oh, sorry, son, I can't think straight.

These two guys took her away. I could hear gorses halloping up the street.

Were they wearing bumblebee-striped uniforms?

Naw, one old guy had a beard, and the other looked nervous, but they weren't wearing sunglasses. They said they weren't sure they'd make it. Said it'd be easier if they left me here; they knew you'd be coming to get me. The Trooper let them go; I think he doesn't know what he's doing.

The Sandstorm Trooper loosened his uniform's belt and was scratching his crotch. Hey, he said, have a look at the TV, hic, it's sure somepin.

The demonstrators surrounding SM had grown in number, or so it seemed to Boyd.

Gee, Dad, what's that sign mean, *Fuck Guv'na Brush?*

Just as Boyd was about to explain, a deep male voice announced, Good people, please rise for the first stanza of our Valley's anthem, *Sunrise Gold.*

The video of street marchers cut to a shot of a yellow-and-black flag striped like a bumblebee, with what looked like a stinger in the upper left corner but was actually a switchblade's glittering tip. A well known soprano belted out the beginning, accompanied by a Jew's harp and someone blowing over a piece of tissue paper pressed to a comb:

O stand and behold
Our sunrise gold.
It's so lovely and lush
We must thank Guv'na Brush.

The anthem's strains died out as the image of the flag, Old Bumblebee, cut to a close-up of a man's beardless face. Sonny broke the silence: Who's he, Dad?

Sssh, Boyd said. Listen up.

At a podium in front of SM's arched portico, the speaker was expressionless. Monumentally dead-pan with one squinted eye that looked weirdly evil, his face resembled one of the stone countenances Dolly used to sculpt, in the early stages of her hammer-and-chiseling.

Greetings, or should I say good evening? Un-fortunately, the Guv'na is busy doing his business. Call me his mouthpiece, whatever. It's not evening, I realize, and it's sure not the end of the day when it comes to everything y'all care about. Some Looters have spread rumors about the Guv'na's death. Some bozos claim he never existed. Well, friends, in the words of the Guv'na's dear, departed comrade, that's a pile of *merde*. But I'm not here to speak French. I'm here hoping y'all carry on with me, learning the truth that shall make us free—of what? you wanna know. Free most of all of Looters who would trade our riches for rags. Word has it a band of the scruffiest of these darkies has beaten back a team of our finest troops. Word has it that, bright and early this morning, the Guv'na's Chief Spokesman and Head of Internal Goings On, plus a number of his elite Sandstorm Troopers, were outnumbered, ambooshed by a group of male and female Looters. Think of it, Valley pals, these scraggly dirt bags use women, as well as men, to do their fighting. This, as y'all know, is topsy-turvological, as the Guv'na's *Good Book* tells it like it is in Article Twelve:

> *Wouldst thou be a headless hen?*
> *Leave thy fighting to the men!*

Sorry to spread the news that two fellow Valley-ites have joined forces with Looters and have brung about the death of the Guv'na's Chief Spokesman and Head of Internal Goings On. These two bad guys wear disguises, but what they want is clear as the kitchen sink: to take over. Do me a special favor and look at their photos.

The TV cut to wanted posters of Hayes and Boyd in disguise, with rewards of ten thousand Bees for information leading to their arrest.

The speaker continued: I wanna say the turncoat on the left, George Hayes, once my crusty employee, was taken into trustody this afternoon; his son's also being held for questioning. But I wantcha paying attention to the photo on the right. This Bill Boyd from Rattlers Parish is still out there, loaded with switchblades and razors, rocks and whatnot. Hey, he rides—and, some say, fornicates with—a Wild Valley Nag. In his heart he's bestial as well as bonkers. You wanna be careful when he turns up. Too bad this Looter-lover's father-in-law was the Guv'na's buddy, a doc who saved the Guv'na's life during the Battle of Honor and Hope in the First War of Excision. If not for that good sawbones, the Guv'na might not be around today. I may be called Boss, but he's my boss, the boss of all bosses.

God bless The Valley! Now please do me a special favor and listen to soprano Carrie Aria's version of the great last words of our anthem, *Sunrise Gold:*

> *So brave and so bold*
> *Is our sunrise gold*
> *That we valiantly rush*
> *To relume Guv'na Brush.*

Huh? *Relume*? What does *relume* mean, Dad?

The Sandstorm Trooper in the bumblebee-striped uniform put on his sunglasses. He tried to belt his trousers, but Boyd twisted his arm behind his back. Now why would you want to do that? he said.

Look, Mister, I'm, hic, just trying to get dressed, said the Trooper.

Why bother? said Boyd. Imitating the guard, he slurred, Whyncha lemme borrow your duds?

While Sonny looked on, Boyd forced the Trooper out of his uniform and tried it on. Not bad, he said. It's way too big in the middle and too short in the legs, but it'll do.

He bundled his own mountain lion skin outfit into a ball, grabbed Sonny's hand, and headed for the swinging doors.

But, hic, what about me? the Trooper said, stripped to his skivvies.

Even bumblebees need to rest their stingers! said Boyd, pocketing his beard and hairpiece.

OK, the Trooper said, and reached for his bottle under the table.

At the front desk the gussied-up receptionist displayed a yellow-toothed smile that rivaled Mrs. Kissman's mouth. Glad you found the kid, she said. I love you without your beard, and that uniform does you proud. Let me know if I can do you any other favors, Johnny—what did you say your name is?

Boyd and Sonny were already out the door.

It's great to be with you on Windy again, Dad, the boy said. Boyd had unbundled his lion skin garb and laid it out on the horse's back as a blanket.

They'd been riding east, but Boyd had seen smoke and had swung through Rattlesnake Alley. From time to time Brush Patrol Guards had mopeded past. Maybe it was Boyd's clean-shaven face or his bumblebee-striped uniform. Maybe it was something else that Boyd thought he'd seen in their mopeds' helter-skelter maneuvers. Considering their hasty turn-abouts, stopping and starting apparently at random, the Guards all seemed to be drunk.

When a squad of Sandstorm Troopers tried to exchange greetings with Boyd, Sonny produced a fake sneeze and spoke up. Without a single spoonerism, he said he was deathly ill from anemia, and a nice Sandstorm Trooper on a horse was rushing him to Desert Center Brushpital for a skin transplant. The Troopers giggled and let them pass.

Wow! Dad! Sonny said, look what happened to Rattlesnake Alley.

Amid the stink and fly ash, they peered at the row of burned-out huts and wickiups, the smoldering frames of mopeds and bicycles in front yards. Having grown up sheltered by Grandma B during the Wars of Excision, Boyd had been lucky to avoid scenes of destruction like this. On the *Ancient History Channel* reporters who replayed footage of a scene like this would refer to it as *a war zone*. Now Boyd understood the phrase as if he'd coined it, as if the smoke were personal. To be sure, the neighborhood had been an eyesore, but was this the solution? Was it an accident? Had some kid been playing with matches?

Ho, someone said. It was the softest *Ho* Boyd had ever heard.

Who goes there? Sonny said.

Ho, it's just me.

My God, it's you, Boyd said. What happened?

They came by on mopeds, dowsing everything with petrol.

She was holding onto something—a rag doll. Her face was black with soot, and her clothes were in shreds.

Hop up here and ride with us, Boyd said.

What's your name? said Sonny.

Now we are three, Boyd thought, trying to remember his grandmother's words. If we consider Mrs. Kissman loping down side streets past the last Broil Station in Rattlers Parish, then we are four. Just as Mindy had called him Little Bro, Sonny might one day talk about Little Girl as his sister. He might say, Ho, Little Girl, have you been to the mini-mart? And she might reply, Ho, Sonny, I've been to the mini-mart to buy a fresh hen.

What nonsense! Fresh hens had gone the way of the railroads. In the olden days you could purchase a quarter of a fresh roasted chicken aboard a train's dining car and have it served to you by a uniformed waiter at a table decked with a white cloth. Today even at barbecues, poultry had to be defrosted and was already cut into bite-sized pieces. Mrs. Kissman would steer clear of The Chicanery, thanks to Boyd's urging. But nobody cared about whole chickens anymore. The Chicanery was far enough from Rattlers Parish not to be smelled by townies, and, in most Valleyites' estimation, chickens were manufactured items, ready-to-eat Mick's entrees. As to their eggs, Guv'na Brush had long ago declared them inedible:

> *Of chickens you may eat the legs*
> *And thighs and breasts, but not the eggs.*

The sky again lowered over the eastern Valley. With Little Girl in front and Sonny in the middle, Boyd urged Mrs. Kissman into the canter he knew she liked. But as they found themselves downwind of Cactus Vale, Sonny said, Dad, this is weird.

Little Girl piped up, Yes, doesn't it feel different, Dad? Suddenly she was calling Boyd Dad.

A sultry air mass enveloped them. A weather front, or whatever it was, seemed to cling to Cactus Vale and Teepee Village, close to the base of Mount Marvelous. The dense atmosphere didn't smell bad, but it was as if a wool blanket descended over them.

Mrs. Kissman must have sensed it, too, with a nicker Boyd had come to understand as *Qu'est-ce que c'est?* Maybe she had picked up her French in Grandpa A's corral, just as Boyd had, despite himself, osmosed some of the old man's lingo.

Well, kids, I don't know what's blowing down from the foothills, but it's sure easier to bear than the cold, Boyd said.

Little Girl's flimsy garments hadn't been lost on Sonny, who gripped her around the waist as they rode through a pungent gust. Wow! Dad! What's in the air?

Smells like a rotten egg, Dad, Little Girl said, holding her rag doll to her chest. I know. I stole an egg from my neighbor who worked at The Chicanery. He said there were all these eggs lying around. The workers were supposed to put them in compactors and spread the stuff on cactus gardens, to make the plants grow—the white eggs made better fertilizer than brown ones. But I was cleaning his house one day, and I found lots of eggs in a basket by his TV. So I brought one home and put it a paper bag and forgot about it for a long time until one day I opened the bag—and it smelled like this.

Boyd noticed how thin Little Girl was, almost as stick-like as Suzy. When Sonny heard her story, he pulled her closer to him. Gee! he said, can you play miniature golf?

A few kilometers ahead half a dozen parked mopeds blocked the trail up Mount Marvelous. Boyd knew a smaller trail south of the blockade, so he nudged Mrs. Kissman behind a grove of wild agaves and proceeded into the foothills. He eased her into a steady walk as the trail wound between shrubs and rocks. At one point all four of them disappeared into a ravine loaded with chaparral, but the path was clear. Mrs. Kissman's sure-footedness, even as it was getting dark, made Boyd think that she must've plodded up this very trail as a Wild Valley Nag. As a filly, she might've accompanied her herd up here, warding off bobcats and mountain lions with bone-cracking kicks from her rear hooves. In a sense, she and Boyd were fellow explorers, he with his Leica, she with her hunger to graze for mesquite pods, wild flowers, and hidden springs. Sure, he'd left his camera at the schoolhouse, but she was not some photo of a nag; she was a genuine horse with real spots.

The trail soon broadened over a saddleback between two hills. For a time they rode exposed on the ridgeline. Except for the high-pitched squeal of a hawk, the hillside was silent—no putt-putting of mopeds, no shouting of Brush Patrol Officers and Sandstorm Troopers. Before the minuscule foursome disappeared into the shade behind the neighboring ridge, Boyd gazed far off at the sun going down over the Great Ravine fifty kilometers away.

Would you look at that! he pointed.

Wow! What is it, Dad?

Little Girl clutched her doll and didn't say a word.

Even Mrs. Kissman glanced westward and sniffed the air.

Boyd scratched his cowlick. The whole damned Great Ravine was clogged with black stuff.

Is it a storm? Sonny said.

I don't think so; it's blacker than that, said Boyd.

It's pouring down into the desert, Sonny said.

It's thicker than that sandstorm on Thursday, said Boyd.

It's smoke, Little Girl said. Can't you see, there must be a giant fire west of the Great Ravine, and the wind's blowing the smoke into The Valley.

It's bigger than a brush fire, said Sonny.

No, Little Girl said, that's precisely it. It's a *Brush Fire!*

Mrs. Kissman veered to the right behind the ridge. As they climbed, Boyd tried not to think of Desert Center. He tried to keep his eyes on the trail and avoid images of demonstrators who'd flung down their posters and taken up torches soaked in petrol. Photographer that he was, he couldn't bear to think of himself snapping shots of Valleyites and Sandstorm Troopers hurling rocks and shoving switchblades into one another's bellies, slitting one another's throats. How could he stand by, like a reporter from *The Evening Star Wrap-up*, and take pictures of Sandstone Manse aflame? He had no affection for its principal resident, but Boyd didn't relish the thought of Guv'na Brush charred like barbecued chicken.

Higher they climbed, and higher—until the ever-larger chaparral bushes merged with a forest of lodgepole pines. They entered a shadowy grove; snowy patches covered the russet pine-needle floor.

Ha! They won't be able to find us here, said Sonny.

Not in this evergreen hideout, Boyd said.

It was completely dark when they reached the entrance. Someone cried, Who goes there?

Only then could Boyd make out a bunch of ragged figures with their arms arched back, ready to hurl rocks.

Ho, Boyd here.

Ho, Boyd.

Ho, Adze. Ho, Karim. Meet Sonny and Little Girl.

Ho ho ho, and a kettle of tea! said Adze. You sure look good in a bumblebee-striped uniform.

They dismounted, and Karim gentled Mrs. Kissman back toward her stall while Boyd's small group made its way down the central passageway.

Wow! said Sonny. I'll bet I'm gonna find Mom here! His voice rose: "Mom, are you here?"

Is this a dream, Dad? Little Girl said.

In the lamp-lit dining room Pete and Chicken Shit slapped Boyd on the back, then exchanged high-fives. Chicken Shit made places at the table for the newcomers. Sonny hadn't glimpsed his mother yet, but he would soon be swept up in her arms and, without a spoonerism, would exclaim, *I love you so much, Mom*!

Chicken Shit tapped Boyd on the shoulder. Are ya hungry, pal?

Karim and Adze stood behind the kids' chairs; Karim had already handed Little Girl a new set of rags, which she'd slipped over her old ones. Yes, Mr. Boyd, a-are you hungry?

Well, not exactly.

I think I know what you mean, said Adze. We were a little worried about the bad air; I don't know if you smelled it riding up here. It's bothered us all afternoon; I hope it's not what I think it is—Karim thinks he knows for sure. Anyway, we set up special rooms for you and Dolly.

Me and Dolly? But I thought you knew we aren't rooming together—

Yes, we know you aren't, ahem! Boyd wasn't sure he liked the sound of that *ahem!*

Why don't you let Karim take you down the hall? We'll see to it these young people get dinner and are settled in for the night. From the ruckus this morning, it looks as though we'll have our hands full of rocks tonight. But the Guv'na's men don't have our advantage up high.

Karim led Boyd farther down the dark passageway. You k-know, Mr. Boyd, we missed you. But now that you're b-back, I feel better, not afraid, almost as though my m-mother were still alive. Tonight w-we decided to empty Cave W. Here is your s-special rock r-room.

It was doorless, but a thin silk curtain had been drawn over the entrance. Boyd wondered how Adze and Karim had come upon contraband silk, a scrim half-hiding the lamp-lit room behind it. He thought he heard paper crackling and glimpsed a glowing thingamabob. He fingered the mole on his left cheek. He hadn't shaved, and his real beard was rough. His cowlick was as stubborn as the mane on a Wild Valley Nag—though, come to think of it, a Wild Valley Nag like Mrs. Kissman wasn't stubborn.

Ho, she said, when he parted the translucent curtain. You sure look like a yellowjacket in that bumblebee-striped uniform.

Ha, he said.

Yo ho and a bottle of wine, she said, pointing to a small teacart. Instead of a kettle, an uncorked bottle sat alongside two long-stemmed glasses.

How did you—? How did they—? Boyd said.

She moistened her lips. She was wearing her school uniform. Her pageboy was the color of sunset. I was about to ask the same question to you? But I'm guessing you rode up here on your spotted—

Yes, Mrs. Kiss—I mean, Windy wended and wound her way home.

So this is your home.

I haven't a hat to hang, but yes.

I also say yes, young man.

Young man?

You're two winters younger than I, remember?

I've always liked older women.

I'm sort of maternal, don't you think?

D'accord, as my father-in-law might say.

Of course, you're really a papa. I don't have kids.

By now Boyd had joined her on the—he'd never seen anything like it: a sofa that had opened up into a bed with sheets and blankets. He poured red wine and sat alongside her, trying to hold himself back. Easy does it, Mrs. Kissman, he told himself.

You know, I haven't kissed you hello, he said.

I noticed, she said.

I'm dying to.

By now we have a history—or should I say a *kis-story?*

Your words are sweet, he said.

I like the way you say the word *sweet,* as if you could put it in your mouth and suck it like a chicken bone.

Bleagh! he said, raising his wineglass.

To The Valley! she said.

To us! he said, and sipped.

Ah, Zinfandel.

Never heard of it, but I like the way you say its name, the way it smells and tastes, the way it makes me think I'm, you know—

What an idiot I am, he thought, as he scooted over on the sofa bed. I'm cock-a-doodle-dooing like a rooster, but I can't say a hundredth of what I'm thinking.

Don't think, she said, as if she'd read his mind.

Then he closed his eyes; they puckered their lips, and she gave him her tongue, as he gave her his. They were in one another's heads all at once, reading the ridges on the roofs of their mouths, deciphering the intricate whorls of tenderness around one another's lips, spelling out a tactile dictionary. It was as if they discovered, in a thousand square kilometers of wasteland, a palm grove and a pool they could dunk their heads in, gulping down such sweet quantities of water they could savor its brackishness as well. He tried not to think, as she'd told him, but he kept hearing her say they had a *kisstory*, kept thinking that he wanted them to keep licking and lipping like this until the evening star and all the dead eyes in the sky went out. If they had a past, would their future not be far behind? Part of him wanted to guffaw at the absurdity of this question, but another part of him succumbed to it in utter seriousness.

Just as a yucca blossoms with a cluster of white flowers, Boyd's mind bloomed with the snapshot of an unclothed man and woman locked in an infinite embrace. They were nestled against each other on a sofa bed—or was it a roughly hewn block of marble?—with the woman's left arm wrapped around the man's neck and the man's right hand resting on her left thigh. Mouth to mouth, they were so entwined that Boyd couldn't make out their facial features. Their eyes seemed to be closed in what must have been rapture, but Boyd wasn't sure. Inasmuch as he ached for them to shift positions, for him to mount her or for her to sit astride him, lost in ecstatic thrusts, he couldn't unlock them. They were sculpted in stone, and they would be kissing forever.

The flickering image of himself and Cathy Vallée as stone lovers brought Dolly to mind. She had never sculpted a man and woman kissing, much less holding hands. The closest she came to this was a bronze cast of two children—you couldn't tell their gender—tossing a ball between them. With closely cropped hair, wearing unisex clothes, their expressionless faces peered across a space of perhaps three meters. One of them had tossed a ball the size of a grapefruit, but you couldn't tell who was the thrower and who the catcher; both figures' hands reached palms-up, about to catch the ball, which hovered airborne halfway between them, held that way by an all-but-invisible wire from the ceiling. Dolly had executed this commission from the Rattlers Parish Art Museum the winter after Sonny had been born. Boyd had thought of it as a celebration of childhood; its title, *Pre-Pubes at Play,* seemed to suggest this. Right now, though, he wasn't sure.

As if to highlight this shutter-blink of uncertainty, the sofa bed shook. It must have been Cathy Vallée fiddling with her buttons, loosening her uniform, even as their lips stayed locked. He began to unzip his leggings, too, a tough task while their open mouths were breathing in sync as their tongues did wonders. So far their mutual inhalations and exhalations made for a delicious dizziness, and if he had his druthers he would breathe in unison with her until he passed out.

But there it was again, a distinct tremble, accompanied by a rumble from deep inside the cave.

No, he wouldn't let her go! Infused with her venom, he wasn't going to stop kissing and letting their kisses lead them to—

Skreak! went the walls of their rock room.

He heard Adze shout something that was blocked out by another *skreak*—and Boyd tore away from her.

What do you—? she began. But this time the sofa bed rattled. The wineglasses and bottle rolled off the table, shattering on the floor, the lamplights flickered, and the silk-curtain entryway fell with its rod in a heap.

They buttoned up. He grabbed her hand and pulled her into the central passageway. By now the rumble from deep within the mountain had grown into a roar. Dolly and Suzy ran from a room down the hall. He couldn't hear what they were yelling but guessed they'd also been caressing.

A mixed crew of men and women who might have also been kissing poured out of innumerable love nests that lined the central passageway. At once the surge became a stampede. As the cave floor shook, it was hard to keep his footing, and Boyd knew that if he or Cathy Vallée slipped, they might be crushed under the feet of dozens of ragged lovers fleeing. Rocks started to crumble from the stone ceiling, and someone collapsed, struck down. Because the electric lights had died, the hall was completely black, and it was impossible to avoid tripping over fallen men and women moaning on the floor. Somehow, with his hand gripping Cathy Vallée's, he made it to the cave's opening—and found Sonny and Little Girl huddled outside.

Adze and Karim had freed the horses that had trampled more than a few potential riders on their way to the cave's exit.

Mrs. Kissman whinnied at Boyd, who mounted her, pulled Cathy Vallée up behind him, and shouted to Sonny and Little Girl to join Karim waiting for them on his roan stallion Abdul. Sonny looked back for his mother before getting on Abdul. Boyd eyed the cave in vain for Pete and Chicken Shit. Dolly and Suzy had mounted another horse, and he heard Adze yell, *Giddyap, people! I'll take care of the stragglers!*

Away they went, trusting their horses' footing, glancing back at the rumbling mountain in the sulphurous air. No doubt about it, these tremors outvied The Valley Quickshake. Whether they would amount to a much-feared Valley Longshake, Boyd had no

idea. Something was illuminating the trail, something brighter than any lamplight generated from
Windmill City. He was still too high on the slopes
to tell what it was, but it lit the snowy downhill path
like intermittent bursts of noonday sun.

Boyd was among the lead horsepeople descending.
All at once, he heard a *thwock*, and the man in front
of him fell from his horse. Another *thwock* brought
down his woman companion, though their lead horse
continued, riderless. Boyd couldn't tell what these
thwocks were, but he heard objects whizzing past
him; one came close to chopping off his cowlick, and
Cathy Vallée, sitting behind him, cried, Oh God, Bill!

This was his signal to nudge Mrs. Kissman into a
plunge, one he never thought she could sustain without stumbling. Right behind the hooves of one of the
lead horses, she nickered and bit its hindquarters to
speed it down the slope—whereupon the half-dozen
lead horses trampled a band of the Guv'na's Brush
Patrol Officers and Sandstorm Troopers who'd been
shooting razorblades from a slingshot contraption
mounted on a dune buggy. If a few horsepeople tumbled from their spooked nags, more slammed into
the Guv'na's troops. Mrs. Kissman cleared the dune
buggy in one leap, knocking over the Troopers' killer
contraption and concussing two razorblade shooters.
Boyd could see Abdul hurdle a couple of mopeds, but
he lost sight of Karim after that. He hoped Sonny and

Little Girl hadn't been *thwocked,* and he didn't know what to think about Dolly and Suzy—couldn't see much around him for all the dust.

What was left of the Guv'na's brigade was probably busy with the horsepeople in the rear, but Boyd's comrades had no alternative except to surge ahead. To return and pick off the remaining Troopers would not only be foolhardy; it would be suicidal. Boyd was far enough from Mount Marvelous to look back and see its summit emit a geyser of sparks. The roar and dazzle of some sort of eruption seemed to be increasing. The Valley floor shook, and once again Boyd feared that Mrs. Kissman would lose her footing. Now there could be absolutely no going back to help the stragglers. Ahead, to the west Boyd peered through the dark at the Great Ravine clogged with something that looked like smoke and, beyond it, the unmistakable flicker and glare of conflagration.

My heavens, look at it, Bill!

Uh-huh, Desert Center's on fire!

A cataclysmic explosion behind them turned their heads in time to see the snow-and-lava-capped summit of Mount Marvelous roar up through the clouds and vanish, leaving the decapitated mountain to pour a molten bowl of flame down its slopes. Boyd was too far away to see evergreens snapping under mudslides and avalanches. He could only imagine sinewy Adze, with his lank hair, in his sheepskin garb, hurling a stone at a boulder about to crush him—or holding one last book in the lightless library about to collapse—if his lungs hadn't already vaporized in the super-heated steam.

Ah, God! he said.

If Cathy Vallée said anything, he couldn't hear it. Mrs. Kissman had ears, and she was galloping full-tilt. It was only a matter of seconds when all of them—

—were overtaken by a dust cloud fanning out from the mountaintop's blowup, followed by a gigantic ear-punishing slam that turned The Valley floor into a trampoline bouncing up and down, up and down, until Boyd thought for sure Mrs. Kissman would break her fetlocks and clatter to the ground, snapping her neck and killing all three of them. That the thingamajig careening down from the sky and crashing to The Valley floor was the summit of Mount Marvelous, Boyd was certain. It caused a stupendous explosion that would leave, Boyd knew, a crater at least a kilometer in diameter.

Lucky that he was able to calculate anything. Aswirl in a sandstorm as ferocious as the one he'd witnessed last Thursday, he felt more fortunate with every cough that meant he was still alive. Cathy Vallée had spit up something, but she was thankfully still gagging, and Mrs. Kissman huffed in mini-eruptions of her own but hardly slowed.

For what seemed like hours, they rode west—or Boyd hoped it was west. The volcanic rumbles and roars never stopped, but gradually the dust abated, and they re-emerged onto the dim Valley floor, side by side with horsepeople who looked as though they were asleep on their mounts, or weeping—he couldn't tell. He couldn't see Karim or Abdul, much less Sonny and Little Girl. He patted Mrs. Kissman's rump, and, as if she were buoyed by the prospect of fresh air, she tore off toward the Great Ravine and outraced the dust cloud still curling over itself in devilish whorls behind them.

Years later, when he understood the concept of *years,* he would think of this Tuesday evening in late winter as more than an exodus. Although he had escaped, he would come to think of these events less as a fleeing-from than a marching-towards. To be sure, nearly half his comrades didn't make it through the explosion and impact of the mountaintop slamming onto the desert. And surely a quarter again as many horsepeople died back at the trailhead, thanks to the *thwocks* of razorblades, rocks, and knives hurled by the Guv'na's Sandstorm Troopers. But he'd made it, and from here on things would get better. That they didn't immediately improve no longer riled him. Years later he would sit back, listening to guitar music, with a book in his hands, and say the words *history* and *kisstory* over and over until they blended into one sound.

Right now, he thought of nothing but his family—*his little family*—making tracks over pebbly outcrops and arroyos. He yelled their names—Sonny, Little Girl, Karim, Dolly, Suzy—but there was no response. The drumming of horses' hooves, the increasingly distant thunder rumblings of Mount Marvelous, which lit the sky with on-again off-again sunbursts—these were all-encompassing. Cathy Vallée clung to him, mumbling from time to time; in the din he couldn't make out what she said.

When his ragged friends looked north and saw the rusted train rails clear as noon in the volcanic light show, they stood up on their horses and waved without sound. They knew where those rails led, and they slowed to give their mounts a rest. Behind them fire, ahead of them fire. Boyd imagined he could hear people nickering with joy.

I think we might make it, he said.

That's where I spent my honeymoon, she said, pointing to a firestorm of evergreens on the Great Ravine. Despite the flames, the smoke wasn't impenetrable; Boyd was surprised he wasn't coughing. And at some distance he noticed Dolly, who had suffered from asthma. She waved to him, seated behind Suzy on what looked like a roan mare.

The ragged group found a gravel road and proceeded at a steady canter, largely unbothered by the Guv'na's men. Twice, a band of Sandstorm Troopers approached them on mopeds, calling out, Who goes there? But when the uniformed officers fiddled with their sunglasses and saw how long the line of horsepeople stretched, they revved their engines and putt-putted away.

Boyd tried to hold himself back and not slip through time's cracks once again. He'd glimpsed Karim and yelled for Sonny; as a result, Abdul rode alongside Mrs. Kissman.

Wow, Dad, that blast was something, Sonny said. Little Girl said that whatever crashed down on us was Guv'na Brush's punishment.

I was wondering about that myself, said Cathy Vallée.

So w-was I, Karim said.

Well, now that you think so, Little Girl said, I'm not sure.

What do you mean, dear? Cathy Vallée said.

Well, if two out of three people agree on anything, I assume they're wrong. What do you think, Dad?

Boyd tried to deflect Little Girl's question. If it wasn't Guv'na Brush's punishment, what else could it be? he said. What else could the destruction of Mount Marvelous mean?

Oh, Bill, you don't really believe that, do you?

Yeah, Dad! What a lot of chickenfeed that is, Sonny said.

Look, I don't say I know anything for certain, but

what we've seen—I'm not sure I know how to explain it.

I a-agree, said Karim.

Little Girl wiped her nose with one hand and held up her rag doll with the other. Well, then, I disagree, she said.

Know what? Sonny said, tightening his grip around her waist, I think I'm gonna stop calling you Little Girl. You need a better name.

Don't you dare! she hissed. I never had parents, and my name has always been Little Girl.

But what will happen one day when you grow up? said Cathy Vallée.

I'll still be called Little Girl. Just wait and see.

Boyd noticed Sonny put his other arm around Little Girl's waist, and he grinned—or was it a sneer?—nuzzling her hair. For that matter, the horse's clippety-clopping had reached below his own belt. What with Mrs. Kissman's warm withers and ribcage rising and falling underneath him and Cathy Vallée's arms ringing his waist, he felt himself rise to the occasion.

In due time they reached the base of the Great Ravine. On both sides of the coulee brush fires flared, in low-lying juniper as well as lodgepole pines higher on the slopes. Fortunately, the roadside vegetation had escaped the flames, and as they slowed to a brisk walk uphill, Karim was the first to notice it.

Ah, c-can you smell it?

Boyd sniffed, overwhelmed by the odor of smoke, charred wood.

No, not that s-smell. There's another smell behind that one.

Sonny pretended to sneeze. Oh, I see what you mean. Dead skunks.

No, silly, Little Girl said. That's not what he means.

But when Cathy Vallée quizzed her, Little Girl grunted and appeared to sulk.

They all felt it, though. Boyd didn't need to say anything. Little Girl's face lit up. Mrs. Kissman and Abdul neighed and tossed their heads. Sonny said, Wow, Dad! And Cathy Vallée leaned forward, grabbed a handful of Boyd's hair, and kissed the back of his neck—which made his whiskers bristle, the mole on his left cheek itch, and his cowlick stiffen in synch with—

How wonderfully ludicrous it was to ride through a light rain, nursing a hardon. Sure, the rain was sooty, and it dowsed everyone. But Karim had been right; it carried with it an aroma of more than fly ash. Mixed with pine tar and creosote, it hauled a wagon-load of fragrances: damp soil, wild flowers—perhaps the salty tinge of a distant body of water.

Boyd had never been much in the olfactory department. Compared to Mindy he'd been a no-nose. She was able to smell Grandma B's dinner sizzling in the microwave while they were still outside. Mindy knew whether it would be chicken thighs or livers. If she was blindfolded, she could smell the difference between the fronds of a fan palm and a palmetto, the flowers of brittlebush and desert chicory. When they hiked the gullies and arroyos west of Rattlers Parish, she would say, Whoa, there's a bobcat around that bend; can you smell her?—she's in heat. Even Grandma B admitted she knew of no one with a schnozzola like Mindy's—that was the word she used, *schnozzola*. Grandma B said that in her own grandmother's day there had been a comedian with such a large proboscis that one of his routines on TV had been to sniff a goblet full of some kind of pulque, whereupon the pulque would disappear up his schnozzola all at once. She wasn't sure of the big-nosed comedian's name but guessed it might have been Chimmy Door Auntie. Some animals had sniffers more sensitive than their eyes, and Mindy was right up there with the dogs and mule deer as far as Grandma B could tell. Which made the day that Mindy returned home from school with a bloody nose all the more painful. Not that the kids who beat her up ruined her sense of smell. If they'd mocked her about being a *darky Looter*, they hadn't affected her status as the *Number-one Nostril in The Valley*, as Grandma B dubbed her.

Sonny must have been reading Boyd's mind. Know what, Little Girl? he said. I think from now on I'm gonna call you Li'l Sis—because you're like my little sister, you know. Now that Jilly's gone, you and I can do stuff.

Little Girl was silent.

What do you think, Li'l Sis?

Little Girl harrumphed.

That's not a bad name, dear, Cathy Vallée said. And Sonny's older than you, isn't he?

He is *NOT*, Little Girl said. I'm older than him, and he knows it.

Sonny was silent.

I still think it's kind of nice that he wants to call you his sister. Sometimes I think of Bill and me as—

Don't say it! Boyd yelped.

What about you, Karim? Sonny said. Did you ever have a girlfriend?

What, me? Well, yes, I had one long ago, but I don't know whether anyone wants to hear about her.

Boyd noticed, as he had once before, that Karim was no longer stuttering.

Karim continued: I lived with my mother in Cave W, you know, until I got too grown-up and I moved in with the men. But in Cave W there was a woman; I'm embarrassed to say what happened.

Aw, c'mon, Karim! said Sonny.

OK: I was just the same age as you, Sonny, when this woman used to go to a spring outside Cave W to bathe. It was summer—I know you don't know what the word *summer* means, but believe me, it was hot.

She didn't have another woman or a man or any children, and she was almost as old as my mother. She used to wear layers of rags. One afternoon behind a rock I counted four layers she peeled off her. Black as lava stone, the stuff Adze called trap rock. Black as the crag jutting over the pool where she bathed. I couldn't stop looking at her. Day after day. One day a raven landed on top of my rock, the one I was hiding behind. He perched there, looking at the woman, and he made his stutter, *Cr-r-uck, cr-r-uck.* By the time the woman turned in his direction, he'd flown off, and she saw me there behind the rock. Well, you k-know, Mr. Boyd, she w-was n-n-naked.

Hey! Sonny interrupted, I saw a naked woman, too!

Little Girl nudged him hard in the ribs.

What's up, Li'l Sis, haven't you ever seen a naked man?

Enough! Boyd snapped. They were approaching three dirt trails that branched off from the main road, and Boyd worried about an ambush. But no bumblebee-striped uniformed Troopers lay in wait.

Too quietly to be overheard, Cathy Vallée pointed out the trail that led to her honeymoon cabin. Sure, the woods were ablaze now, but back on that ridge once upon a time there had been cabins, with superb views of The Valley. Each cabin had wooden rocking chairs on a wraparound deck. You could sit there and look off toward Windmill City. On most days you could gaze out and let the railroad tracks lead your eyes to Mount Marvelous. The only problem was Johnny Fusspot. Even then he was more interested in stringing beads and making necklaces, than in—

—I'll be honest with you, Bill, in all those days we honeymooned on the ridge, we hardly kissed. He said he worried about getting sick from the water. I could never cook his chicken right. The one time we slept together—I'm ashamed to tell you this—he called me skinny.

Skinny? Boyd whispered. You're not skinny!

He said I needed to gain weight. But even then I liked to run ten kilometers before breakfast. I shouldn't say this, but I've never been fond of Mick's breakfast food.

Me neither, Boyd said.

I shouldn't say this, but I like my body. It's tough. It gets things done.

Boyd thought of her wasp waist, her unclothed thighs, which he'd never seen, her slender ankles that poked out from underneath her school uniform. And—boing!—there he was again, with a stiff, staring truncheon!

He wanted to say, Oh, Cathy, make me immortal with a kiss!

Instead, he thought of Dolly and Suzy. He wiped rain off his brow and nudged Mrs. Kissman toward the final crest in the road.

***

Four times while they rode the last kilometers to Desert Center, groups of yellow-jacketed Brush Patrol Officers attacked on mopeds. Boyd heard *thwocks* and saw five men and three women tumble from their horses that shied and then loped off into the darkness. Eight people down and four riderless nags make a dozen sadnesses, Boyd calculated.

In the saddle between two mountains to the north and south, Desert Center, once a glitzy bastion, had become a disaster zone. As Boyd entered the city limits, he saw families on mopeds packed with belongings, putt-putting in various directions. A woman with a small child belted to her bike's banana seat couldn't get her engine to rev; she tried to jump-start it again and again. A man slapping his cowboy hat on his thigh rode through a mud hole. A bearded geezer and a woman who reminded Boyd of Grandma B had tied their mopeds to a wagonload of birdcages, with canaries, parakeets, a mackaw; they kept pace with the horsepeople and pulled alongside Mrs. Kissman. The geezer called out, Ho, who goes there?

Bill Boyd and Cathy Vallée!

Ho, Bill. Ho, Cathy. My name's Dallas Mallon; my wife's name is Birdy.

No need to go through the never-fear-Govnor-Brush-is-here stuff, Boyd said.

No, sir! Me and Birdy salute you with make-believe high-fives, though. He raised his right hand and laughed, Where you from?

Rattlers Parish—well, no, we're from the west slope of Mount Marvelous.

That so? Can't see her from here, but we heard she blew her lid.

Uh-huh. Looks like the lid's off the kettle up here, too.

Yup, Desert Center's on its way to becoming one of those ruins like, you know, Chicken-Its-Uh in old Mexico. Maybe someday we'll see it on *The Ancient History Channel*!

Just then, a squad of Sandstorm Troopers pulled alongside in muddy Miramar mopeds. Boyd expected a fusillade of *thwocks* but received a chorus of slurred *Ho's* before the mopeds sped off, slip-slopping around a corner.

Cathy sniffed the air. Did you smell pulque? she said.

The rain started to let up. Inasmuch as they'd welcomed it when it came, they *whewed* its passing. The huge clock on Police Headquarters had been smashed; its hands had been removed, along with its cuckoo apparatus, so that it made Boyd think of a glass eye in the middle of the building's forehead. On second thought, despite the late hour, nobody could see the dead eyes of the Guv'na's supporters in the cloudy night sky. Further down Bristle Boulevard, the towering Cathedral of the Splendiferous Spires appeared to be untouched. When Boyd passed beneath its large stained-glass window, however, he saw that someone had removed the panel of The Brush Babe's Baptism so skillfully that the rest of the window hadn't shattered. Faithful disciples surrounded a large puddle where a pastor seemed to be plunging an invisible infant into the water.

Boyd was imagining how nice it would be to immerse himself in a tub of hot tea with Cathy Vallée—when Sandstone Manse came into view.

Oh my God, Bill! she said.

Isn't that where we got taken the other day? said Sonny.

Dolly and Suzy had caught up with them. That's right, Sonny, thanks to your Grandpa A, the bumble-bee-striped boys let us go.

I'm so glad you're here with us, Mom! Sonny said.

Will you quit whining like a baby! Little Girl said.

But Sonny had begun blubbering. You wouldn't understand, Li'l Sis. You never had a mom.

Right! And I'm not wasting my tears either.

Enough! Boyd snapped. Look at SM, all of you. We're lucky we missed the party!

The hulk of Sandstone Manse looked as though it had been firebombed by revelers. Too many pulque bottles aflame, with petrol-soaked rags as wicks, had been flung at its oversized redwood entryway, charred and crumbling. The manse's arched portico had collapsed, and the words engraved above it had been reduced to, *Bles Is Th Loot*. The first floor of the redbrick façade, long the pride of architects and construction workers from Teepee Village to Camp Wonderful, had caved in. Many of its bricks, baked from Valley clay, had tumbled onto Guv'na Brush's gold-leaf statue, decapitating and breaking off its left hand that gripped the bullwhip. Curiously, the headless, one-armed Guv'na was still holding the Bible in his right hand, though every bit of gold leaf had been stripped from his clay underpinnings.

Whoa! Boyd said. Why don't you all wait under the awning of that Mick's Bistro across the street. I need to see this for myself. He slid off Mrs. Kissman.

But Dad! you might get hurt!

Oh, hush up, Little Brother, Dad'll be OK.

Bill, please be careful. It's treacherous over there; things could fall on you, Cathy Vallée said.

Don't w-worry, I'll w-watch out for everyone, Mr. Boyd.

Without a word Dolly and Suzy joined Boyd's group across the street while the procession of horse-people continued to plod past them.

I'll be right back, Boyd said. This horse line is so long we'll fit right back in.

He waved goodbye, jogged to the downed chain-link fence, and hopped over its barbed wire. On the ground, like a giant scorched golf ball, Guv'na Brush's head lay face upwards. Discolored as it was, his countenance still wore its characteristic half-smile, half-sneer. Boyd maneuvered between the collapsed arches and gave the crumbling redwood entryway a shove. Rather than falling off its hinges and bringing down the ceiling, it teetered and opened with a groan. Inside, although everything was dark, some faint streaks of light from Mount Marvelous still flashing, followed by distant peals of thunder as well as light from another source Boyd couldn't detect, shone on what was once the chandelier with its dozens of five-watt bulbs in smithereens on the floor. The oil portraits of Guv'na Brush had turned into charred caricatures. The marble staircase still ascended in the shape of an hourglass, be it ever so fire-blackened. Boyd decided to give it a chance, aware that it might crumble, bringing the cathedral ceiling down on his head. But behold! when he started to climb, the marble steps neither crumbled nor creaked. It wasn't as though he used stairs every day, so he was especially careful, mouthing Cathy Vallée's words about falling objects.

On the second-floor landing two hallways branched off, each with its own fallen chandelier. Somehow, up here the propane gas lamps affixed to the walls had not been destroyed, which explained the source of the weird half-light he'd seen downstairs. Even if the roof had collapsed, there must have been an attic to bear its weight. As far as Boyd could tell, things had fared pretty well up here. One hallway had a yellow carpet stained by soot; the second sported at least a dozen black rug remnants lined up end to end. Both hallways led to doors painted yellow and black respectively; their brass doorknobs glowed under gas lamps in wall sconces.

Boyd stared down both hallways, thinking of something Grandma B had read him about a parting of the ways. His decision to try the yellow door first had less to do with symbolism or esthetics than with the black-carpeted hallway's having taken a greater hit from the fire; its floor was littered with shards of glass and fallen plaster, whereas the hall with the yellow rug was basically intact. For an instant he thought he heard music, though he wasn't sure where it came from. He could've sworn he heard a song sparrow, but it must have been something else. At least he didn't hear the *Who goes there?* of a bumblebee-striped uniformed Sandstorm Trooper in sunglasses!

He crept over the yellow carpet like a firecat—*I am a firecat*, he said to himself—but the weighty imprint of his desert boots on the rug may have been responsible for the lamps flickering. For the umpteenth time during the past week, things slowed to a crawl. It was as if he were a character in a snapshot or a slide struggling to be in an old-fashioned movie. When one leg lifted, the other fell, but there was no continuity. His arms splayed in opposite directions, and he was caught, mid-stride, going nowhere. He needed to take a step, he knew, but he felt frozen in some interstice, timeless as the smashed clock on Police Headquarters. Yet it was late, getting later with every heartbeat. For all he knew it was midnight

WEDNESDAY

when he reached for the brass knob but had the sense to knock on the yellow door. He stood back and waited another infinity for an answer. He crouched, his head full of comparisons, when a voice from behind the door called,

I know you're out there! Don't be shy!

Boyd turned the knob. From an antique phonograph, a tinny rendition of *I'm Just a Vagabond Lover* greeted him like a high-five. He could feel it in the palm of his right hand. He could smell it like the incense he'd savored in Myrna's teepee house winters ago. What was it about this music that made him feel queasy, as though the evening star and all the dead eyes had gone out but he was still teaching a photography class at Bee Rush Academy? What was it about this place, a sizable room with the biggest bed he'd ever seen—it was circular, rumpled, with super-bright yellow sheets and blankets—that made him feel as if he was looking straight at the sun?

Who was this man sitting at a writing desk under a floor-to-ceiling photomural of a Joshua tree? He motioned Boyd to come closer, and as Boyd did so, the man began ever so slowly to smile. He didn't get out of his chair or go through formal greetings. Only his smile seemed to recognize Boyd who, looking again, saw the smile morph into a sneer, then implode into a smile again—until the morphing and implosions were indiscernible, and the man's face turned into a mask of perfect ambiguity.

I knew you'd come, he said.

I'm not sure I—

I know, you're not sure you're seeing the real me. For a while there, you weren't sure I existed. But look at me. Come closer. Smell my cologne.

Boyd cringed.

I'm a little smaller in person than I come off on TV—which is almost never—and I haven't much hair left. For a while there you foxed us all with your beard and hairpiece. I use a hairpiece under my cowboy hat in public. But now who cares?

He put down a pen he'd been using and took something out of his desk drawer. He held it to his head with both hands and brushed his meager locks in slow strokes.

That's better! he said. Would you care to join me? You look as though you could use a trim. I'd trade Sandstone Manse for a head of hair like yours.

Sir, I expected you to be—

I know, you expected me to be a mighty fortress or something. You expected me to be surrounded by my honey-loving bumblebee-striped Sandstorm Troopers. Alas, half of those stinkbugs budded out on me, and the other half drank themselves blotto and slit one another's throats. No doubt you've seen their bodies rotting all over The Valley.

No, sir, I haven't.

And please don't call me *sir*. Makes me feel like a fusspot. I'm just an ordinary bloke. He replaced the hairbrush in his desk drawer.

After everything you've done, sir, how can you—

Call me Rudy. I mean, nobody else does, and there's nobody else left, except— But look, before we turn this twosome into a swinging party, won't you please sit down, yes, over on that chair by the table, and have a cup of tea. The kettle's brimming, tea-bags are swimming, the cups are hymning—no, that doesn't make sense. What rhymes with *brimming* and makes sense in context? Dimming? No, the lights may flicker now and then, but the cups are not dimming. I spend far too much time rhyming, but rhymes prevent crimes, *n'est pas*? How else to keep things in order?—ordered rhymes for disordered times! How else can an ordinary bloke like me keep things from falling apart? This last week's been hell—pardon my French—but you've got to give me credit for keeping the lid on The Valley until now. If I'd flinched like a ninny, don't you think those Looters would have wrecked things long before now? Let's face it, your average Teddy in Teepee Village and Cally in Cactus Vale are far happier with my *Good Book* than with a library full of dangerous ideas. Do you think your buddies Pete and Andrew give a fig about high-toned concepts like freedom? I'm talking about more than literal handcuffs; I'm talking about freedom to think and act responsibly, from the heart—only I am capable of that. Eons ago many thousands of kilometers east of The Valley a philosopher who loved to walk, and was therefore named Play Toe, wrote about leaders like me. Pete and Andrew walked off and are OK, by the way. I've seen to it that Hayes and Willy were released along with Hayes's new friend Ruthie, and that stupid Rhode Island Red, that Boss I myself installed at Windmill City, is probably hiding right here under a junkpile in Desert Center.

Boyd sipped his tea and sat back in an overstuffed chair with armrests. For some reason, perhaps because he was awed by the man who sat before him, Boyd fell silent. He felt as if he might crumble like a TV-dinner tin plate.

The man locked eyes with Boyd. Even as you sip, hundreds of Valleyites lie rotting under the moon— oops, I forgot, you're not supposed to know what the moon is. Even as we sit here as politely as kings, thousands of Valleyites will be bored as capons; they won't know what to do with themselves when they wake up this morning. You and I could shoot the breeze till dawn, but do you think more than a dozen Valleyites could carry on a conversation and talk about ideas for more than two blinks of a Bighorn Sheep? No, back in the Stone Age when I was a boy I went to a theater and saw what they called a movie about a long-ago, faraway place named Vee Enna. It featured two men stalled high atop a Ferris wheel—I know you've never heard of such a gizmo. One man says to the other, Look at all the people down there on the ground; they're tiny, unrecognizable dots; who would care if any of them stopped moving? Well, I'm the one who has allowed some to keep moving and stopped others. I'm the one who sees to it that those dots are dead eyes that stay put in the night sky forever after their productive lives as my followers down here. I may have that Vee Enna movie wrong because it's been so many years ago—oops, I forgot, you don't know what the word *years* means. I think you can connect the dots, though. Because of facelifts and transplants, I may not look as old as I am, but it's been a scad of winters since I sat in that theater on Flatbush Avenue. I can hardly sing it anymore:

> *Fegedaboud Flatbush Avenoo,*
> *Fegedaboud Prospect Pahk.*
> *Heah we ah out West,*
> *Not in East Noo Yawk.*

Not bad for an octogenarian, huh? But I was always a mimic. I could croon like Frank Sinatra in my day. My mother used to say, Thomas, someday you'll be a real Wolfe—ha! Ain't that hilarious. And here your father wrote the supposedly authorized biography of Guv'na Brush, AKA Rudy Newhouse. Either your dad was trying to dupe his readers or he didn't know what he was talking about—but then how could he know stuff that was top secret? I went out of my way to cover my tracks, knowing there would be poseurs like your father, trying to unmask me. Well, you may be the third person in The Valley to hear the truth, which will make you yadda yadda. Rudy Newhouse is my *nom de guerre*; I made it up. Thought it was more memorable and euphonic than my real name, which is, guess what? Thomas Micks, Jr. I kid you not, I went by Thomas Micks so long I felt I was turning into a slimy mixture for chocolate pudding, like the Gowanus Canal. After the insurrections I headed out here with my Newhouse moniker. Come to think of it, your dad might have known that. He might have known more about me than he let on, maybe more than I knew myself. I'm not sure, but this may be why he wrote that bogus biography of me and why so many people believed it: because it's easier to believe a lie than confront the you-know-what, which will make you you-know-what.

Boyd twitched in his chair. It was getting late. What about Cathy Vallée and the others outside?

Why was he sitting glued to his chair? Why couldn't he say anything?

Smiling and sneering, the old man continued: Right now I bet you're thinking about that gorgeous broad, Johnny Kissman's wife. What a chump Johnny was. I heard he got caught in his moped's power chain on the way here and got, well, chumped up! That old letch Heetclit told me all about you and guess-who breaking into his closet, smooching in the teachers' lounge. I care about education, let me tell you, most of all when it comes to Numero Uno, *moi*! I knew Heetclit way back when. He's even older than yours truly. Gives me this story about growing up in Hell's Kitchen, looking at some storefront window, and traveling out here to escape the cold. What a pile of nag poop! My bumblebee boys gave me info the guy grew up in L.A., did his hitch way back in the Mideast Wars, and settled in The Valley. Fell head over heart for your girlfriend's mother on a trip she took out here; then, when she died, fell head over heart for her daughter. Hah! he sure is something, that Heetclit, the wheeziest geezer you'll ever sneeze at.

Boyd faked a sneeze.

'Smatter, got a cold?

No, I just can't believe this. She's outside waiting for me.

Lucky you! I guessed as much. Listen, if I had world enough and time, I'd tell you more about Heetclit's escapades. But since there's no help—alack, the servants have amscrayed—let's just sit awhile longer.

He paused to sip his tea before opening a large, falling-apart old book, in which Boyd glimpsed hand-writing, faded chicken scratches.

Listen to this: *The day is deepening into dusk as the winter light straggles half-heartedly through our faded dining room curtains. Thick draperies of mist, like the black plumes of a hearse, still twist over the wet expanse of asphalt. Wilted by a continuous downfall of rain, they are something like a soft weeping. Really, these colourless days get on my nerves. They dawn half-heartedly into some dispirited grey light and drowse away into a still deeper grey. Hardly a jot of brightness out there. Just the dank pavement, the refuse-clotted snow heaps, and the run-on, indifferent hours.*

What do you think of that? he said.

I don't know what to think. I don't understand it, said Boyd.

Ah, *the run-on, indifferent hours!* How they pass by. It's not as though they reach out for us like the limbs of that Joshua tree in the wall photo.

Or take this, a description of a man who the writer says, *will, in time, be my second son: He will have long since made up his mind on every subject conceivable and, when conversation so demands, he will simply open a secret drawer that holds the solution to the problem and will proffer it with an air of invincible authority.*

His mind will be a filing cabinet in which eternity and the price of chicken gumbo are pigeonholed in adjoining compartments.

Only a person who saw through the veil of time, only a visionary, could have written those words. I knew you were coming, so I took out his old journal. I've been trying to write something of my own in response. Do you happen to know who wrote what I just read you?

Boyd shook his head.

No, I didn't think you'd know. Well, let me put it this way: if you think Old Man Boyd was a writer, this guy was a monument; as we used to say, he was the best thing since sliced bread. He never published a syllable during his lifetime, but he far surpassed your father. In fact, who do you think your dad learned how to write from? Two bits he never mentioned this man. Do you think you're ready to learn the truth?

Boyd squirmed in his chair. He felt like a chicken about to have its head chopped off, yet he couldn't do a damned thing.

Just then the door swung open. The man chortled at his desk, And now we are three!

The person who stepped over the threshold looked so familiar it was as if Boyd had known her all his life. Still, her gray, stringy hair, her long witchy nose, her hunched back gave away nothing. She appeared to have come in from the rain after a night on the town with a Sandstorm Trooper who'd abused her. She looked like the spitting image of Grandma B but younger, and infinitely more frazzled.

Ho, he said—at least he was able to speak!

Apparently, she was as surprised to see him as he was to see her, because she stared at him, shaking her head in denial. At one point she slammed her brow with her fist.

'Smatter, cat got your tongue? the old man said.

But nothing could get her to say Ho.

The old man continued, Here I am at the end of my whatsis, at the close of my heyday, getting ready for my swan song but nonetheless still breathing, babbling, braying like a Wild Valley Nag. It's not as though I've sat at this desk for thirty years, waiting for Mr. Photogenic to arrive with his tall, dark good looks—he's taken so many Handsome Lessons he's got three PhDs in the cuties! It's not as if I've slurped tea and scarfed chicken a la king, hoping to meet the man I've had my eye on for decades. No, don't get me wrong, buddy, I'm not into the man-to-man shtick! It's just that you and I have a lot in common—and I'm not talking about cameras! My pal your father-in-law—what did you call him, Grandpa A?—was dead-right when he said you're too interested in details; you need to come out from behind the viewfinder and smell the Mick's. My woman friend and I here haven't had your problem. As a matter of fact, we're well equipped in the smell-the-Mick's department. We've let our noses do the work, so to speak, for seventeen years now, haven't we, hon?

The gray-haired woman trembled, whether in ecstasy or rage Boyd couldn't tell. Her dark face glowered.

Hey, Missy, when I'm talking to you, I expect you to answer. One minute I may call you *hon,* the next I may turn into Attila. My bullwhip fell through the cracks when that last band of Looters torched my jail cells. But you know my moods can turn on a dime— forget about these stupid Bees we use in The Valley; give me a good, old-fashioned Roosevelt dime! So lemme hear it, Sister. Now!

The gray-haired woman stopped trembling and began to pace the yellow carpet in figure eights, stooped, with her hands clasped behind her back:

OK, you asked for it so you're gonna get it! You're right: It's as if we've smelled this moment forever; my nose knew it would happen. We've been waiting for him to come knocking for too many years, and when we had him in jail the other day we were hoping he'd stay and join the family business, but he didn't. He gave us a rain check, and here he is with us tonight, even though the poor guy doesn't know what's what, and maybe he never did. Maybe he never opened his soulful brown eyes except behind the lens of his Leica to shoot canyons and cacti while I focused on the big picture. Maybe he was a blindsided Romantic in love with thick, ropey love while I learned the ropes and got in the thick of things. But then he was born during the Fourth War of Excision's last skirmishes. How could he know about Sandstorm Troopers fighting Looters night after night, or hear the thud of a rock smashing a skull, the hiss of a switchblade slitting a throat? He was a babe in arms, waah waah, nursing when I was a kid in my sandbox who happened to witness a yellow-jacketed Brush Patrol Officer and a Looter go at one another in the neighbor's yard. How they ever met up there I'll never know, even if those were the final days of the Third War when we still thought we could excise evil. But the thud of a skull, the hiss of a throat being slit can't be excised, which is why I continue to cry for those two dead men—and have learned to cry for all the dead sons of bitches rotting under the desert sun, waah waah! I'll never s-stop c-crying. Please s-stay with us tonight, d-don't leave us, L-l-lit-t-tle B-b-b-r-r— D-don't leave us, B-b-b—.

Boyd put down his teacup and fidgeted, aware of the mole on his left cheek. It itched, and he ached to scratch it. Why was he sitting, motionless, mute as a molehill—certainly no volcano—unable to utter a word? This woman was someone he'd known, that's for sure, yet she might have been a stranger skulking by a garbage dump not far from The Chicanery.

He longed to say something like *Do you remember the day we hiked with Grandma B to the salt flats south of the golf course?* Or *Where were you all the winters I went outside under the evening star and prayed for you to come back from wherever you'd gone?* He was shuddering like a windmill, like Old Forty-nine permanently out of whack. Was this because he cared too much about the woman and the old man? Because he'd never really been able to say what he was feeling? Or because, deep down, he relished situations in which the odds were stacked against him until he couldn't stammer a syllable, the pressure was turned up too high to resist, and all the chairs he ever sat in were booby-trapped?

As if he heard Boyd's thoughts, Thomas Micks, Jr. pressed a button, which activated steel cuffs that circled Boyd's wrists, clasping them to his chair's armrests at the same time as his ankles were cuffed to the chair's legs.

Naughty, naughty! he said. When Big Sis invites you to stay, it's bad manners to say no. As Article Thirty-four in my *Good Book* states:

> *Of all bad folk, the meanest will refuse*
> *Kind invitations to sip tea and schmooze.*

The woman kept winding a strand of her gray hair around and around her forefinger as she continued to pace. Tee hee, she giggled, isn't he a riot? Little Bro, he means you no harm. Why do you think you weren't drafted during the wars? You probably don't remember much of what went on back then. Who do you think gave you a special deferment all those years? I realize it's hard to hold your teacup with your wrists cuffed, but we thought you might have the courtesy to stick around just a bit longer. There's something you should know before we— Well, I'll let Tom take over; we women aren't great in the final-moments department.

Boyd struggled in his chair. He uttered nothing more than a grunt.

Thomas Micks, Jr. *tsked,* Wow! That was some grunt. Reminds me of a pig on its way to a deli; I prefer chicken cacciatore—but I digress. It's a wise rooster who knows where he got his cock before his head gets chopped off! In your case, Bill, you have a lot to crow about when you consider yours truly. My revels may have ended—well, not quite—but I've had somewhat of an illustrious career. That marvelous passage from the journal I read you just a minute ago, the one about dusk and mist: the man who wrote it was a fellow Kings-County Anglophile, Thomas Micks, Sr. from Sheepshead Bay. Oh, how I loved the name of that place, how I yearned to bay like a bighorn sheep—but sheep don't bay, do they? Later TMS moved our family a bit to the northeast, but I believe he always carried the image of a sheep's head in his mind, and that image foreshadowed my residence here in The Valley where I've been a good shepherd. Anyway, from the minute my papa got hold of a pen as a boy, he was a scribbler. He read writers nobody ever heard of: Dorothy M. Richardson and Edward F. Benson. He steeped himself in the poetry of Algernon Charles Swinburne. But above all he worshipped a writer named Joseph Conrad, which wasn't even the name the dude was born with, and he had to learn English from scratch, which isn't all that different from you and me as infants. But from day one you were surrounded by people saying, *Bill-this, Bill-that* in English, so it came as second nature.

The woman stopped pacing. You're digressing, she said. Tell him the best part. We haven't much time.

The best part, yes. Let me tell you the best part. As you know, my real name is Thomas Micks, Jr. It so happens that Thomas Micks, Sr.'s other son's name was Catsby Micks. Catsby and I were separated when our father re-married after Catsby's mother got killed in a plane crash—you don't know about planes, and there's no time now for a *crash course*! Anyway, my older half-brother moved about six kilometers northeast to Bensonhurst while I stayed home and played with my toy soldiers. There was one special soldier I thought looked like General MacArthur, and—

Tom, dammit, you're digressing. Get to the point! the woman shouted.

The point. Ah, yes, the point. Well, I bet you remember your Grandma B. Much as I cared for the good doctor who saved my life in the Battle of Honor and Hope—I'm referring to your fusspot papa-in-law, *requiescat in pace,* ha ha!—I was positively smitten by your grandmother. You cannot believe how luscious that woman was in her prime: ink-dark, Elizabeth-Taylor hair, cocoa-colored eyes that made me feel I was gazing at an Aztec princess. Smart, too, was she ever smart! She could add up columns of numbers in her head and steam homemade chicken dumplings like I'd never tasted. Best of all, she loved to read: poems, stories, plays. She could tell a story so well you could visualize everything she said. Although she could never remember the neighborhood where I was a kid—she mispronounced it as Can Ah See or something—the woman was a fucking genius, if you'll *pardonnez-moi.*

We've only got a minute, Tom. Tell him, for chrissakes!

Boyd flexed and flopped, tongue-tied in his chair.

OK OK, I know time's up for us. To make a short story long: when my big bro Catsby met your Grandma B at a candy store in Bensonhurst one morning, he told me she flipped his banana split. She whipped his cream into a lather with the maraschino cherry on top when he asked her name and she answered, *Why, Beatrice Boyd, but it was originally something different in Mexico. What's yours?* From then on they were inseparable. To my horror, they got hitched at the Kings County court building, and wouldn't you know it, my big bro decided to use his wife's surname—he was a feminist or something. He starts calling himself Cat Boyd, which, with a Brooklyn accent, sounds like some kind of mimic thrush. Nine months later guess who pops out of your Grandma B?

The gray-haired woman answered: Our father who art in heaven.

Well, Micks continued, I made sure the great Catsby got his comeuppance. I won't tell you how, but we all carried switchblades and razors back then during the insurrections, and there were plenty of acres in Flatlands to rot on. I made sure your grandma got settled into a condo out here in The Valley, so she could take care of my nephew and I could use the metric system as they did in old Europe. I could sing, *Down in The Valley, The Valley so low / Late in the evening, hear the train blow*—ha, that's a good one! Your Grandma B spurned me, but I wasn't about to sic my bumblebee boys on her. After all, I cared—correction, I care—about my little family.

Boyd mustered every bit of energy, trying to burst his steel cuffs.

Now Bill, don't you think it's time to cry Uncle?

From deep within SM Boyd could hear something like distant thunder: a series of muffled thuds. From the burned-out basement jail cells to the ruined first-floor gallery, it sounded as though propane containers were exploding.

You've wired—

That's right, dear boy, I've wired the Manse to go poof.

I'm sorry it had to be like this, Little Bro, but Great-Uncle Tom's got a certain charm. Plus, you'll have to admit, SM's definitely an improvement over our smelly old condo; there are no kids from Rattlesnake Alley beating up on me, calling me a *darky Looter* here. I haven't been able to resist Tom or his minions, with my tubes tied and all. Incest may not be best, as would've been the case with you and me, Bill, but Uncle Tom's pleasure palace has been no cold-water cabin. Now it's time to say bye-bye.

She lurched toward Boyd but never made it. The gas lamps in the bedroom flickered as the walls shook, throwing Mindy and Micks to the floor. The impact of the armchair crashing to the carpet didn't break Boyd's cuffs. Bound to his overturned chair, he had a millisecond of photographic clarity, in which he saw himself as a child being covered with an iron quilt by Grandma B. Then he exercised every flicker of concentration and flexed his muscles with a sustained glottal *nnng*. He gulped air and slammed his eyes shut like that famous Biblical strongman he'd seen on *The Ancient History Channel*.

He heard four *thwangs* and rolled over onto the carpet just as the gas lamp over the bed blew out of the wall and shot a white stream of flame across the room. On his feet, he leaped over Mindy and Micks sprawling on the tea-stained carpet, and dashed across the room before another gas lamp exploded. He cracked open the bedroom door to find a wall of black smoke in the hallway. Down on all fours, he elbowed himself like a lizard into the hall, whipping around the corner where the stairs met the landing. He couldn't see, he could barely breathe, but he could feel his way down the first couple of steps—when an enormous explosion upstairs lifted him bodily and lodged him between two marble posts holding up the banister in what he guessed was the narrow middle of the staircase. Again, he flexed, like the famous Biblical strongman. The air wasn't breathable, and he needed to huff for a final push. Pinned there, he glimpsed what he thought was the final snapshot image he'd ever see before lapsing into unconsciousness: it was of himself caught in the wasp waist of an hourglass dripping grains of sand on his head for all eternity.

Then it was as if Mount Marvelous blew its top all over again. He felt the marble posts split like kindling, the staircase give way beneath him, and the first floor collapse, plunging him into the basement, where he lay curled in a tight ball, covering his head with his hands. He felt his cowlick stand up straight, so he knew he must be still alive. On hands and knees he elbowed his way over what felt like jailhouse bars, wheezing, unable to smell what must have been corpses rotting under the dirt and debris.

Aware of the continual grinding of marble and sandstone, of wooden joists and steel beams, he scuttled on his elbows over bricks and boards up the remains of an exit passage to the rear door that had been blown wide open, the same door that he'd used days earlier when he broke out of jail with his companions.

He ached all over, but he sprang to his feet and threw himself into what used to be an alley; the neighboring building had collapsed into a hill of crumbled mortar and broken glass. It wasn't easy climbing over this shifting mass, so he slid back down and darted behind the base of a stone portico just as SM let out a cacophonous sequence of squeaks and booms, only to collapse—from its topmost cupola and sandstone turrets—into a mini-mountain of dusty rubble. Much of the mess shot toward Boyd, who held his breath and prayed the stone portico wouldn't fall on top of him. When he opened his eyes, he could see the Guv'na's statue still standing, but it was buried up to its headless neck in wreckage.

He shook himself like a mutt from Rattlesnake Alley, removed glass slivers from his forehead, and limped across the street. The awning outside Mick's Bistro had fallen to the pavement, along with the building's façade. Where were Cathy Vallée, Sonny, and the others? The only remnants Boyd could make out, nearly covered by debris, were three dust-coated droppings evenly spaced from each other, headed in one direction—though it was too dark to follow the imprint of horse tracks.

As he looked south, he could see a few dead eyes poking out of the clouds. The rain had stopped, but it had cut down on the dust swirling everywhere. With the dead eyes' faint glow and sporadic glimmers from Mount Marvelous still erupting, Boyd began his slow journey in the wee hours.

Not one moped cruised the streets. A group of drunken locals stumbled up to Boyd, chanting, *Fuck Guv'na Brush*! They tried to enlist Boyd into their ranks, and when he refused they yelled, *Well then, fuck you and the horse you rode in on*! Much as he was pissed, he had to laugh. He hobbled through downtown Desert Center, marveling at its apartment houses' broken windows, its looted shops. When he reached some condos, he noticed they, too, had been fire-ravaged and ransacked. Here and there several wickiups stood, but no smoke from woodstoves emerged from their black chimney pipes.

At the city's outskirts he stooped to catch his breath. He wanted to lie down by the road and cry into his bandana. He was pooped enough to snooze for a week, though that wouldn't solve anything. Neither would sleep bring him any closer to wherever they'd gone. They: Sonny, Cathy Vallée, Mrs. Kissman, and the others.

Thinking of Karim, Boyd felt better. As long as Karim led the others, they would be all right. Boyd was all right, too. You can be anything you want if you want it hard enough, someone—was it he himself?—had said. Now, for the first time he believed these words. No matter that Mindy and Thomas Micks, Jr. had been buried alive. They had wanted things enough, and they'd gotten them, at least for a while.

Boyd thought he heard the wind crooning *Don't Fence Me In*. It could have been a mockingbird that never came to Sonny's birdhouse, cooing, *Don't Mention Him*. It could have been Sonny, with his baby talk and spoonerisms, saying, *Don't Wrench a Limb*. Any way Boyd put it, the melody was catchy. If Guv'na Brush were around, perhaps he would write a brand-new Article for his great-nephew:

> *Remember how I always did and will*
> *Look out for you, my darky Looter, Bill.*

He gazed over the dark plateau and started walking. Faster he strode, and faster, until he was jogging uphill past roadside mesquite. The air was fresh out here. Blowing in from the west, the wind was in Boyd's eyes, ears, mouth. At least it carried none of the dreck from Mount Marvelous and Desert Center. Up here the air was thinner than in The Valley, but Boyd hated to think of any survivors gasping the clotted air down there. Grandma B had once told him that the Great Ravine, which widened into a plateau, eventually sloped down south of Desert Center, but all he had was her word.

Now, more than ever, words seemed meaningless. If Great-Grandpa Thomas Micks, Sr. pored over writers like Joseph Conrad, what did that matter? Sure, Great-Grandpa had described the winter dusk in a faraway city where snow lay in dirty heaps. He had blabbed about *the run-on, indifferent hours,* but what good were his words now that Boyd was a roadrunner? He would probably be running like this for hours, and who could expect the hours to be anything but indifferent? When he was younger, Boyd used to think time would add up to something. He believed that if he worked long enough on his photos, he would get better and even eventually become well known. After all, Guv'na Brush's *A-1 B-listed* sculptors had time on their side. Over many winters they had distinguished themselves and accepted commissions. As Grandma B had said, quoting Guv'na Brush,

Great leaders who arise and climb
Leave chickweed on the sands of time.

Boyd wondered about his great-grandfather, Thomas, an exquisite stylist but a failed writer. Having faced an apparently blasé readership, he sired two sons, one of whom went on to father Old Man Boyd. But even if Boyd's dad had authored a best-selling biography, it turned out to be inaccurate. Had Old Man Boyd also been a failed writer, or had he deliberately falsified the life of Guv'na Brush? Had Old Man Boyd perhaps known the truth about his Uncle Tom—and buried it under the myth that Rudy Newhouse was obsessed with power and Leghorn Chickens—a myth that became a reality? Certain things he'd said about Uncle Tom had been right on target, but why had Old Man Boyd ignored his uncle's real name and his thwarted love affair with Grandma B? Why had Old Man Boyd as a son completely omitted any mention of his father Catsby?

Boyd popped with sweat, but he shivered to think that one day Sonny might omit mentioning him. Not that Sonny was cut out to be a writer. But what if he eventually became a papa—with Little Girl or Jilly as a mama—and he never said a word to his child or to anyone about Grandpa Bill? Why would a son do that to his father unless the father had done something evil to his son—or else had neglected to do something important with his son, like show his son love? What if Boyd never saw Sonny again? Would Boyd's disappearance warrant Sonny's excising him from their family history?

The Wars of Excision hadn't removed Looters from The Valley—far from it! But there were other private wars more successful in their goal of stamping people out. Mindy had written Boyd off, finally, just as Grandma B had rejected her deceased husband's younger brother as a suitor. Had she known about Thomas's fratricide? If so, she gave no evidence of this to Boyd while she was alive. On her deathbed in the Rattlers Parish General Brushpital, Mindy and Boyd had gathered at her side to hear her murmur, *Don't doubt Thomas,* but Boyd had thought she might be alluding to the Bible. Right up to her last words, though, Grandma B had buttoned her lip, deriding Guv'na Brush as was her custom. It wasn't safe to say such things as

> *No law can make us love the*
> *Man known as our Guv'na.*

Her irreverent rhyming couplet about her brother-in-law notwithstanding, who had any idea how she really felt about Tom, AKA Rudy, AKA Guv'na Brush? Who knew whether she'd been fibbing when she told Boyd about his great-great-grandfather's Ess You Vee, as well as Boyd's great-great-grandparents' experience aboard the Cannonball Express? What about great-Uncle Tom's story about his sister-in-law Beatrice, Grandma B, originally having a different name in Mexico?

For that matter, Cathy Vallée's mother had apparently taken to the grave the details of her relationship with the *wheeziest geezer you could ever sneeze at*, AKA Mr. Heetclit—not that Cathy herself had been altogether candid with Boyd about the school principal.

Boyd was so sick of AKA's that he decided, if he ever saw her again, to rename Mrs. Kissman, to call her Horse. Simply and clearly, Horse! Like Little Girl, who could have chosen a dozen *noms de* whatsamajiggy. As moody and small-framed as she was, she could easily adopt the name Dollyette! Ridiculous to think of himself as Boyd, when half the time he felt like a kid younger than Sonny. Maybe he should drop the final *d* and reinvent himself as *Boy*!

Oh boy, he thought, you're really something, Mr. Bee. At first you feel like everybody's hero; next thing you imagine yourself the way you were as a baby during the Fourth War of Excision. Better not to think about this shit—yes, I can say *shit* now that Guv'na Brush has been crushed!

He picked up his pace, uttering the word *shit*, then shouting it so loud he thought he could hear it echo off the surrounding mountain walls. He relaxed into a brisk jog and chose another mantra. Every time his left foot hit the gravel road, he would say Cathy; every time his right foot touched ground he would say Vallée. After a while the image of her naked, motioning him closer, faded, and his mind went blank. Not entirely blank of course: even as he tried to empty it of all thought, he caught himself imagining that this blankness was the same *run-on indifference* which must govern the dead eyes, those dots in the sky. The evening star had by now long vanished to wherever it went in the early morning. But the dead eyes remained open, blinking up there. The sky had undoubtedly gained two more sets of eyes tonight, Mindy's and Guv'na Brush's. No use to try and find them, but Boyd knew they were there. He only hoped Cathy Vallée, Sonny, and the others—his own little family—were not up there, too.

Before long the road narrowed and began to slope in a downhill straightaway whose distance he couldn't judge; still, his lungs felt the difference. Strangely, no mopeding troops or marauders followed him. Not one headlight beamed in the distance, and when he looked back now and then, no one was there. How many times he'd carried his camera to desolate arroyos to photograph a solitary cottonwood, though not on this byway southwest of Desert Center. If it wasn't the most popular route—and Boyd had never ventured on it—everyone knew this was the only way to Camp Wonderful.

To speak of wonder! There it lay, a hundred meters ahead, alongside the mound of what appeared
to have once been a garbage dump. Boyd had seen
the camp's giant searchlights. In a special feature on
The Evening Star Wrap-up, those lights were capable
of pinpointing a jackrabbit a kilometer away, as well
as flushing out a Looter or an escaped Sandstorm
Trooper. Tonight the giant beams weren't brightening anything; only the glass caps covering their unlit
bulbs reflected the ambient light from the sky. Boyd
counted four-legged platforms, the camp's watchtow-
ers, and recalled a news story about an uprising that
had been quashed by the Guv'na's Troopers stationed
atop these towers. With mini-catapults, loyalist rocks
and razorblades had decimated the camp insurgents,
whose leaders' throats had of course been slit and
their bodies draped over the barbed wire electrified
fence to sizzle and disintegrate.

As Boyd approached the fence, he sniffed the be-
ginnings of something. By now familiar, the smell
of decaying flesh met his nose, and he sneezed for
real. He assumed there would be corpses outside the
fence, but when he passed the central gatehouse, he
glimpsed what he first thought was a slagheap. On
second thought, he saw it was unmistakably a pile
of bodies in bumblebee-striped uniforms. He wasn't
close enough to detect a skull, but the white tips of
bones protruding through jackets and leggings was

evidence enough. In some cases, no flesh clung to those bones; the stench was so overpowering that Boyd took to the open desert and jogged parallel to the road.

Wow! Sonny might have said. All Boyd could do was study the ground in front of him, hoping not to trip over a snake hole. He continued at a slower pace like this for a kilometer or so before returning to a sandy desert track. He had now entered the restricted territory west of Camp Wonderful known as Erewhon. No *Evening Star Wrap-up* feature had televised anything about Erewhon, supposedly known for its wolves, cougars, and dangerous insects. The only mention of it Boyd had picked up in all his winters was the proverb,

> *Don't go to Erewhon, the Guv decrees,*
> *Or you'll earn Bees galore, yea, killer bees!*

Boyd shuddered to think of wandering into a swarm of those buggers. Once, while photographing hives outside of Rattlers Parish, he had stepped into some flowering mesquite. The result was three days lying swollen in bed, while Dolly bathed his bee bites in chicken broth. The itching had made him delirious, and for a while Grandpa A thought Boyd might succumb. He could still hear his father-in-law leaning over him in bed, saying, *Quel dommage!*—before daubing Boyd's bites with balls of cotton soaked in Dolly's urine.

Something hissed from behind a boulder. Something else hooted from a live oak. And a rising chorus of crazy yip-yaps from nearby made Boyd think of Sonny and a pack of school kids pretending to be wolves. He paused to squint at a piece of scrap metal that looked as though it had been lying half-buried in the brush for scores of winters. He stooped to read a faded metal insignia that seemed to glow in the dark: NASA.

Although the path was all but non-existent now, he stepped up his pace when the downhill straightaway leveled out. From afar a tiny luminous eye—was it a cat's?—peered up at him. It was at least three kilometers away, but with every step he took, it grew larger. He thought he might be better off if he resumed his jog through the desert. Here and there rocks and tumbleweed branches littered the way. Without his moped and Leica, in light too dim to shoot anything, Boyd felt a second wind carry him towards the light aimed at him just as brilliantly as a search beam trained on a Looter.

The closer he approached the light source, the larger it got. Less than half a kilometer away, he heard what sounded like the tick of a grandfather clock. He wondered how much time he had left before he'd join the owners of all those other dead eyes in the sky.

Perhaps a few seconds awaited him before he'd be with Mindy and Guv'na Brush.

Then he heard it for sure, a voice. "Hey!" it shouted. "Hey you!"

The ticking clock turned into a putt-putting he recognized. Boyd was flush up against a barbed wire fence that stretched north and south as far as he could see. On the other side of the fence, a voice called out again, but softer this time, "Hey you! Need a lift?"

Later, perched behind him, clasping his ample gut, Boyd realized how simple it all had been, the barbed wire fence he'd scooted under with signs facing west: STAY OUT and NO TRESPASSING. The rotund man who wouldn't give Boyd his name said he was out for a *midnight spin*—whatever that meant! He'd seen smoke and what he thought were lightning flashes, accompanied by distant thunderclaps.

"Know what? I thought it was fireworks. Them kooks in The Valley: you can never tell what they're celebrating or confiscating. We've heard how they light Roman candles and cherry bombs when they feast on one another. I don't care for cannibals myself, but if they wanna keep down the population by roasting babies and such, I say, 'Live and let live!' I'm a Right-to-Lifer myself, but when it comes to kids outside the womb, I say, 'If need be, light the stove!' Them Valleyites all have hare lips and no teeth, so you can't blame them for doing mean and ugly things."

Boyd sat silent as the moped whizzed west.

"Yeah, man—what did you say your name was? Boyd? You're sure scruffy, but you look normal enough to me. All you need's a bath, so I'm guessing you're one of us, not one of them Valleyites. I mean, where's your harelip, ha ha! But the way that Valley guy, the leader, you know—what's his name? Guv'na Something-or-other—the way he fenced off the place a gazillion years ago and raised hell with any of us when we tried to hop the fence and say hello, you know, like, 'N'yellow, how're you doin' today, neighbor?'—I mean, like, the guy's fuckin' loco in the coco. But then what can you expect after what happened fifty years ago? I guess we're all lucky to be alive. I heard on KNN that there are thirty-four barbed wire territories in the States, every one of them with their loony-tunes Guv'na or Emperor Whosamajiggy."

There was no traffic on the road, less potholed and wider than any in The Valley. But dawn appeared to be breaking in the East. When Boyd glanced behind him, the sky was pink, and there were fewer dead eyes watching from their observation posts. The moped putt-putted much faster than any Miramar bike. Boyd estimated they were driving about seventy kph. By the road a sign read *Riverside 10 miles.*

"Sir, are we coming to a river?" Boyd said.

"A river? What? Oh, that sign, huh? Well, maybe there's a river, but if so I wouldn't know about it. Sit tight, and we'll get you some coffee. You look beat."

Boyd stayed silent as the day got brighter. The road widened, and he saw mopeds parked outside a petrol station. A red and green sign with a ridiculously decorated mini–fir tree read *Holiday Gas.* He thought it might have referred to The Valley's main holiday, Midwinter Sunday. The rotund man lowered his kickstand and parked his bike among a bunch of others.

"C'mon in, let's get a cup of joe!"

Inside, there was a counter just like any Mick's, but there were also chairs and tables with checkered tablecloths. "Siddown, pal. Give 'er a rest!"

A woman in a stained apron approached the table. "Whaddle it be, boys? The usual?"

"Yep, and give us some of that, you know, hummus and black beans, willya, sweetie?"

Boyd saw a nametag over the woman's left breast: *Meg.* He saw three young guys in heavy sweaters enter and join the crowd of men in identical hooded pullover shirts with insignias that spelled out the word GENTRIFY. He heard an obese man, even more rotund than his new friend, yell behind the counter to someone in back of a see-through partition, "Hey, Tony, get the lead out! We need H and BBs for two hungry tigers!" At first Boyd smelled something like the grease he'd sniffed in the cave on Mount Marvelous with Adze, but, no, come to think of it this odor made him think of something he'd scarcely experienced: the smell of roots and herbs.

An attractive brunette with a wild blue streak in her hair winked at him. Seated at a table with another man whose back was turned to Boyd, she was wearing a skirt shorter than any he'd ever noticed; he could see above her knees.

"Sir," Boyd said, "have you heard of a woman with red hair named Cathy Vallée?"

"Cathy who? Vallée, you say? Nope, can't say I have."

"What about a kid by the name of Sonny? Sonny Boyd?"

"Nope, but this is a big place. What's he, your brother or something?"

"No, sir, I'm just trying to locate some people on horses."

"People on horses? You must be kidding. Everybody uses mopeds around here."

By now Meg had returned with two steaming cups of an aromatic tea-like beverage. Boyd was about to taste his when the brunette with the blue streak, who'd been winking and batting her eyelashes, made a kissing motion with her lips, directed at him. Her leather-jacketed companion whipped around and glared at Boyd. Then, before Boyd's friend could fork down one mouthful of beans, the leather-jacketed man stood up and roared, "Who the fuck're you, big boy?" Before Boyd could answer, the man pulled a huge knife out of a sheath on his belt and barged across the room, slashing the air.

"Sir—" Boyd began, but there was nothing he could do except slam the leather-jacketed man's wrist with one hand, causing him to drop the knife, and smash the man square in the nose with his other fist.

"I'm so sorry, sir," Boyd said, standing over the man, who had fallen to the floor in a widening puddle of blood.

The obese man behind the counter picked up some sort of thingamabob and spoke into it. Boyd's companion, hissed, "C'mon, let's get the hell outta here."

They fled out the door, but not before Boyd's friend tossed a banknote onto the counter; it appeared to be ten Bees.

Outside they mounted their moped and roared away at ninety kph with Boyd's arms wrapped around the other man's gut.

"Whew, that was a close one. That guy was out of his gourd. I mean, what did you do to piss him off? I was hoping to treat you to breakfast, and we end up on the road like in that old novel, what's its name. I'll tellya, it reminds me of the time when I was a young hunk like you. I was thin and good-looking—well, not as good-looking as you, but I was OK. I lived down in San Diego for a while, trying to restore a carrier they'd brought up from the bottom. I was one of the last of the shipbuilders, but nobody was building new ships those days. I sure knew how to handle a wrench and tighten a lug nut. Well, that damned carrier was minus half her flight deck, and a great big hole had tore the hell out of her hull. It was larger than any torpedo could make I'll tellya. Most of the boys thought she'd scraped a reef on her slide before she got stuck on the continental shelf. How the hell those anchor clankers re-floated the sucker was beyond me. But anyways I and a crew of ironworkers, mechanics, and fitters had been trying for fourteen months to fix up old Hillary Clinton so she could be, you know, shipshape. Every night after work I'd hit the Dockside Bar & Grille for a couple of tofurky sandwiches and beers. I had my eye set on a waitress named Patty. She had red hair like that what's-her-name, that Cathy you mentioned. Lord, when Patty brought me and the boys tofurky, she put mustard in my teakettle, if you know what I mean. Her hair was so red I could taste it. And she kept calling me Hon. I love that, when somebody calls me Hon. My Aunt Sammy used to call me that after my mom and dad died."

Boyd whipped his head around. No one was following them. The road had begun to fill up with mopeds going in both directions, just like Rattlers Parish during rush hour, except there was a lot more traffic here, and everyone was zipping along at ninety kph.

"Anyways, one night at the Dockside Bar I was in a sweat. That day we'd worked real hard to lay down a section of flight deck. But what was making me sweat was this: I'd bought Patty a box of dried fruit: dates, figs, desert stuff like that. It happened to be Valentine's Day, and I had one of those heart-shaped boxes I'd bought for the fruit. I'd written her a little poem:

> *I'm sure not natty,*
> *But I love Patty.*

Not bad, huh? It may not be William Shakespeaker, but it's got, you know, feeling. Well, so's I give her the poem and the box of dried fruit after the boys and I pay our checks and all of a sudden this pipsqueak bolts out of the kitchen, screaming, 'You mother-fuckin' son-of-a-bitch!' and then before I know what's going on he pulls out this tiny pistol and shoots me square in the breadbasket and I don't know anything after that till I wake up in the hospital with the biggest bellyache I had since my Aunt Sammy and I got food poisoning from peanut butter and alfalfa sprouts sandwiches in Bakersfield. But— and here's the thing—when I finally got stitched up and sent back to the docks, I put on weight and realized I could, like, do the same thing with myself as I was trying to do with that old carrier Hillary Clinton. You won't believe this, but I started to have dreams at night, and they weren't about Patty; they were about flying. Not that I was an airplane pilot, but that I could float way up there in the sky on my own, that my arms were, like, wings."

"Very interesting," Boyd said. "But where are we going?"

"You'll see," said the man.

Boyd saw plenty that morning: petrol stations named PDQ and Joey's Fuel Hole; zipped-up mopeds driven by men and women decked in flashy footwear that his new friend called "running shoes"; kilometer after kilometer of moped dealerships featuring brands other than Miramar; emporiums whose signs advertised Vegans Vee Are and Take-out Falafel—one moped's attached wagon already had a line of people waiting in front of it for Meatless Tamales, whatever *they* were; humongous establishments, Discount Donuts and Have a Seat 'n' Eat, which attracted parking lots full of moped moms—many of them roly-poly—with their kids in tow; a tiny chapel next to a gigantic upright wooden post with a transverse wooden pole near the top, across the street from what could be a prayer hall with a tall, skinny tower that housed balconies from which a recorded man's voice cried out a kind of song; a dilapidated building with a sign calling it a Public Library surrounded by men marching, carrying posters that said WAGES, NOT PAGES.

"Sir, are there stores around here that sell cameras?" Boyd said.

"Are you kidding? We got digital, hominal, Grain-a-berry—you name it."

"Are they expensive?"

"Naw. But why would you want a camera?"

"I'd love to buy a Leica."

"Huh? Leica? Never heard of it. All we got are Nebuchadnezzars; Kodaks and the rest went out of business a gazillion years ago. A good Nebuchadnezzar digital could run you a hundred Rudolphs. But why would you want one? You don't have a family or anything."

"Well, I—"

"Me? After what happened with Patty, I quit caring about settling down and having kids, you know? All that horseshit about families? You can dump it in East LA as far as I'm concerned! When I retired from shipbuilding, I got into something much more interesting."

"What's that?" Boyd said.

"You'll see," said the man.

As they zipped west, petrol stations and shop clusters gave way to stretches of what looked like rubble-strewn war zones next to taller buildings made of steel and glass. Many windows were smashed, and the buildings looked uninhabited.

"What happened here?" Boyd said.

"These high-rises? What the quakes and so on didn't hit, the Herbivarians did."

"The Herbivarians?"

"Oh, c'mon, Boyd, don't tell me you never heard of the Herbivarians?"

"I'm sorry, sir, I've never heard of them."

"Well, I'm not gonna give you a history lesson. But I'll tell you one thing: this used to be a burger-loving nation. It *used* to be!"

At last the man pulled into an empty parking lot. Boyd smelled something strange.

"OK, Mr. Know-nothing, get a whiff of this."

"What are those pictures of animals and the black goop behind the fence?"

"Ha, you don't know, do you? Can't you read?"

"Well, yessir, it says, 'La Bre Tar Pi,' but that doesn't mean anything. Is it another language?"

"No, dumb ox, it means the sign's been vandalized—again. Probably the Herbivarians."

Another three mopeds pulled into the parking lot. A man and woman approached the fence with a boy who looked to be Sonny's age.

"Gee, Pop, did the tar really swallow that woolly mammoth?"

"Yup, and it said, 'Jump in' to that saber-toothed tiger, too."

Still another two mopeds parked, and a woman clad head to toe in a flowing dark blue garment led a dark-haired girl to the fence. The woman spoke some words through a mesh that covered her mouth. Boyd couldn't understand what she said.

"Don't ask *me*," the fat man said.

As they mopeded west, Boyd looked to the right and thought he glimpsed something familiar, though he didn't know where he'd seen it—was it, as Grandpa A said, *déjà vu*? In fact, he wasn't sure if he saw it at all; it could've been one of those mirages he thought he'd seen quite a bit lately. So many buildings had been reduced to rubble that they afforded unblocked views of the distant terrain. On top of a scrubby hill perhaps ten kilometers away a broken-down sign seemed to spell out HLYWOD in white letters. Boyd didn't dare ask his new friend about what he saw—or thought he saw. As though he read Boyd's mind, the fat man crooned,

> *I'm putt-puttin'*
> *With nuttin'*
> *To say to you.*

The boulevard seemed to go on forever, and the man sounded as though he was whistling. In the noisy, fetid air Boyd couldn't identify the tune, but it made him think of Myrna and Cathy Vallée. The farther west they drove, the more densely bunched-together the shops and small condo-like dwellings became. The almost seductive scent wafting from a building called Vegetarian Noshery met the fresh air mixed with mist blowing from the west, while mopeders and pedestrians proceeded at a statelier pace than they had a kilometer or so back east.

"OK, buddy, here's where it's at. As you can see, it's sure no disaster area," the man said, hopping off the bike and lowering his kickstand.

Boyd slid off the banana seat. He smelled salt in the air, but the mist was thick, and it smelled good.

"Where are we?" he said.

"Oh, let's just call Santa Monica paradise!" his new friend laughed.

"But I can't see anything."

"Why, sure you can. Look at these benches. See these date palms? What about these ground-hugger trees—can you believe how twisted they are? Can you guess what's booming down below? It's too far down, and the wind's blowing too hard to hear it, but it's down there, buddy. Believe you me, it's been down there a long time, slapping the sand. My guess is that it's gonna be there a gazillion years from now."

Boyd listened. He heard the chirrup of a bird perched in a tree nearby.

"Hey, Boyd, did you hear that chickadee? Weird: they're not so common around here. Hey, what about those two over there? They're a couple of goldfinches flying in that special way they have, up and down like roller coasters. The wrens and woodpeckers'll soon be making babies, you know. I gave up on Patty, but I'll never give up on these little suckers. Plus the big ones, the condors up north of here—I love those buzzards! Anything with wings makes me go cock-a-doodle-doo!"

"I had a wife who could peep and trill like a song sparrow."

"Oh, yeah? Well, I can squawk like a goose, warble like a verdin, *brrp-brrp* like a robin. I can make the thin whistle of a cowbird and the stomach-grumble of a rock dove. About the only bird I can't mimic is a whippoorwill because they don't grow here."

Boyd had umpteen questions he wanted to ask his new friend, and it was still early.

"Well, buddyroo, I've gotta head up the coast. There's this conference of condor watchers camped out up there. Preservationists, they call themselves, and I wanna be in that number! I wanna count every one of those ugly mothers and make sure no Herbivarians put them in cages. So I'll say adios and good luck to you!" When they shook hands, he pressed what looked like a twenty Rudolph banknote into Boyd's palm.

Boyd waved goodbye to his friend, but the mist enveloped him so fast there was no time for formalities. The putt-putt of his moped blended with the chirrup of chickadees, goldfinches, and the salt air whooshing through branches.

He took a seat on a bench by the parapet. It was too misty to see anything right now, but he would wait. Soon he would be able to peer down from the cliff-top park at sand unlike any he'd seen in The Valley. He would hear water crests—were they called waves?—breaking, handclapping as they hit the land's edge. He would gaze, as if from an eagle's aerie, at the wide deserted arena, and the windblown thingamajig topped with a white triangular bandana floating on the blue out there would be like one of those ships his new friend had spoken about. He would think of his little family, which had recently become littler—though not really. He had lost Dolly, but he'd gained Cathy Vallée. Wherever she and Sonny were, Little Girl, Karim, and the horses would be near.

He would let his mind linger on them, especially on Cathy Vallée and the feeling of her flame-redness inside him. He would imagine himself lying beside her, pressed to her lips—she who'd been childless, a reader. He would think of her reading a book to him and the others in folding chairs on the sand, with waves breaking, clapping hands on the shore. He would imagine another shore, the one in the book Cathy Vallée was reading—and hear waves breaking on every page, over and over, clapping hands in the book.

His little family:

He would rise like the mist and go find them.

JAMES REISS grew up in New York City and northern New Jersey. For many years he was Professor of English at Miami University in Ohio, as well as Founding Editor of Miami University Press. He is the author of several collections of poetry, including *The Breathers, Riff on Six: New and Selected Poems*, and *The Novel*, as well as the editor of *Self-Interviews: James Dickey*. His work has appeared in such places as *The Atlantic, Esquire, The Hudson Review, The New Yorker, The New York Times, The Paris Review, Poetry, Virginia Quarterly Review*, and *Slate*. His surname rhymes with "peace." He lives near Chicago. This is his first novel.

CPSIA information can be obtained at www.ICGtesting.com
Printed in the USA
LVOW11s1746270716

498005LV00007B/740/P